# ALREADY GONE

(A Laura Frost Suspense Thriller —Book One)

BLAKE PIERCE

## Blake Pierce

Blake Pierce is the USA Today bestselling author of the RILEY PAGE mystery series, which includes seventeen books. Blake Pierce is also the author of the MACKENZIE WHITE mystery series, comprising fourteen books; of the AVERY BLACK mystery series, comprising six books; of the KERI LOCKE mystery series, comprising five books; of the MAKING OF RILEY PAIGE mystery series, comprising six books; of the KATE WISE mystery series, comprising seven books; of the CHLOE FINE psychological suspense mystery, comprising six books; of the JESSE HUNT psychological suspense thriller series, comprising fifteen books (and counting); of the AU PAIR psychological suspense thriller series, comprising three books; of the ZOE PRIME mystery series, comprising six books; of the ADELE SHARP mystery series, comprising ten books (and counting); of the EUROPEAN VOYAGE cozy mystery series, comprising six books (and counting); of the new LAURA FROST FBI suspense thriller, comprising three books (and counting); of the new ELLA DARK FBI suspense thriller, comprising six books (and counting); of the A YEAR IN EUROPE cozy mystery series, comprising three books (and counting); of the AVA GOLD mystery series, comprising three books (and counting); and of the RACHEL GIFT mystery series, comprising three books (and counting).

An avid reader and lifelong fan of the mystery and thriller genres, Blake loves to hear from you, so please feel free to visit www.blakepierceauthor.com to learn more and stay in touch.


ISBN: 978-1-0943-9077-2

**BOOKS BY BLAKE PIERCE**

**RACHEL GIFT MYSTERY SERIES**
HER LAST WISH (Book #1)
HER LAST CHANCE (Book #2)
HER LAST HOPE (Book #3)

**AVA GOLD MYSTERY SERIES**
CITY OF PREY (Book #1)
CITY OF FEAR (Book #2)
CITY OF BONES (Book #3)

**A YEAR IN EUROPE**
A MURDER IN PARIS (Book #1)
DEATH IN FLORENCE (Book #2)
VENGEANCE IN VIENNA (Book #3)

**ELLA DARK FBI SUSPENSE THRILLER**
GIRL, ALONE (Book #1)
GIRL, TAKEN (Book #2)
GIRL, HUNTED (Book #3)
GIRL, SILENCED (Book #4)
GIRL, VANISHED (Book 5)
GIRL ERASED (Book #6)

**LAURA FROST FBI SUSPENSE THRILLER**
ALREADY GONE (Book #1)
ALREADY SEEN (Book #2)
ALREADY TRAPPED (Book #3)

**EUROPEAN VOYAGE COZY MYSTERY SERIES**
MURDER (AND BAKLAVA) (Book #1)
DEATH (AND APPLE STRUDEL) (Book #2)
CRIME (AND LAGER) (Book #3)
MISFORTUNE (AND GOUDA) (Book #4)
CALAMITY (AND A DANISH) (Book #5)
MAYHEM (AND HERRING) (Book #6)

**ADELE SHARP MYSTERY SERIES**

LEFT TO DIE (Book #1)
LEFT TO RUN (Book #2)
LEFT TO HIDE (Book #3)
LEFT TO KILL (Book #4)
LEFT TO MURDER (Book #5)
LEFT TO ENVY (Book #6)
LEFT TO LAPSE (Book #7)
LEFT TO VANISH (Book #8)
LEFT TO HUNT (Book #9)
LEFT TO FEAR (Book #10)

**THE AU PAIR SERIES**
ALMOST GONE (Book#1)
ALMOST LOST (Book #2)
ALMOST DEAD (Book #3)

**ZOE PRIME MYSTERY SERIES**
FACE OF DEATH (Book#1)
FACE OF MURDER (Book #2)
FACE OF FEAR (Book #3)
FACE OF MADNESS (Book #4)
FACE OF FURY (Book #5)
FACE OF DARKNESS (Book #6)

**A JESSIE HUNT PSYCHOLOGICAL SUSPENSE SERIES**
THE PERFECT WIFE (Book #1)
THE PERFECT BLOCK (Book #2)
THE PERFECT HOUSE (Book #3)
THE PERFECT SMILE (Book #4)
THE PERFECT LIE (Book #5)
THE PERFECT LOOK (Book #6)
THE PERFECT AFFAIR (Book #7)
THE PERFECT ALIBI (Book #8)
THE PERFECT NEIGHBOR (Book #9)
THE PERFECT DISGUISE (Book #10)
THE PERFECT SECRET (Book #11)
THE PERFECT FAÇADE (Book #12)
THE PERFECT IMPRESSION (Book #13)
THE PERFECT DECEIT (Book #14)
THE PERFECT MISTRESS (Book #15)
THE PERFECT IMAGE (Book #16)

THE PERFECT VEIL (Book #17)
THE PERFECT INDISCRETION (Book #18)
THE PERFECT RUMOR (Book #19)

**CHLOE FINE PSYCHOLOGICAL SUSPENSE SERIES**
NEXT DOOR (Book #1)
A NEIGHBOR'S LIE (Book #2)
CUL DE SAC (Book #3)
SILENT NEIGHBOR (Book #4)
HOMECOMING (Book #5)
TINTED WINDOWS (Book #6)

**KATE WISE MYSTERY SERIES**
IF SHE KNEW (Book #1)
IF SHE SAW (Book #2)
IF SHE RAN (Book #3)
IF SHE HID (Book #4)
IF SHE FLED (Book #5)
IF SHE FEARED (Book #6)
IF SHE HEARD (Book #7)

**THE MAKING OF RILEY PAIGE SERIES**
WATCHING (Book #1)
WAITING (Book #2)
LURING (Book #3)
TAKING (Book #4)
STALKING (Book #5)
KILLING (Book #6)

**RILEY PAIGE MYSTERY SERIES**
ONCE GONE (Book #1)
ONCE TAKEN (Book #2)
ONCE CRAVED (Book #3)
ONCE LURED (Book #4)
ONCE HUNTED (Book #5)
ONCE PINED (Book #6)
ONCE FORSAKEN (Book #7)
ONCE COLD (Book #8)
ONCE STALKED (Book #9)
ONCE LOST (Book #10)
ONCE BURIED (Book #11)

ONCE BOUND (Book #12)
ONCE TRAPPED (Book #13)
ONCE DORMANT (Book #14)
ONCE SHUNNED (Book #15)
ONCE MISSED (Book #16)
ONCE CHOSEN (Book #17)

**MACKENZIE WHITE MYSTERY SERIES**
BEFORE HE KILLS (Book #1)
BEFORE HE SEES (Book #2)
BEFORE HE COVETS (Book #3)
BEFORE HE TAKES (Book #4)
BEFORE HE NEEDS (Book #5)
BEFORE HE FEELS (Book #6)
BEFORE HE SINS (Book #7)
BEFORE HE HUNTS (Book #8)
BEFORE HE PREYS (Book #9)
BEFORE HE LONGS (Book #10)
BEFORE HE LAPSES (Book #11)
BEFORE HE ENVIES (Book #12)
BEFORE HE STALKS (Book #13)
BEFORE HE HARMS (Book #14)

**AVERY BLACK MYSTERY SERIES**
CAUSE TO KILL (Book #1)
CAUSE TO RUN (Book #2)
CAUSE TO HIDE (Book #3)
CAUSE TO FEAR (Book #4)
CAUSE TO SAVE (Book #5)
CAUSE TO DREAD (Book #6)

**KERI LOCKE MYSTERY SERIES**
A TRACE OF DEATH (Book #1)
A TRACE OF MUDER (Book #2)
A TRACE OF VICE (Book #3)
A TRACE OF CRIME (Book #4)
A TRACE OF HOPE (Book #5)

# CHAPTER ONE

Laura tensed her fingers around the grip of her gun, trying to make sure it wasn't going to slip out of her sweaty hands. She was only one of many agents and cops surrounding the farmhouse, but that didn't mean she could let her guard down. She had to be ready.

Around them, a field of overgrown wheat whispered softly in the wind, the only sound that broke the silence of the loose circle of men and women. Each of them was focused on the farmhouse, the peeling paint on the doors, the smashed and boarded-up windows, the hole in the roof. A couple of crows wheeled lazily overhead. Laura tensed her hand again, loosening and then tightening her fingers to ensure her grip.

She glanced to her side, where her partner was watching on with grim silence, his eyes trained on the special agent in charge. Most of the agents were also turning their eyes that way, waiting for the go-ahead. The silence from inside the house was eerie.

Biting her lip, Laura tucked a loose strand of her blonde hair behind her ear as it threatened to stir in the breeze. She felt like there were ants crawling under her skin, the anticipation almost too much. There was so much at stake. If they didn't do this right, the man who had kidnapped the governor's daughter would have time to do some serious damage.

She was glad she didn't have the responsibility of being the one to decide when and how to storm the building—but at the same time, she itched at the lack of control. She had been on dozens of raids over her career, but never where a child's life hung in the balance like this.

"The longer we wait, the more risk he sees us," Nate hissed under his breath, only audible to her. Laura nodded almost imperceptibly. The kidnapper was almost certainly armed. How long were they going to give him before they went in?

Nate shifted restlessly beside her, and she glanced up at him instinctively. Nathaniel Lavoie, her partner of several years at the FBI, was not good at operations that required secrecy. His six-foot-two frame stood out in the average crowd, towering over her. She stood level with his shoulders, which were currently tense and corded, his muscles all flexed in readiness. A bead of sweat stood out here and there on his black skin, but he was all focus, his sharp brown eyes fixed on the house. That put her at ease, knowing he was just as alert as she was. Laura took a deep breath to try to steady herself, concentrating on watching for a hand signal.

When she looked back at the special agent in charge, a flare of alarm went through her. He was holding up a megaphone. No—surely this wasn't right? There weren't enough agents on the ground yet. They were still waiting for backup. If they had to go in, Laura thought the better option would be to storm the place, not give him any time to react. If they gave away the element of surprise, the kidnapper could end up seriously hurting the kid…

Or just coming out with his hands up, Laura reminded herself. Her heart was beating hard and painfully in her chest. She kept picturing her own daughter, Lacey, with a gun to her head, in spite of her determination not to. Lacey was about the same age as the governor's daughter, who was around five years old. Not that Laura was entirely sure the picture in her head was accurate. They grew fast at this age. Would Lacey look different since the last time Laura had been able to see her? The pang of pain that hit directly in the center of her chest was so sharp Laura had to swallow hard. She breathed the fresh country air deeply, trying to steady herself again. Now was not the time to allow in the heartache that came with thoughts of missing her daughter's life.

"This is the FBI!" The voice blaring through the megaphone made Laura jump, and she immediately refocused an intense gaze on the house. On the side door that she and Nathaniel had been assigned to cover. "Come out now with your hands up. You're surrounded!"

There was silence. No movement. Laura resisted the urge to move, to shift her weight to the other foot. She glanced out the side of her eye briefly to see her superior lifting the megaphone again. Something throbbed between her eyes. A distant pain.

No. Not now. Laura tensed her jaw, trying to hold off the vision. Not now, when they were all relying on her to cover the side door. If the kidnapper came out that way and she wasn't on the ball, and he got past them, if Nathaniel couldn't cover him alone, if the child died because she was out of it, Laura would never be able to forgive herself.

The pain intensified rapidly, like something exploding inside her forehead. No. Laura tried to hold on just a little bit longer.

"This—"

The pain was suddenly gone, along with her vision and hearing.

*Laura saw the killer driving his car along a narrow country lane, between overgrown fields on either side of the cracked concrete. Her view was grainy, distorted, like she was looking through a window smeared with dust and dotted with raindrops. She was floating above him. He had a pinched look to his face, his hands gripping the steering wheel so tight his knuckles stood out white. He looked up ahead, and Laura saw what he saw: the farmhouse rising out of the fields in front of him, the roof and then the windows of the upstairs, the walls…*

*And the agents, milling around in their dark blue windbreakers. Moving in and out of the house. Shaking their heads and gesturing. The sun glinting off a radio.*

*The killer hit the brakes hard, then twisted and put his arm around the back of the passenger seat. He floored the accelerator in reverse, the engine revving up noisily as he threw the car backwards as fast as he could. Laura heard the pant and whine of his panicked breath like it was right in her ear as he reversed all the way to the last turning, sweat running in beads from his forehead. He looked forward again for just one glance, saw that nothing had changed. No one was racing down the lane after him. There was no noise, no flash of light.*

*He swung the car around in the turning, completing a ragged circle and then firing the car in the direction he'd come from, raising only a brief puff of dust from the back tires before he was gone. Laura felt it hit her face, smelled the burning rubber.*

*She blinked and found herself inside the car. Alone in the front seat, the man laughed in disbelief, then focused on driving again. He'd gotten away. One moment more of inattention and they'd have been able to take him in. But he was free.*

*And Laura knew they were never going to get a second chance to stop him.*

Laura gasped, blinking hard against the too-bright sun as her head throbbed. The inside of her mouth both tasted and felt like sand, as it always did after one of her visions hit.

"Are you all right?" Nate whispered, his eyes still trained on the house as he leaned only slightly closer to her.

"Headache," Laura fired back. Her eyes were moving desperately, tracking the scenery around them. The kidnapper had been able to see the front of the house. That must have meant he was coming from her right—and there must have been a hill—*there*, behind the cluster of agents opposite the front door.

What if the vision was wrong? Laura knew they weren't always accurate. She saw what could be, not necessarily what would be. And if it was wrong, and the girl was inside the house…

If she messed up now, the girl might die. There weren't enough agents on the ground to cover all of the exits alone.

She had to move, and fast. She thrust her gun back into the holster by her side, knowing it would only slow her down as she ran, and broke formation, sprinting at a diagonal angle from the farmhouse. She felt rather than saw Nate move instinctively to reach for her, holding her back from breaking formation, his fingers closing on air. She knew the others around her were staring as she went. She heard the agent in charge shout her name. It didn't matter.

Laura plunged into the tall waving wheat, taking a direct route as fast as she could go. The thin fronds whipped at her elbows and around her body, and she knew if she put a foot wrong and went down it was all over. Behind her, she heard the command from the special agent in charge to go in. She ignored it. They were all going the wrong way, and she had no time to convince them of that fact.

Laura was almost at the road, her progress hampered by the incline of the hill. She was almost at the top. Where was he? The agents were coming out of the house below when she threw a glance over her shoulder. There was no one here. Was the vision too late?

Too early?

Laura spun in the middle of the road, her breath ragged and burning her lungs. There was no sign of the car. Below her, she saw two agents exiting the house, shaking their heads. She'd been wrong. The vision had been false.

Not only had she jeopardized the mission, but she'd been wrong. She was going to get her ass handed to her—and she tasted bile in her mouth as she wondered if she'd maybe given him a chance to slip away… There was no sign of Nathaniel by the side door. Had he followed her? Had he left the side door unguarded?

She heard it first. A thin, reedy kind of noise. The way the land was built here was all wrong for acoustics; the hill gave her little view of the land on the other side, where the road vanished into trees, and everything seemed to absorb sound and bounce it around her. Her pounding head didn't help. But the sound made her turn, and it almost wasn't enough notice.

She had barely begun to move when she saw it. The car, cresting the ridge, coming directly into view and driving right for her. She was close enough to see his face through the windshield, to see the moment he spotted the FBI logo on her chest.

She still had a chance. She threw her body forward, ignoring the complaint in her lungs and the sting in her calves, her eyes trained only on the car. She could see him moving, putting the car into reverse, throwing his arm across the back of the seat. It was almost too late—

Laura hit the edge of the wheat field and launched herself through the air in one last-ditch effort to stop him from getting away. She landed solidly on the windshield, spreading her arms and legs in search of a hand- or foothold and managing to cling on desperately to the bodywork as the impact knocked out the last breath in her body. The car was already moving, wind whipping in her ears and sending her hair flying into her eyes as she clung on for life, not having thought her way through to step two of this desperate leap.

The car was speeding up, just as she had seen in her vision. Laura gritted her teeth and clung on, feeling the strain in her cramped fingertips, how she had to use all the strength in her body to hold herself down and not fly off like a paper bag caught in the wind. She could hear him shouting something through the windshield, but the rush of the wind in her ears and the roar of the engine right under her were too loud to make out the words.

She became aware of movement close to her head, to the window of the driver's side rolling down and an arm coming out of it, and she braced herself for him to hit her. But before he could reach her, a massive, juddering shock pitched her away from the windshield and off the car completely.

Laura slammed down her arms to absorb the impact and rolled across the hard surface of the old road, not breathing again until she managed to lie still. Even then she couldn't rest—she heard the rev of his engine and instinct threw her to the side, off the concrete, into the wheat. If he came at her and ran her over—

But the revving stopped, and Laura looked up, managing to make out through her spinning and roiling vision that the car was not moving. It was stuck, she realized from this angle, one of the back wheels spinning uselessly in the air while the front was lodged in a low ditch at the side of the road. She'd managed to throw him off course enough to stop him. Which was good, because from all the spinning and the motion on top of her headache, she was pretty sure she was going to throw up.

Laura put her hand out to stabilize herself and came up with a handful of dirt, her fingers sinking into the dry soil. The sound of a door opening made her look up and see the kidnapper jumping out of the car, his face twisted in rage. He was lanky, all sinew, tall enough to eat up the distance between them with long strides. She only had time to register the fact that he was holding something dense and dark in his hand before she dodged out of the way.

He growled at her, an inhuman snarl without words, and swung again, quick and heavy, aiming right for her head. Laura knew she couldn't keep evading him. She was trapped unless she got to her feet. The only thing she could do was to roll forward instead of away, launching herself at him, a facsimile of her earlier leap for the car.

The kidnapper fell to the road with a cry, his legs tangled around her body as he plunged back, allowing her to trap his feet. She fought her way out and got up, ready to cuff him—but before she could even get her bearings, a sharp blow to her thigh had her crying out and going down, her knee giving way.

"Fucking bitch," the kidnapper spat, scrambling up and over her. One of his hands pinned her shoulder in place, his weight preventing her from shifting. He lifted the club into the air, and Laura tensed.

There was no way she could pull herself out of the way of the blow.

# CHAPTER TWO

Laura's only hope, she knew, was to use his momentum against him. She grabbed the handcuffs from her belt and in one motion, snapped one side around the wrist that held the club and pulled down hard on his arm as she did it.

She managed to avoid the club smashing into her nose by the thinnest margin. She felt the air move around it, the small spray of dirt fly over her face when it hit the ground.

The kidnapper stumbled and tried to pull back, but she had him now, and she tugged as hard as she could against the cuffs. She used all of her body weight to smash his fist against the hard surface of the concrete until he dropped it. The impacts ran heavy through her arms and shoulders, leaving aches that Laura ignored, adrenaline flashing through her and drowning out the pain.

She had the training, and she didn't need to think. Laura took advantage of his focus on freeing his right hand to flip him over, grab his left hand, and pull it across. The second cuff snapped into place behind his back, and Laura panted for breath, using her weight to keep his legs down while her arms pushed down on his to stop him from struggling.

She looked up at the car. It had seemed empty in her vision. Now, too.

"Where's the girl?" she asked, her voice as ragged and hoarse as her breaths. Arresting him, reading him his rights—that could wait. She needed to find the girl.

He was still trying to struggle against the cuffs and throw her off. Silently, Laura prayed that Nate had followed her, that he was coming over the hill even now to help her keep him restrained.

"The girl!" Laura shouted, the effort cracking her throat. "Where is she?"

The kidnapper looked at her sideways, his head twisted to one side and forced against the dirt. She could see the whites of his eyes, rolling with the effort of trying to get free. A sneer came over his face, an imitation of a grin. "It doesn't matter," he said. "She won't be alive much longer."

Laura felt her heart plummet like a stone.

Her vision had shown her the wrong thing. The girl wasn't here.

And Laura had no idea how to save her.

"Laura!"

She looked up to see Nate jogging toward her, breaking into a faster sprint as he took in the scene.

"Radio it in," she called out to him; it was unnecessary. He was already pulling the radio off his belt as he approached, his gun still drawn and pointed steadily at the kidnapper's head as he pressed the call button.

"Sir, we have the suspect," he reported, rattling off a quick description of their location. He turned briefly to wave until the figures down near the farmhouse waved in response, and Laura saw them bursting into motion. They were on their way to help.

"How did you know he was here?" Nate asked, putting both gun and radio away as he knelt beside her. He grabbed hold of the kidnapper's cuffed wrists, allowing her to get up and move away as she caught her breath.

"I saw the trail of dust," she lied breathlessly, gesturing off to the side. Now that she had stopped moving, she felt it: the blow of her body against the windshield, the jolts through her arms as she forced the club out of his hands, every point of contact she'd made against the ground each time she fell. Above it all, the headache, throbbing so violently she felt sick.

Nate looked at her sharply. "You okay?"

"Had a few knocks," Laura said, gulping in the fresh air as fast as her body would take it. Water. She needed water to hydrate herself, stop the headache getting worse. "I'm fine. Focus on him."

"Lavoie?" That was another agent, coming up the hill toward them and then jogging up the road.

"I've got him here," Lavoie said, nodding at Laura. "Agent Frost took him down. We should take him for questioning."

"Urgently," Laura cut in, seeing the special agent in charge coming into hearing range—along with the others who had been gathered around the farmhouse. "He said something about the girl—that she won't be alive much longer."

"Where is she, you scumbag? Huh?" Nate demanded, giving the man a shake, but he seemed to have gone off somewhere inside his own mind. He only wheezed slightly in response, his mouth hanging open and his eyes hooded. Nothing changed when Nate hauled him to his feet, handing him over to a pair of cops who quickly began the interrogation.

It all washed over Laura like the light breeze that was still making the wheat whisper below. She was finding it hard to think through the throb of her headache, the burn of the pain points all over her body. She felt tiredness come, tried to battle it. Something wasn't right. The girl.

"Hey." It was Nate again, standing in front of her, one arm hovering just beside her elbow as if ready to catch her. "You doing okay? Really?"

"I just—this isn't right," Laura said, looking up at him. He was something she could focus on against the too-bright sky, the loudness of the voices around her. "She's in danger."

Nate glanced behind him; as he twisted, Laura saw past him to the police car that had pulled up. The suspect was being pushed into the back seat, ready to be taken off. Questioned, probably for hours. The girl didn't have that kind of time. From what he'd said, the way he'd said it, Laura knew. He'd been serious. She was dying, right now, and Laura had no idea what that meant.

"Good work, Frost," their boss said, nodding at her as he got into the front seat. The car started. Laura didn't even have time to formulate a reply. They were gone. Around her and Nate, the other agents and police officers were heading back to the house or checking the car over. Wrapping things up.

"I need to see," she said, half to herself. Another vision. That was what she needed now. If she could somehow force it to come—but there was no way. She had never been able to trigger them exactly—she could only create the right circumstances and hope. They came unbidden and unasked for, like a bolt out of the blue. Laura saw the girl's face behind her eyes, but it was only a fake, the memory of the picture she'd seen in the briefing. If only she could have another vision, now, right now—

"See what?" Nate asked, ducking his head down to her level, shadowing over her with concern. "Laura?"

Laura made an effort to center herself, to think through the mud and jagged rocks at her temples. She was acting suspiciously. She needed to try to be normal.

"The farmhouse," Laura said, managing to make a connection at last. Yes. The farmhouse. Maybe if she went down there and walked around, it would trigger something. Right now, she was removed from the scene—done with it, maybe. She could easily get in a car with Nate and drive out of the area, and the scene would be dealt with by someone else. She wasn't involved enough.

She had to put herself right down there, in the middle of it. The kidnapper's lair. Maybe then it would come. She had to try.

"It's already been checked over," Nate said, reaching for her arm. "Boss wants us back at the precinct with everyone else. Come on. We've got to head out."

"No," Laura said, loud enough that Nate quickly turned, blocking her from the line of view of the other agents who were still around them.

"It's an order, Laura," he hissed under his breath. "He wants us to go debrief. Come on."

Laura had to ignore him. Even if it meant more explaining later. Even if it made him angry with her. She pushed past Nate and started down the road, even though she was bone-weary in all of her limbs. The vision followed by the chase and the fight had hit her harder than usual. But there wasn't any time to rest and recover right now. Not when the girl was in danger. Not when her life could be ticking away, minute by minute.

Nate caught up with her halfway down the hill. Laura walked down the road this time, taking the easier path, still walking as fast as she could. Frustratingly slow. She forced her body to move, to carry her there, keeping her gaze focused on the farmhouse ahead. Everyone had left in favor of checking out the car and the arrest. Someone would come back, keep the scene secure, search for evidence, but it would be too late.

Laura was the only one who could act now. She could feel it in her gut. If the kidnapper didn't talk, and she didn't think he would, then Laura was the girl's last hope.

"What are you hoping to see?" Nate asked, falling in with an easy lope beside her.

The road flattened out as they reached the bottom of the hill, heading on in a straight line for the farmhouse. "A clue," Laura told him, keeping it vague. She had never told him anything about her visions; she didn't expect him, or anyone, to understand. They had been partners for a few years, and she would trust him with literally anything else, but that wasn't the point.

The point was she needed him to trust her, and not to start thinking she'd lost her mind. He had always trusted her before, since their first assignment together when her hunches proved right. She only hoped he would do so again now.

She forced herself into a jog, almost at the door now.

"You think she's somewhere around here, is that it?" Nate asked.

"He was coming back here," Laura said, wrenching the door open and bounding through it, into the interior of the building. "There must have been a reason for that."

Heading inside the farmhouse was like having a candle pinched out. The bright sunshine of the outside world was gone, barely filtering in through cracks around the shuttered windows, places where the boards of the exterior walls had shifted and left gaps. Rays of light burst through the gloom like shards of glass, brilliantly illuminating the dust that hung in the air.

Laura's eyes adjusted to the gloom quickly as she glanced around, her head stabbing with pain every time she encountered one of the rays. From the front door, a set of stairs led upward, two doors led to the left and right, and one final door was ahead at the end of the hall.

"This place is about ready to fall down," Nate observed, following close behind her. "I'll take a look up there real quick. Maybe he kept her in one of the bedrooms, might find a clue up there."

Laura nodded distantly. "I'll check down here," she said, more out of habit than any real meaning.

She heard Nate's booted footsteps thud on every stair on his way up to the second floor. She closed her eyes to drown them out, trying to think. Nothing was happening. The only thing she could feel was the pain in her head from earlier, not the new pain she wanted to bring on. Wanted desperately. No matter what it would cost her, it could save the girl's life.

Laura reached for the nearest door and shuffled inside the room, closing the door behind her. She shut out the sounds of the outside, the bright light from the doorway, the fresh air. Everything. She took a deep breath of the musty-smelling atmosphere inside the room, closing her eyes and letting her senses take over. One, smell: the decay of a place that has been left abandoned for too long. The scent of the outside fields.

Laura reached out another sense, acknowledging it, then letting it envelop her. Listening. Not to the sounds in the distance, or even Nate's heavy footsteps above her head. The room itself. The settling of floorboards. The soft silence of a place out in the middle of nowhere. Laura breathed deep, then held her breath to listen for a beat.

She was building a cocoon around herself, a shell of sensory input. One that centered her in the moment, pushed her into deeper awareness of her surroundings. And with it, sometimes, the visions. If she could trigger it like this, she might still have a chance…

Laura wrenched her brain back from the possibilities, focusing again. Musty air. Almost-silent room. She reached out without opening her eyes, until her hand landed on the surface of the wall nearest to her. A hollow feeling. A thin wall. Dry, peeling wallpaper that threatened to crumble under her touch. A texture that spoke of repeated damp in the winters, drying out over the summers, over and over again. Years.

Laura breathed deep, listened, and felt—the stab of pain between her eyes—a short, sharp rush—

*The girl was gasping for breath. Laura was inside the space with her, a tiny space and so tight, hovering just inches away from the girl's face. She was streaked with both tears and dust, dry and yellow, caking her skin and hair. She took another rasping inhale now, ending on a shudder, a whimper.*

*She was so alone. Laura wanted to reach out, but she couldn't—she was only an observer here, devoid of form. Of corporeal touch. The girl's face was screwed up with fear and sadness and pain, pain in her little chest as she struggled to breathe, pain in her hands where she'd tried to scratch her way out…*

*Laura's eyes drifted to those hands. They were coated with dust, caked under the fingernails. Somewhere above them, Laura heard the sound of a man's voice. Nate's voice. Calling out Laura's name. It made her look up, and she saw the girl's face. The blonde hair streaked with dust, just like Lacey's hair. Blue eyes like Lacey's, bright and vivid in the darkness.*

*Her blue eyes were closing. Slowly, gently. The little chest was pumping up and down one last time, but there was no oxygen for it to take in. Her chest deflated like a slow balloon, and Laura hovered helplessly over her, and it did not rise again.*

Laura gasped out loud, her eyes flying open. She was dripping with sweat, and it felt as though a bucket of ice had been poured over her. The thudding pain in her head drove her to her knees as she cried out, then dizzily reached for the floor to push herself up again. The color of the dirt on the girl's face, under her fingernails. It matched the color of the dirt out there, around the house. But she wasn't outside. If she had been outside, they all would have seen the disturbed ground already.

The vision was prescient, but not always by much. And Nate had spoken in the vision—had said her name. That meant the girl wasn't far away.

And it meant she didn't have much time at all. Maybe thirty seconds. Maybe less.

The little girl was running out of air.

# CHAPTER THREE

The door beside her opened, and light from the hall poured in, momentarily blinding her. The stab of pain into her head at the light was almost too much to bear. "I heard you call out," Nate said, but Laura was already turning away from him.

"She's here," she said, leaning down, hurriedly moving forward with shaking hands and legs, looking for any sign of disturbance, any mark on the floor. There was a caved-in sofa, no mark in the dust beside it. It hadn't been moved. Neither had the armchair, the seat fallen in on a lopsided angle. Laura stumbled behind it, looking for a sign at the back of the room.

"What? Where?"

"I don't know—under the ground," Laura said, continuing her frantic search of the room. She kicked up the corner of a bedraggled old rug, and a clump of the fabric came apart from the whole. It was rotting. No way it had been moved any time recently. She felt sick to her stomach, the pain in her head was so bad. She had to keep going.

"Under the ground, like, buried?" Nate asked. He didn't ask her how she knew. He never did. That was the blessing of having Nathaniel Lavoie as a partner: he never asked. He just trusted her. Any other partner would have forced her to either confess or lie her way out of things by now. But Nate trusted her "gut instinct," and even as he asked the question, he, too, was turning to search the rest of the room.

"Buried in a—a box," Laura told him, turning frantically and racing for the door. There was nothing here. The living room was empty. Somewhere, somewhere in the house, she was there… Laura crossed the hall, almost tripping and then using the momentum to fall to her knees, tracing her hands over the floor in every direction as she moved.

"Like a coffin?" Nate raced after her, yelling as he took off for the door at the end of the hall. The kitchen, probably. The door Laura had chosen led to a dining room, at least judging by the table and the single chair, and one or two pieces of rotting wood that hinted at other pieces of furniture long since gone.

Laura's eyes traced patterns in the dust. Footsteps, all over the room. Maybe he'd taken the chairs elsewhere, or used them as firewood in the night. He'd been in here, a lot. Was that a disturbance in the dirt floor? Laura scrambled toward it. No—it was packed tight here, tight like the passage of time and many feet had done it. There was only a scuff where some old chair had been driven into the ground as it was broken up. God, why couldn't she think? Her head was throbbing—if she could just think—

"Hey? Do you hear me?"

Laura's back stiffened. Nate. He was waiting for her response. In a moment, if she didn't give him one, he would call out her name.

She stood and bolted for the kitchen, pure adrenaline and fear driving her legs forward, crashing toward where she'd heard his voice. This was it, she knew. This was the moment she had heard in the vision. It had to be. If they didn't get to her now—

Laura burst down the hall. Nate was standing by a group of rotting wooden cupboards down around a rusted oven, surrounded by discarded trash and bits of broken furniture. The second she saw it, she knew. There was a whole row of busted cupboard doors, and then one that just so happened to be intact, carefully closed while all the others hung off their hinges. Not only that, but the area around it was a little less dusty and cluttered, the door just a little more clean. Laura didn't have the time to examine it for other signs, but she knew they would be there.

She dove forward, falling to her knees on the floor. She slid a short distance closer to the intact cupboard, completely out of control. She yanked the door open as fast as she could, looking inside for exactly what she knew she would find. The dirt here was less tightly packed, a slightly different color. It had been disturbed recently.

"She's here!" Laura half-screamed, frantic, seizing hold of the first thing her hands fell on. A section of corrugated iron that looked like it had once been the roof of a chicken coop or something similar. The whole roof was lying in shattered pieces on the floor, close by the oven, but this piece was the right size to scoop dirt out of the way.

Laura set the piece of iron to the ground and dug a deep gouge through the earth, throwing a clump of soil behind her. Nate barely dodged out of the way with a grunt, then set to his own knees, tearing at the remaining corrugated sheet to fashion his own digging implement.

Laura scrambled to the side to let him in, shouldering her way in through the other broken cabinets and tearing a rotted wooden board out of the way. It came away soft in her hands, leaving another opening into the space where Nate had started to dig. She scooped another mound of earth from her new position inside the ruined cabinets, still seeing nothing below the dirt.

On his second frantic dig through the earth, the iron glanced off something that made a dull thunk.

"Laura!" he called, drawing her attention to the discovery—but it only made her blood go cold. That was the sound she had been waiting for. The sound that meant the girl's time was almost up. Even now, she was breathing her last struggling breath.

Laura cast aside the corrugated iron and began to work with her hands, scribbling at chunks of loose dirt and flinging it out of the way. The object in the earth was some kind of metal lid. Laura hoped and prayed there was no lock, invisible under the rest of the dirt. As Nate dug another shovelful that exposed even more of the metal object, she dug her fingers through the earth at its sides, scrambling for the edge. Finding it, she pulled with all her might, lifting both dirt and lid until there was a thin space beneath it.

Space for precious air to flow inside.

She heard a faint cough from inside and gasped with relief, struggling to lift the lid further. It was jammed under more earth at the far end, where they hadn't yet managed to clear it. Nate pushed more of the dirt out of the way, his thick arms bulging as he strained to lever the lid up.

It wasn't coming.

He swore out loud as his fingers unearthed a lock, attached to the far end of the metal box—the coffin, Laura's mind recognized with horror. This would be a coffin if they didn't get her free.

"Hold on," Laura said, hoping the girl would hear her. "Just hold on! We're getting you out!" Her fingers were aching from the strain of holding up the lid, the sharp metal edge biting into her skin. Laura didn't care. She would endure the pain for as long as it took. She wasn't going to let the girl's only source of air disappear.

Nate pulled his gun out of the holster at his hip and used all of his strength to bring the grip down against the lock, yelling with effort as he did it. Reverberations shuddered through the metal, making Laura bite down on her own lip against the pain in her hands. She tasted blood. The lock budged, just slightly. It was probably the only thing in the kitchen that wasn't falling apart with rust. Nate hit it again, another scream of effort ripping out of his throat.

The lock came away. Laura wasted no time. She pushed upward firmly, using all of her strength to lift the lid on the box.

As it opened in front of her, Laura could finally see the girl. She was lying there on her back, just like in Laura's vision. She was dirty and dusty, crying and gasping for air. Laura swallowed back a sob herself. Nate took the strain of the lid as she reached down, spreading out her arms to either side, enveloping the girl in an embrace as she lifted her out of the metal box and into her arms.

"You're okay now," Laura said, cradling the girl against her chest as she half-tumbled out of the cabinets and back into the more open space of the kitchen. "It's okay now. You're safe. You're safe." She panted for breath even as the girl did, screwing her eyes tight shut while the kid couldn't see her face. Tears streaked down across her cheeks, relief and horror and the delayed force of the pain in her head. Above them, she heard Nate taking out his radio, standing a few steps away to bark out the news to the rest of the team and request an ambulance.

And it should have been a happy moment. A moment in which Laura felt she had won. She had saved the girl's life, right as she was on the brink of losing it. She had used her vision to stop a death. The death of a little girl, just like her own daughter.

But that wasn't what she felt. Instead of the growing relief and joy she had felt when she first saw the girl, something else took over. As Laura cradled her to her chest, she felt the encroaching chill of something dark. Something that she couldn't name, but she could feel it running icy fingers down her spine. The girl—there was something wrong with the girl. There was something wrong with her future. The darkness wasn't over.

Laura could feel it as real as if the entire room had been plunged into darkness. There was more night to come.

But, exhausted as she was, there was no vision. Only the feeling of a chill running through every one of her bones, plunging her into icy water. It was a…darkness around this girl.

Laura had no idea what that meant. She was safe now, for today. She could see that clearly.

But not for long. Somehow, inexplicably, a darkness was still before her.

The girl was still in danger.

## CHAPTER FOUR

Laura hugged her arms across her chest, tapping the empty polystyrene cup against her upper arm. Instead of the hospital's sickly overhead lighting and the faint smell of antiseptic, all she could think about was the feeling of darkness that had rolled over her when she'd held Amy. The fear that even now was still making her heart race.

"You want another coffee?" Nate asked, making her look around. Laura hadn't even realized he was there. There was still a little dust in his dark coiled hair, buzzed neatly across the top of his forehead.

"Probably best not to," Laura said, giving him a wry look. She was already wired, energy thrumming under her skin. It didn't sit well against the bone-weary exhaustion she otherwise felt, or the headache still pounding away so strongly in her temple she couldn't see straight.

"I would agree," Nate laughed. Laura couldn't find it in herself to laugh back.

The hall of the ward behind them was buzzing with activity, as was the small waiting area just a few steps away. Other feds were milling around, both the personnel from the scene and those who had been brought in to assist after the fact. They were all waiting for news, and for the call to leave. This investigation was just about wrapped up; they wouldn't all be needed to stay and interrogate the kidnapper or search the grounds of the farmhouse. The local cops could handle that.

"She's going to be all right, you know," Nate said.

Laura looked at him. "What?"

"Amy. You saved her life," Nate said, nodding his head forward at the window they were standing in front of. The blinds were drawn across it. Behind it, they both knew, the girl was being checked over by the doctor.

"Yeah," Laura said, trying to sound convincing. "I know."

She hadn't been able to shake the chill that had fallen over her at the farmhouse. She knew that something was wrong, but until she had a clear vision that actually told her something, she didn't know what to do. What could she do? There was no clue in her mind as to the nature of the darkness that awaited the little girl.

Perhaps there was a medical emergency about to happen. Something untreated, undetected, that would risk her life. If so, there was nothing Laura could do that the doctors wouldn't be able to. Or maybe the kidnappers had planned a raid on the hospital, if there was more than one accomplice, and she was about to be put in jeopardy once again. Maybe they were going to target her father, the governor, directly this time, and Amy would be caught in the crossfire. But there was not much Laura could do about that either, since she didn't know what quarter it would come from or if that threat was even real.

Or maybe it was something else entirely, something she couldn't even think of, and that was where the problem lay. When her visions—or in this case, feelings—were so vague, she had no direction to go in.

Only continual frustration, and the horrible feeling that something bad was going to happen that she couldn't stop.

And that was even if she was right. She had been so exhausted, so stressed out. The fear over this little girl's life, just like her own Lacey's, had been so strong. What if it had only been her own worry and fear creating a sensation that wasn't really there? That would explain everything, and allow her to at last relax. But she couldn't relax. Not while there was any chance that the girl was not out of harm's way.

She needed to get close to Amy again—to see her and touch her. That was the only way she could get another vision to trigger, the only way she could hope for more details.

"Agent Frost!" the familiar voice called from behind her, prompting Laura to turn away from the blank window. "And Agent Lavoie. Congratulations, both of you."

"Thank you, sir." Laura dipped her head in acknowledgment of the special agent in charge's words. He wasn't a man she had worked with before; multiple agents had been pulled in from the field for this urgent case, and she didn't know most of them. He was balding and had obviously begun to put on weight since being promoted to a less fieldwork-oriented position.

"How did you do it?" he asked, leaning in conspiratorially close even as he kept his voice raised. Laura caught a whiff of stale cigarette smoke wafting from his tailored black suit. "Did he give you a little hint before we took him away?"

"No," Laura said, then cast her eyes down to the pale beige tiles of the hospital floor. "He just said the girl was going to die before we got to her. We thought it best to check the farmhouse out, and we found her by chance."

"Hmm," their boss said, looking them both over with a too-wide smile. His teeth were yellow and brown, stained from years of smoking. "That's good. Because keeping evidence to yourself just so you can get the glory of the case—well, that's the kind of thing I don't like to see at all."

Laura looked up sharply. "No, sir," she agreed. "Neither do I."

Although, she thought, it wasn't as though she had a leg to stand on. Sure, she hadn't been given a clue by the kidnapper and kept that to herself. But she had been given a pretty big clue by the universe, or whatever it was that controlled her visions. And that, she certainly hadn't shared with anyone.

He must have seen the doubt in her face, the small tinge of guilt. His faced twisted just a little, until his smile was no longer a smile but a sneer. Then he turned and swept over to the others, congratulating them on the finished case.

The door to Amy's room opened, and Laura turned with her heart leaping into her mouth. Her skull also lurched with the movement, but she ignored it in favor of concentrating hard on the figures leaving the room for news.

"Thank you, Doctor," the man in the gray suit was saying. He looked frazzled, his white shirt crumpled and creased, his hair disheveled. Laura couldn't judge him for that. He was the governor, and it was his daughter who had been missing for the last three days.

"Don't mention it. Just don't tire her out too much today. If she gets enough rest, we'll be able to let her come home tomorrow," an older man in a white coat said, nodding politely to everyone before hastening on his way to see another patient.

Laura read the signs, her eyes tracking urgently from face to face. The mother's eyes were red from crying, but she was sniffling now and the sides of her mouth were turned up just fractionally. The governor seemed tired, yes, but relieved. As if they were through the worst of it.

Amy was going to be okay.

Laura felt her shoulders ratchet down a level, the tension and apprehension flooding out of them just slightly. She was out of the woods. Although there was still the question of that dark cloud, at least she was safe right now.

"You're the man who found her, isn't that right?" the governor was saying, pointing at Nate.

"Oh—well, it was myself and my partner, Agent Frost," Nate replied, pasting his customer-friendly smile on his face as he turned to gesture toward Laura. A smile he only dragged out when having to deal with important people connected to cases. She wished he wasn't using it right now, and especially not turning it toward her. "Actually, she did all of the work. I was just backup, really."

"Oh, thank you," the governor's wife said, her voice halfway to a sob again, as she stepped forward. She clutched Laura's hand between her own, despite the fact that one of them was also holding a decidedly damp handkerchief. "Thank you for saving our baby."

Laura flashed a weak smile up at the woman and her husband. It was the most she could manage with the threat of danger still hanging over Amy, and the opportunity to talk to her again so close but so far. "Just doing our jobs."

"And some," the governor replied, giving her a look with raised eyebrows. He was the kind of man who always seemed more than slightly impressed with his own words. "You gave us our daughter back, Agent Frost. I'm going to keep my eye out for you, and that's a promise. There's a promotion coming your way."

Laura nodded gratefully, though she didn't believe a word of it. People always made big, slick promises when they were in that first flush of relief. Everything would be back to normal soon enough. "Thank you, sir."

The governor nodded and made to step past her, but Laura saw her chance and couldn't miss it. Hardly knowing what she was about to say, she turned after him and raised a hand, preventing the couple from moving past her. "Actually," she said, "I was wondering if it would be all right for me to talk with Amy."

"Why's that?" the governor asked, the slight beginning of a frown poised to overtake his amiable expression.

"Just to make sure we understand everything," Laura said. She was mostly making it up as she went along. Someone would be assigned to talk to Amy, yes—but not her. It would be an agent who was trained in dealing with children, who knew how to speak to them and tiptoe around trauma. "It won't be too much for her. I want to make sure she's all right, and we haven't missed any injuries, or anything like that." She kicked herself inwardly for not having come up with a better excuse, but it was the only thing she had been able to think of. She was going to have to run with it now.

"Isn't that the doctor's job?" the governor asked, but then the storm cloud that had been threatening his face cleared. "You know what, let's go ahead. I'd rather be sure our little girl is all right."

Laura held up another hand to stop him from moving forward. She knew she was risking a lot—the governor had enough power to directly impact her career, as he'd just pointed out—but she needed to see if another vision would come. "It's important I speak with Amy alone," she said. "If that's all right."

The governor hesitated, glancing at his wife. After a moment, he shrugged. "Sure," he said. "Whatever it takes."

# CHAPTER FIVE

Laura nodded and turned to walk into Amy's room, ignoring the fact that Nate was watching her with an obvious question in his eyes. She could explain to him later. Tell him how she just wanted to make sure the girl really was okay, how she felt responsible. He would accept it. Laura knew he wouldn't question her then, and he wouldn't stop her now.

She felt a painful squeeze in her chest at the sight of the small five-year-old body in the middle of the hospital bed, cleaned up and dressed in pajamas now. She was bandaged up and tiny, and her large blue eyes were sleepy as she watched Laura come into the room.

Laura took a breath before moving forward, needing to center herself. She'd recovered somewhat from her double visions, if not entirely. The coffee had helped. She just hoped it would be enough to allow her to trigger a new one—to let in the warning that little Amy so clearly needed.

"Hey there, Amy," Laura said, keeping her voice low and soft. She made herself smile, so the girl would be reassured and not afraid. "How are you doing?"

"You're the lady who got me," Amy said, her head moving on the stack of pillows she was in danger of being dwarfed by.

"Yes, I am," Laura said. She sat down in the chair by the bed. "I just wanted to check that you're all right."

"Yeah," the girl said, pushing herself upright in bed, her halo of blonde hair tumbling down her back. "I was so happy when I saw you!"

"You were?" Laura asked, smiling. Amy reached out, and Laura obliged her by taking her hand, moving to sit on the edge of the bed so she could reach. She was so small. Just like Lacey. Laura blinked back unexpected tears at the thought of her daughter. Something about Amy's hand in hers brought a wrench to her heart. Maybe it was because she'd been so afraid for her, because she'd fought so hard to save her life. They had a bond now that was new and strange, and Amy's immediate and natural affection only made it seem all the more real.

"Yeah. I was really scared, and then you came and said it would be all right." Amy leaned forward a little, shuffling to the edge of the bed. "And now I saw my mom and dad again! And the bad man's gone. And the other man said you made the bad man go away."

Laura could only smile. She could see that the girl was a born chatterbox. But the vision she had been waiting for wasn't manifesting, not even at the touch of her hand. "I did," she said. "You don't have to be afraid of the bad man anymore."

*I think*, she added mentally. Because she really couldn't be sure. Not when the vision stubbornly refused to come.

Laura tried to figure out how she could force it. There was nothing now. Not even that hovering darkness. Maybe she really had just made it all up, born out of a frantic mind. It had felt very real at the time. It had felt like a vision that couldn't get through. But maybe she was wrong.

"I thought I was going to go away like Grandma did," Amy said, her voice quiet and low. "Until I saw you."

Laura bit her lip, her heart breaking all over again. "Your grandma went away? Where'd she go, to heaven?"

"Yeah." Amy paused, looking down at the sheets of the bed. "It didn't feel like I was going to go to heaven. It felt bad. It hurt. And I was really scared about going away."

Laura squeezed her hand silently. There wasn't much else she could say. Her heart ached that Amy would know that kind of feeling. That she had come face to face with her own mortality at such a young age.

"But then you came," Amy said, looking up and into her face. "I knew I was going to go away. I knew it. But you stopped that from happening. You changed it even though I knew."

"That's what I'm here for," Laura said, putting on a brave face for her. "To make sure that doesn't have to happen to you." Inside, she was mulling over those words. Thinking about destiny, even though Amy was too young to know a word like that. That was what she was talking about. The ability to change destiny. Was that what Laura was doing?

"You're like a superhero," Amy said earnestly. "Do you take care of bad men all the time?"

"Yes, I do," Laura smiled, patting Amy's hand. She thought about sitting in bed with Lacey at nighttime, reading her a story. That kid always had more questions than Laura had answers.

Laura pushed aside the thoughts of her daughter and the pain that came with them with impatience. Sitting here, trying to force a premonition… this was useless. There was no point in trying any longer. She had done what she had to make the optimal conditions for a vision. She'd rested a short while, taken painkillers for the very worst of the headache, caffeinated herself. She'd cleared the room to keep all those people from clouding the vision, causing confusion and interference. But nothing had happened.

"There are lots of people just like me. You see this badge?" she said, wanting to at least put Amy's mind at ease before she left.

Amy peered forward at the FBI letters stitched into the front of Laura's jacket. "Yeah?"

"That means I'm from the FBI. It's our job to make sure little girls like you are safe," Laura said. "So, if you ever see the bad man again, or you ever get scared, you can ask your mommy to call the FBI or the police, and someone will come help you. And if you're on your own, you just dial nine-one-one. Got that?"

"Yeah, I knew that before," Amy said, sounding a little uninterested in the process. "But you're special. You're my guardian angel. Mom said I had one but I didn't know what you looked like before."

Laura laughed. She pulled away from Amy's hand, sensing that she no longer needed quite so much comfort. "I don't know about that. But I'm happy that you're okay now."

"Will you come visit me again?" Amy asked, propping herself up on one hand and tilting her head to one side. Her hair swung down over her shoulder, her eyes getting even bigger and wider. "Pleeeeease?"

Laura couldn't help but laugh again. The girl was cute, and Laura had a feeling she was used to getting her own way already. Who could say no to big eyes like that? The thought sent a twinge of regret through her, of pain about her own daughter. She hadn't see Lacey's big eyes for so long. "Well, that's up to your mom and dad," Laura said. "They might not want me to visit."

"I'll ask them," Amy said seriously. Someone had propped a small, fluffy rabbit toy on the bedside table. Amy reached over and picked it up, swinging it by its floppy ears. "I need my guardian angel to look after me. And you can come back and see all of my toys."

Laura's smile was wan this time, her eyes following the rabbit so that she didn't have to answer right away. It was a nice thought, but it wasn't reality. How could it be? Laura wasn't anyone's guardian angel. She wasn't good with kids. She'd failed as a mom, failed completely. She didn't even know what her daughter liked to eat anymore. Lacey was growing so fast, and Laura wasn't there. She'd allowed Lacey's father to get the upper hand, to tear her away from Laura.

No, she wasn't likely to be allowed to see Amy again. There was no reason for her to. As much as Laura had found her heart touched by Amy, she was an FBI agent. She had no connection to Amy's family.

Then again, Laura had no doubt that the governor would give Amy whatever she wanted. And given that he had promised to oversee Laura's career progression, it was possible, just slightly, that their paths would cross again. Maybe they would end up getting to know each other. And if she dared to admit it to herself, Laura hoped they would. Amy was a sweet little girl, and Laura wanted to look out for her if she wasn't going to be able to look out for Lacey.

"I should let you get some rest," Laura said. She'd done what she needed to do. She was convinced, now, that there was no darkness hanging over Amy. It had all just been a hangover, a bad feeling born from the double whammy of the two visions slamming into her brain. The child was going to be all right.

"Wait," Amy said, arresting Laura's motion as she made to stand up. "I want a hug!"

Laura paused. Well, that was to be expected, probably. She'd held Amy close when she pulled her out of the box, after all. It was the only way children really knew to show affection. She gave Amy a warm smile and shuffled to the edge of her chair, keeping herself at the right height for Amy to throw her arms around her neck.

And that was when she felt it. A sharp pulse of pain behind her eyes, like an electric shock. Laura drew in a sharp breath, her arms tightening around Amy's tiny form—

*Amy was lying against the pillows in her bed, surrounded by stuffed animals. It was early in the morning, and she was playing with her toys as daylight filtered through the curtains. Laura could only just make out the scene.*

*There was some kind of noise out in the hall, beyond the room. Shouting. Crashing. An angry voice cursing, rising and slicing sharply through the air. The governor. Laura knew his voice, even if she couldn't turn the vision around and look at his face. The edges of the scene were completely out of focus. She couldn't sharpen it, no matter how she tried. She was still tired.*

*Amy looked up at the sound and hugged her stuffed bunny closer. Laura found herself turning now, slowly, as the sound continued. Turning and moving until she was behind Amy, looking over her head.*

*The door to the bedroom was closed—but then it burst open with a loud clatter, slamming back against the opposite wall.*

*"No, let her alone, it's not her fault!" A woman, the woman Laura recognized as Amy's mother, said. She was frantic, pale, hurrying after her husband.*

*The governor filled the doorway like a wall of rage, his face red and twisted, his hands swinging in fists. "She drew on the papers—and she needs to learn!" he yelled, spit flying from his mouth. Amy cowered back from him. "She needs to be punished!"*

*He was brandishing something in his hand. Pieces of paper crumpled now in his fist. A child's drawing of a distorted pony in purple pen on the front of one of them. That was all Laura made out before the governor cast them to the ground, stomping toward Amy with furious movements.*

*"No, please," his wife begged, rushing forward and taking hold of his elbow, trying to pull him back. "Don't—"*

*Her voice was cut off as the governor slammed his elbow sharply back into her chest, throwing her off and making her stumble into the door before dropping to the floor. She clutched at her chest, and Amy cried out, afraid for her mother.*

*"Now, it's time for you to learn your lesson about messing with important things," the governor said darkly, starting to undo his belt and pull it off his waist, pulling it between his hands until it formed a kind of club.*

# CHAPTER SIX

Laura shuddered with shock as she came back to herself, the pain in her head turned all the way back up. But that wasn't the thing that was making her feel sick to her stomach. That wasn't why she wanted to keep hold of Amy and walk right out of the hospital and never look back.

"Are you okay, miss angel lady?" Amy asked, trying to pull away from her. Laura realized she was holding on tight and let go, allowing her to rock back onto the bed.

"Yes," Laura said, attempting to smile brightly. Inside, she could barely keep it up. She just wanted to cry. She couldn't tell this girl what was waiting for her at home. She couldn't tell the doctors. What was she supposed to do to stop this from happening? "Yes, Amy, I'm fine. I'll come and visit you soon, okay?"

"Yeah!" Amy cheered, but even as she sat back against the pillows, Laura could see that she was halfway to falling asleep. "We're going to have a tea party, and the best time, and you can meet my doll."

"I will, honey," Laura said, turning to go, because she couldn't keep up the smile any longer.

She only had a few steps between the bed and the door. Only the time it took for her to open it before she had to put the mask back on again. She couldn't explain to anyone what she had just seen. Couldn't tell them how she knew that Amy would be abused. If she told them about the vision, she'd be laughed out of the room—even more so, given the governor's power.

Laura walked the few steps toward the door, losing control over her face. Inside her chest, her heart was breaking. She could barely stand to walk away. But she had to.

As her hand rested on the door handle, Laura made a promise to herself. She would visit the governor at his home, as early as next week. As soon as she could. It was the only way she could live with walking out of that hospital and leaving Amy behind.

Laura opened the door and stepped outside, smiling up at Nate and the governor's wife, studiously avoiding the eyes of the man she knew now to be a monster.

"Everything all right?" the governor asked, his tone sounding falsely bright.

"What?" Laura asked, then remembered her ruse. "Oh, yes. Everything's fine." It made her want to bite out her own tongue to say those words, but she had to play it safe. She'd been here so many times before—knowing something that she couldn't possibly know. She couldn't accuse him yet. There was no evidence. If there had been signs of long-lasting physical abuse on Amy's body, the doctors would already have seen them.

This was new behavior. Something that would start soon. And until it did, there was no way she could stop it. Child Protective Services wouldn't take Amy away before the abuse happened. Laura's mind raced for a way to get the child out of that environment, but she could think of nothing.

"Are you sure?" the governor asked, making Laura look up sharply in spite of herself.

He was studying her closely, she realized. She must not have been controlling her voice, or her face, as well as she thought.

"Quite sure," she said, then forced herself to take a deep breath and put on an even bigger fake smile. "Thank you, Governor. I hope you're able to bring Amy home as soon as possible."

"No, thank you," he said, with a slight narrow angle to his eyes that told her he still wasn't convinced she was telling the truth. With his arm on his wife's lower back, he turned back to go inside, leaving Laura to clench her fists in the corridor and use all of her willpower to avoid running after him and tearing Amy out of his arms.

She would do it—but first, she had to figure out how.

***

Laura stared at the empty wine glass on her kitchen counter, trying to find the strength in herself to put it away.

If she didn't put it away, it was going to sit there waiting to be filled. And if she kept looking at it, wishing it was filled, she would go out. She would walk or drive to a store somewhere outside of the radius of those she had asked not to serve her. She would pick up a bottle—maybe three bottles—and bring it home, and she would fill the glass.

And she would drain it. And she would fill it again. And she wouldn't stop until she was so drunk she missed a few days of work and a few days of memories, and she knew deep inside it still wouldn't be enough to stop herself from remembering what she'd seen in that hospital.

Laura let out a long, low sigh, then forced herself to get up right when she'd exhaled every last gasp from her lungs. She drew in another hasty breath as she snatched the wine glass up and shoved it back into the cupboard it came from, so hard it almost smashed. She slammed the door closed and leaned on the kitchen counter for a long moment before turning to walk out into the hall.

Laura headed for her cramped, ramshackle living room, needing to be as far away from the kitchen as her small apartment would allow. The apartment was always supposed to have been temporary; Laura couldn't bring herself to upgrade it to something more careful, because that would have meant admitting defeat.

Besides, getting a decent apartment on a single wage in this city wasn't easy. Not even for an FBI agent. Given the way the alcoholism had ravaged through her savings, Laura counted herself lucky to have been able to scrape together the deposit for this place, furnished with cast-offs and donations as it was.

She glanced out the window, taking in the skyline, thinking of all those people out there. All of them managing to have a single drink and then stop. They were crowding in bars and restaurants now, she knew, somewhere out there in the DC evening. She envied them. She wished she could be one of them.

Laura reached into her pocket and pulled out the forty-five-day chip she had received almost two weeks ago. One and a half weeks, to be precise. Just a few more days, and she would be back at the sixty-day mark of her sobriety. Visions like these, like the abuse of Amy at the hands of her own father, always threatened to drag her back under. To drown her. Especially when she couldn't do anything about them. So many times she had beaten her demons, or thought she had, only to fall back into old habits.

She was trying not to let them. Not this time.

There had been a time, a couple of years ago, when something like this would have sent her into a destructive spiral without end. She would have drunk herself into a stupor for weeks on the back of this, maybe even months. Even half a year ago, she might have fallen off the wagon with such speed and violence that it would have shocked even herself. But now, things were better. She was getting better.

At least, forty-five days' worth of better.

Laura still wasn't perfect. She knew that. But this case was so close to her own heart. When she looked at Amy, what she was really seeing was Lacey. And more than anything, she wanted to be with her daughter.

Spurred on by that thought, Laura opened up her laptop and tapped out her password, opening it up to a full-screen image that she used as her background. Herself with Lacey, when Lacey was about three years old. She was so tiny then. Laura remembered that day, when they'd gone to the beach to show Lacey the sea for the first time. They'd had ice creams and built a sandcastle, and laughed. And then Laura had snuck away to get herself a drink, and Marcus had caught her, and they'd had a screaming match that ended with a silent and sullen drive back home.

Laura opened up her browser and logged into Facebook, typing "Marcus Amargo" into the search bar. He came up as the first result, and she clicked on his profile, ready to send him a message.

It wasn't as though she hadn't sent him hundreds of messages before, but that didn't mean she was going to give up. She could just tell him that she was almost at sixty days again. She knew he'd said so many times he wouldn't let her so much as see Lacey from a distance until she got to the ninety-day mark, but maybe he would soften up when he saw that she was trying.

Laura frowned at the screen. Where was the message button? Actually, where was half of Marcus's profile? She couldn't see anything. Not even recent posts or pictures. She'd been hoping he had posted something about Lacey recently.

She clicked around, her heart rate steadily speeding up as she search for anything she could grasp onto. *No.* No, this couldn't be happening. This couldn't be true. He'd…

He'd blocked her.

Laura stood up, throwing her hands to her head, spinning in a circle as she panicked, her breathing coming short and fast. Marcus had blocked her. How was she supposed to talk to him now? How was she supposed to get Lacey back?

She knew she was never going to be granted full custody of Lacey after all of the problems she'd had. Her alcoholism was a matter of court record, and she had to accept that. But she'd hoped that at least visitation might be possible one day—that she might at least be able to see her!

Tears welled up behind her eyes and streamed down her cheeks as Laura buried her face in her hands. *No*. She was so close. A few more weeks, and she would be there. She would reach the goal that Marcus had set after he'd taken custody of Lacey.

Behind her eyelids, the last time she'd seen her daughter replayed in Laura's mind. The way Lacey had looked so confused, so upset at her mother's tears. The way Marcus had lifted her and carried her away, their daughter looking back over his shoulder. That had been the last time she'd been allowed to speak to her daughter.

The last memory that Lacey had of her was of a woman streaked with mascara and tears, crying great sobs that brought her to her knees, her hair a mess, her clothes stained with vomit, an empty vodka bottle still in her hand.

Laura couldn't let it be that way. She had to fix it. She reached for her phone, intending to call Marcus right away, but she paused and then put it down again. No. If she contacted him some other way, it would only prompt him to block her there, too. She needed to be smart about this. She needed to stay strong. If she proved herself, Marcus might come around. And if he didn't, the court system would.

Marcus didn't understand any of this. He didn't know about her visions; she'd never found the courage to tell him. And when she'd had the vision of him breaking it off with her and taking their daughter away, she'd only been able to drink herself to unconsciousness to block it out. That hadn't stopped it from becoming reality.

She had never been able to give him an excuse for her behavior. He didn't know the burdens she was carrying. The only thing she could do was prove to him that she was fighting them—and that would only be achieved by bringing him that ninety-day chip.

Laura needed to distract herself with something else, stay busy. Prevent the devil from getting to her idle hands.

She sat down on the uncomfortable, lumpy sofa and opened up her laptop again, lifting it from the coffee table. She fired up the tabs she'd last opened in her browser, trying to get her head back into the game.

She needed to do something about Amy. Lacey was out of her reach just now, and that hurt like hell, but there was nothing she could do except wait. She might be able to help Amy today. If she could, she was going to have to.

Laura brought up a search on the governor, looking for as much information on him as she could find. He'd been in various political offices for a few years, rising through the ranks. There were plenty of news stories about him, even some vague whiffs of scandal involving a previous secretary of his. But nothing about violence or abuse, no hint of an out-of-control temper.

Laura tucked her blonde hair back behind her ears, trying to think. She worried her long, slim fingers together, twisting and turning them. If she didn't figure this out, Amy was in for a horrific existence. She needed to do something.

Impulsively, she picked up the phone even though it was late in the evening. Those who worked for the FBI quickly got used to never really being off duty. That was part of the job. The tech department was no different.

"Yeah?"

Laura half-smiled to herself, in spite of the seriousness of the situation. Dean Marsters always answered the phone in the same way. "It's me. Just wanted to pick your brain on something, if you're not busy?"

"For Christ's sake, Frost, it's nearly midnight." Dean paused, then sighed. "Yeah, I'm not busy. What do you need?"

"I'm looking into someone," Laura said, trying to keep it sounding as casual as possible. Maybe she would be able to slide the bombshell of the person in question's identity under the radar. "I wanted to know if there's any dirt on him."

"Dirt?" Dean sighed. "Okay. What scumbag are we dealing with this time?"

"His name's John Fallow," she said, inwardly bracing. "I'm a little concerned about his behavior behind closed doors."

"John Fal—wait. *Governor* John Fallow?" Dean repeated, almost blasting her ear off. "You must be kidding. Frost, this is *so* far above my pay grade!"

"Please?" Laura asked. "Look, the safety of a little girl might be at stake, okay? And, you know—I have my sources, but I need something that will stand up in a court of law."

"I know, I know," Dean replied, sighing heavily down the line again. "You should tell your sources to bring you real, legal evidence instead of having to come to me for it all the time."

"I do tell them," Laura lied. "It's just not always possible." It was a convenient cover story. Dean believed she had some kind of underground network of informants. He never talked to Nate, and she never told Nate who her contact in the tech department was either, and everything worked smoothly. She was able to follow up on her visions from time to time without alerting anyone that she knew things she shouldn't. This one, she knew, was a big risk. There was no source that would have been able to tell her what she'd seen; the family was alone in her vision. But she had to take the risk. Amy needed her.

"All right, leave it with me," Dean agreed. Even though he always sounded grudging, like he was doing her a huge favor—which he was, considering he was putting himself on the line for her—he always came through in the end. "I'll get back to you as soon as I have something."

"Thank you," Laura said. "I owe you a coffee at lunch tomorrow."

"You owe me a coffee *and* a muffin," Dean corrected, before ending the call.

Laura closed her eyes for a moment, leaning her head back on the sofa cushions. She'd set the wheels in motion for Amy. She'd tried, and failed, to contact Marcus, and she knew what she had to do now. Still, she wasn't calm enough for sleep. She felt everything still buzzing around in her head, all the fears and worries and the desperate impulse that told her she needed to *do something*. Maybe going back to her usual search would help to quiet her brain for a while.

The search was something that Laura had been undertaking for a long time now. It had come hand in hand with AA; realizing that she needed to fix herself, needed to get herself back on the straight and narrow. In order to do that, she first had to understand what was going on in her head. What the reasons were behind her slip-ups. Or so they said, at the meetings.

Lauren knew what was behind her slipping up. Every single relapse could be traced back to a particular vision, or to the repercussions of one of her previous slip-ups that was caused by a vision. She knew what it was that she had to deal with.

What she didn't know, what she had never known, was where the visions came from. Why they happened to her and not to anyone else. How she could trigger them, how she could make them more effective. She had learned a few tricks over time—like isolating herself from others, or making sure she was well rested and fed, and putting herself into physical contact with people who could be at the center of them. She had also learned, mostly through trial and error, that the visions only told her about futures that she was personally involved in. She knew, too, that she could affect their outcome—that she could stop the futures she saw from happening.

The only way that she could think of to get to the bottom of all of this was to find someone else who had also been through the same thing. A support group. A mentor. Someone who could give her the answers she so badly needed.

That was why she spent most of her spare time searching online and looking into other people who claimed to be psychic. People who worked as clairvoyants, or claimed to have a big lead that could help a police investigation. Almost all of the time, what she found was someone who was desperate for fame and money, not someone with a real gift like she had. Or curse, as she preferred to think of it.

Every now and then, there was someone who didn't quite fit the pattern. They would be content with working a small-town job, doing psychic readings for a few customers a week. Making hardly any money from it. But even in those cases, Laura had invariably found that the reason behind their perceived reticence was that they just wanted to help a few people. Or they just wanted a little pocket money. Whatever it was, it was never the real thing. It was just cold reading, a whole bunch of fakes deceiving people over and over again.

Laura stared hopelessly at the forum she had found, featuring a thread where people discussed what they thought might have been psychic dreams. It wasn't even a real lead, as far as leads went. Even if she thought any of these people really were psychic like her, she would have to spend hours, if not days, tracking down IP addresses and trying to figure out who they really were. There were ways to figure it all out, but she wasn't in the tech department of the FBI. This kind of thing took her a long time.

And for what? She wasn't going to get anywhere with this. She sighed with frustration, slamming the lid of her laptop closed. A glass of wine looked really good right about now.

And yet. With a growl of frustration, Laura wrenched the lid open again, looking at the results that still had not cleared away from her screen. She had to do this. Even if she knew it was hopeless, she had to keep digging. Keep looking. For the sake of her daughter, particularly tonight but also for the long run, she had to keep searching.

The only other option was to lose herself completely at the bottom of the glass, and Laura didn't want to let that happen again anytime soon. She searched Governor Fallow's name instead, looking for the address for the governor's mansion. As soon as she got the chance, even if Dean didn't find anything, she would go to the governor's house and ring the bell, try to check up on Amy in person. Tomorrow, if she could sneak out of the office early.

She wasn't going to let Amy fall by the wayside. She wasn't going to let her down, the way she had with Lacey.

Laura was going to stop this—and no one was getting in her way, not even the governor of the state.

# CHAPTER SEVEN

Carrie put her key to the door and slipped, fumbling it. She muttered a quick curse under her breath as she fought her tired fingers to grasp the key again and make it into the lock, almost falling through the door as it opened.

She sighed, pulling off her coat and dumping it on the peg by the entrance as she kicked off her shoes. She had the vague feeling she should put them away, but then again, it could wait until the morning. She just wanted to eat something and get into bed. Anything else could wait, and she didn't particularly care what it was. After the shift she'd had, she couldn't imagine anything less than fire or flood that could convince her to put her shoes back on or care about a little mess.

Carrie charged through to the kitchenette and grabbed something down from one of the cupboards. As she did so, she hit her elbow on the side of the fridge, like she had done a million times before.

"Goddamn Albany rent!" she cursed, because that was the cause of the bruised elbow. If she had been able to afford a nicer place, at a lower rent, she wouldn't have been stuck in this tiny little place with its too-close cupboards and its utter lack of space.

She managed to get the packet of mac and cheese down without further incident and shoved it into the microwave. She jabbed the few buttons on the front that still worked until she managed to get something approximating the right time, and set it going, leaning back against the counter with her head in her hands.

Mentally, she was calculating how much time she had left. Just a couple of minutes of microwaving time, then maybe ten or fifteen minutes to eat it with her phone in her hand, looking over social media. Another ten minutes to get changed for bed and brush her teeth, and she could be asleep. But no, wait—she had an early shift in the morning, so she would be better off showering right now to save time. So, another fifteen minutes on top of that. Then she could fall into bed, at last.

A ringing noise rose above the sound of the microwave beside her, making Cassie lift her head. Her eyes instinctively darted to the cell phone sitting on the counter beside her, but it wasn't that. This was a different tone. It was the landline; it had come with the apartment, but she'd never really had cause to use it. No one even had the number, apart from her sister. It was probably either a crank call or a scam.

Carrie let it ring out, ignoring it. There was no point in answering it, and she couldn't suffer any fools with how exhausted she was. They would be getting a real piece of her mind, so she was doing them a favor by not answering. She waited for the microwave to finish, then pulled the hot plastic tray out and dropped it on the counter, wincing and moving fast to avoid burning her fingers.

The phone went silent, and Carrie sighed as she fished for a fork out of her cutlery drawer. Blessed peace. Now she could just eat this as quick as possible, get a quick lukewarm shower, and climb into her lumpy single bed and shut the rest of the world out.

She was lifting the tray over to the table when the phone rang out again, almost making her drop the whole thing.

"Dammit!" she shouted, dumping the tray onto the table and rubbing her forehead. If she'd lost her dinner as well as everything else today, she would have probably lost her mind on top of it. She tried to stay cool for a single second, then gave up and marched through to the hall and the ringing phone.

She wrenched it off the wall and put it to her ear. "Hello?" she demanded, half-shouting already.

"Hello." It was a male voice, unexpectedly calm. "Am I speaking to Carrie Adeline Birchtree?"

Carrie resisted the urge to confirm right away, even though the guy knew who she was. Even her middle name. That wasn't necessarily a good thing. Debt collection agencies would be able to get hold of her full name, right?

"Who's calling?" she asked. It was late, too. Why would a debt collection agency be calling this late?

"Miss Birchtree, I'm with the IRS," he said, his voice low and controlled. "I need to confirm a few details of your latest tax return with you. It seems you may have overpaid your taxes."

Carrie hesitated. No, this wasn't right. It was probably a scam. Debt collectors didn't need to tell the truth, did they? They could straight-up lie to get you to tell you who you were. She didn't yet want to confirm who she was. But then again, if she was going to get a bigger tax refund…

"Do you know what time it is?" she asked, putting off the decision until later. "It's a ridiculous time of night. What are you doing calling people at this time?"

"Ma'am, we tried calling you earlier and your phone wasn't answered," he said. "That's why it's been left to me on the late shift."

Carrie hesitated. A late shift. That made sense. There were probably enough people who needed calling about this kind of thing. Why wouldn't they have a call center working around the clock? She couldn't hear anyone behind him—but then, maybe it was quieter there at night. She wandered back through to the kitchen, the cord on the phone stretching behind her as she stirred her mac and cheese to cool it down.

"Well, please call back again tomorrow," she said. "I'll be able to answer in the early afternoon after I get off work."

"Before I confirm that, can you just confirm for me that you are Carrie Adeline Birchtree?" he asked. "If you're not, there's no point in scheduling a call back."

Carrie chewed the fingernail on her right thumb for a moment, thinking it over. Wasn't it obvious already that she was who he was asking for? If she wasn't, she would have said no and put the phone down. She'd as good as confirmed it already, at least as far as it mattered if someone was trying to track her down. So maybe it was the tax thing. Maybe she could get a little extra money in the bank. It wasn't long now until winter. She could do with a little extra cash, something to keep the heating on longer during the weekends when she was home.

"Yes," she said, at length. "That's me. Look, just call back tomorrow, okay? I'm about to go to bed."

"I can't do that, Carrie."

Carrie froze, her thumbnail halfway back to her mouth. His voice had changed, she could swear it. It was deeper now. Less polite. Like a mask had been taken off. "Why not?" she asked, cursing mentally. She shouldn't have told him her name. This was it, wasn't it? He was going to tell her how much she owed and how much she'd better have ready in the morning, or they'd take everything. Not that it mattered. She didn't have anything worth taking.

"Because I'm right outside your door."

Carrie's head sharply jerked toward the door. No. He couldn't be. Had she heard that right?

"What?" she asked, praying for him to repeat it so she could hear how she'd gotten it wrong.

Instead, a series of beeps rang out from the handset, signaling that the call had been ended.

Carrie pulled the phone away from her head and stared at it, hoping it would give her some kind of answer. There was nothing. She rested it down on the kitchen counter for a moment, trying to think. What was going on here? Some kind of prank?

Maybe she'd misheard him. Maybe he said "I *can* do that," and then just confirmed it and ended the call. How could she have messed those words up? Was that possible? No, she played the words back in her head and they still sounded the same.

He'd said he was outside.

Carrie sprang into action, grabbing a knife from the kitchen and then lunging toward the front door and checking the lock. It was intact, and when she looked through the peephole, she didn't see a thing. She swallowed hard and pulled lightly at the chain, making sure it was properly engaged. No one would be coming through that door unless she opened it.

Carrie made a conscious effort to breathe, realizing she had been holding it to try and listen. There wasn't a sound out there. No one else was around. She was on her own. Wasn't she?

She lifted up a shaking hand to the door and set her eye to the peephole again, straining to make anything out in the dark corridor. The light that should have been opposite her door had blown a bulb weeks ago, and the landlord had made no move to replace it. Carrie swallowed again on her dry throat, pressing close against the door as she strained to see.

Through the pressure of the wood against her fingertips, she could feel her own heartbeat, rapid and wild.

Carrie turned, putting her back against the door for a moment. There wasn't any other way in, was there…?

The windows?

She rushed through the apartment, checking them one by one. Bedroom, kitchen, bathroom. All of them were locked, and the blinds and curtains were closed. She didn't want to open them and look out, in case of what she might see.

Carrie hesitated, glancing around her small space. Despite the fact that she had checked everything, she still felt unsure. The call had sent shivers down her spine, and the longer she thought about it, the more they increased. How had he known her name? If it was just a prank call, she might have accepted that he knew her surname, even her first name. But her middle name? He didn't get that from the phone book.

Come to think of it, she wasn't even in the phone book. Did people still use phone books these days?

Carrie put her cell phone down on the bed for a moment, reaching up to double-check the bedroom window frame, pushing at the handle to reassure herself that it wouldn't give easily. It stayed solid, and she stepped back with a little relief. No one was getting in here.

She returned to the kitchen with a determined stride, trying to feel more confident than she really did. Her dinner was still sitting on the counter. She needed to eat, to shower, to get ready for bed. All of this nonsense about the prank call—it was just nonsense. Just a prank. She couldn't let it derail her whole evening.

She almost managed to convince herself that she believed it. Carrie set down the knife and picked up her mac and cheese, moving it to the other side of the table where she preferred to eat. But her hands shook so badly as she set it down, she nearly spilled some of the creamy cheese sauce over the edge of the tray.

A soft sound outside had her on alert again, her body going stiff. It was only a second later that she heard the smash of broken glass, a symphony of tinkling as it fell to the ground in the bedroom.

In the bedroom. Where she'd left her cell phone.

A strangled cry caught in Carrie's throat as she lunged for the landline, still sitting on the counter where she had put it down. She dialed with fingers that were thick with fear and shaking, her own breath coming out in sobs as she hit the wrong digit and had to clear the number to start again. *He was inside the house.* Then she pressed the phone to her ear, breathing raggedly.

"Nine-one-one, what's your emergency?"

"There's—there's someone in my house!" Carrie wailed, all too aware that saying those words would alert him to where she was. "Please—you have to send—"

"Ma'am, are you able to get out of the house? Ma'am?"

The operator was talking to herself. Carrie was staring forward, frozen, the phone clutched in her hand still but falling away from her ear. He was there, right in front of her, tall and menacing. She had no idea who he was. But he was looking at her in that way, dark eyes boring into her from under a sweep of dark hair, and she knew, just *knew*, he wasn't there for anything good.

He wasn't even wearing a mask. Wasn't he worried about her identifying him to the police, if he wasn't wearing a mask?

Carrie's heart stuttered in her chest as she realized he didn't intend for her to be alive to tell them.

"Ma'am, please stay on the line. We'll be sending someone out to you as soon as possible. Are you there, ma'am? Can you tell me any more details?"

The voice faded out as Carrie lowered the phone, her whole body shaking and her breath coming out in whimpers as she stared at him. He was moving slowly toward her, inch by inch. Her body felt frozen. She managed to back up just a couple of steps, but then her spine hit the fridge, and she was trapped.

She didn't say anything and neither did he. They faced each other silently, him ever advancing, her frozen and shaking and unable to do a thing. Her mind was almost blank with fear and she couldn't force herself to move. It was as if she was a butterfly trapped to a piece of card with a pin.

She thought he would continue moving slowly forward forever, but then he lunged, clearing the space between them so quickly she barely had a moment to react. She screamed, just once, but she couldn't move fast enough to stop him. He wrenched the phone from her grip, and she thought he would hang it up. But even as she flailed to get it back, he made a quick move of his arm, flicking the cord around her neck. The ice in her veins turned to acid as she felt the wire against her skin, lying over her windpipe.

She made to dash forward, to go past him through the tiny space between his arm and the counter, a futile but desperate attempt. He stepped aside and she dashed free, just for a moment—before the cord caught her and pulled her back, coughing already, a tight line branded into her neck where the cable lay.

Carrie's hands flew up and scrabbled at the cord, but somehow, now, it was too tight to move. She couldn't get her fingers underneath it. Something was behind her, supporting her—a body—his warm body, pressing against her back and using her body weight against her. She couldn't breathe. She couldn't get a single gasp of air. She fought against the cord madly, her fingers scoring lines in her own flesh, glancing off the cord every time and never budging it a millimeter. She kicked the floor, feeling him pull her away from it, the weight on her neck only increasing as she was lifted up into the air.

Carrie thought she heard something, someone asking her an urgent question. She couldn't process it. She tried to scream, but the air wouldn't come into her lungs. All she could do was make a desperate gurgle, kicking out with her legs and trying to catch onto the cabinets. She only hurt her shins and knees. In front of her she could see the kitchen, the tiny space with its rickety table and the lone tray of mac and cheese, still waiting for her. She was so tired. There were blank dots dancing in her vision, more of them every moment.

Her fingers fell slack on the cord, then down at her sides. Carrie tried to breathe in one last time, but failed to find any air. The black dots multiplied, covering everything, and the last thing she knew before her final spasm left her body was black.

# CHAPTER EIGHT

"Ah, there she is!" Nate exclaimed, as Laura walked into the bullpen inside the J. Edgar Hoover Building. It was crowded with desks and agents, most of them occupied with their own calls and computer screens. A few of them looked up and grinned at her, and a couple even clapped a few times, which only increased her sense of anxiety. She just wanted to get in and get her paperwork done, and avoid any awkward questions about how she'd found the girl.

"Here I am," Laura replied, without any of his cheer. She tucked her hair behind her ears, hoping Nate would lower his voice. She hated being watched, being the center of attention.

"A coffee for the Bureau's finest child rescuer," Nate said, handing her a cup bearing the logo of a local chain. Not, thankfully, the office's own machine. If he had tried to give her that, she would have thrown it down the sink.

"Thanks," she said, taking it from him and taking a sip immediately to hide her face. It was only divine providence that it wasn't burning hot. She swallowed the bitter liquid quickly, gesturing behind Nate toward their respective desks. She hoped he would take the hint.

Nate turned and led her across the room between desks stacked high with haphazard paperwork, waving a goodbye to the agent he'd been engaged in conversation with closer to the door. "So, good night's sleep?"

"Perfect," Laura replied. Truth be told, she'd slept the sleep of the dead. Yes, she had Amy's fate playing on her mind—but that wasn't enough to keep her up. Not after the exhaustion of three visions, a dead run across a field and up a hill, a physical fight with the kidnapper, and then digging Amy out of the box. It had taken all of her power to stay awake for long enough to get home and into bed. She'd woken up with a start, though, immediately filled with anxiety that someone was going to know.

It was always like this after a successful case. The fear that someone would question her methods. That they would ask a question she couldn't answer.

"Great. You might need it." Nate flashed her a grin as he reached their adjacent desks near the back of the cramped, busy room and lifted up a manila folder. "Paperwork."

Laura groaned. "What is this? Payback from the boss? Extra filing?"

"Maybe," Nate said, and laughed. "No, it's just the standard stuff. I already started mine. Report on the events of the day, the forms to assess whether we've been through any trauma that might make us a liability, et cetera, et cetera. You know the drill. Might take us the rest of the morning, but it's boring enough."

"What a relief," Laura sighed, putting her purse down beside the desk and her coffee cup on it. The hum of conversation in the room was already almost overwhelming, and she had no doubt it would be worse as the day drew on. The bullpen was chaotic, the space too small for so many agents in the square, uniform building of their headquarters. "If there's one thing I love about paperwork, it's when it's boring."

Nate laughed. "Here," he said, handing a sheaf of loose papers from inside the folder to her. Their fingers brushed as she took it, and just for a moment, she felt a chill rising from the point where their skin was in contact.

Laura froze.

She'd felt that same chill with just one person before. It wasn't quite a whole vision, not yet. It was something more distant than that. An early warning.

It was the shadow of death.

Laura couldn't find a way to describe it, the way she might explain it to another person. It wasn't a color. It wasn't a sound. It wasn't something she could see, but then, it wasn't a feeling either. It was somehow physical and yet intangible.

The first time she saw it, it was hovering over her dad.

"You okay there?" Nate asked, regarding her with a puzzled frown.

"Yeah," Laura said, quickly sitting and placing the papers on her desk. "Clearly, I haven't had enough coffee yet. Which my thoughtful partner has already seen fit to solve, so thanks again for that."

Nate chuckled as he took his own seat, grabbing up a pen and going back to work.

Laura pretended to sip at her coffee and study the first page, but really she was looking over the top of her lid at Nate. She was trying to think, trying to quell the rising panic that was threatening to choke off her throat. She had never sensed death around him before. She'd had visions where he was present, yes—but in the course of a crime that they were both investigating. Never on a personal level. She'd never sensed that he was even in danger.

It was hard to imagine him ever being in danger, as well-built and tall as he was. He was sitting in his shirt sleeves now, one big hand cradling the pen as he looked down at the form he was working on.

There was no way he could be in danger. No way. And yet…

Laura swallowed a gulp of coffee past the lump in her throat and looked down, focusing her eyes on the paper. Some of it she could fill in by automatic habit, not needing to think. Her name, her ID, the date. That left her mind free to reel, to try to cope with what she'd just felt.

When she saw that shadow of death over her dad, it had been long before his diagnosis. Maybe before he'd even been sick—she had no way of knowing. But she'd felt that sick kind of resonance in the air around him whenever they touched. It had gotten so she shied away from him, shutting herself up in her room so she didn't have to see it.

Then she had touched him one day and seen him lying in a bed hooked up to a drip on a cancer ward, and she'd known.

She'd been so terrified of what she'd seen that she'd never said a word. How could she? She couldn't tell her parents that she'd had a vision of her father dying from cancer. Not after all the therapy they'd made her go through to stop her "hallucinations."

But now she was faced with the same problem. Something was going to happen to Nate, and it was going to kill her, too, because how could it not? They had been partners for so long, and he was the only person she really trusted. The only person who really seemed to trust her. The only one she could rely on. She needed him. More than that, she *wanted* him to be around. He was strong, capable, reassuring. The one constant that never changed.

And he was going to die. Maybe not right away. But sooner or later, he was going to die, and she was going to know how. Unless she avoided touching him for the entire rest of their career together, which seemed unlikely.

So, could she keep it from him? Right up until the moment he died?

Or would she be able to intervene?

Laura drained the rest of her coffee in one go and set about attacking the rest of the paperwork. She couldn't deal with this right now. She had things to do. Responsibilities. If she didn't get this done, people were going to ask why. She could digest this later, when she was back at home on her own. She could grieve for him then, and figure out what she was going to do. Not now. Not in the middle of the office.

"Hey, heroes!" That was Jones, a short and squat agent with dark hair, walking by them to reach his desk at the very back of the room. "Come down from cloud nine yet?"

"This paperwork brought me down to earth like an anvil," Nate joked, turning to look over his shoulder as Jones passed through.

"That was good work, though," Jones said, raising his coffee to his lips and sipping before lifting it in Laura's direction. His heavy brows jumped up and down at the same time. "You too, Frost. Pretty glad you were there, to be honest. I couldn't stand the thought of that kid dying out there in that box."

"Oh, you've got a son around that age, haven't you?" Nate said. "Yeah, that must have been tough. It was bad enough for me to think about it, and I don't have kids."

"Believe me, whole world changes when you've got 'em," Jones said, shaking his head, one hand on his hip. "Ain't that right, Laura?"

Laura stiffened even more than she already was. "Sure," she said, her tone flat and brittle.

"Jones," Nate hissed, making a flapping motion at him.

"Oh, sorry," Jones said, wincing as he sat down. He wasn't the most socially adept agent in the room, even when he was the only one in the room. "I didn't mean anything by it."

Laura sighed. There was so much on her shoulders. It felt like the weight of the whole world. Her daughter. The governor and what he was going to do to Amy. And now Nate. At least she didn't have another case to work on just yet. A little break might help her to get her mind around a few things.

The phone on Nate's desk burst into life, emitting a shrill ring before he snatched up the receiver. "Agent Lavoie," he said, his expression going serious as he listened.

Laura watched him with concern. The call he was on right now—was that what led to the end of his life?

Every little thing, she realized. She was going to be analyzing every little thing now. Every sign that something might not be right. Every call was going to make her jump out of her skin. Every case would be a potential danger. She didn't want to lose Nate. He was a good partner. A good friend.

Well, as good a friend as someone could be when you only saw each other on the job. She'd never been to his home, and he'd never visited her apartment. They didn't meet elsewhere for coffee. They didn't gossip about their family lives, at least beyond the greater sketch of the need-to-know. They didn't share feelings.

But, after three years of working together, he was still the closest friend she had. And what did that say about her life?

Either way, he was a good person. One of the best. The thought of him no longer being in the world made her feel sick.

"That was the chief," Nate said, pointing a finger up to heaven. To the floors above them, where senior agents had their offices. "Wants to see us in the sky."

Laura nodded, tossing her empty coffee cup into the trash as she stood. "He say what it's about?"

"Time off for our efforts?" Nate said, and grinned as he shook his head. "No idea. But I'd bet he has a job for us."

"Great," Laura said, following him through the bullpen and out into the hall beyond again, trying not to sound as irritated as she felt. She couldn't deal with something else right now, not on top of all the rest. And it wasn't as though she could tell them why she needed time out. She'd hoped for a lull, for paperwork and maybe some mandated counseling that she could space out for.

The muscles of Nate's back moved visibly under his shirt as he led the way. Normally, Laura found it reassuring to walk in his shadow. He was a powerhouse; people stepped out of his way. They didn't mess with him unless they had a death wish. In his wake, Laura was also protected. She didn't have to shout to be heard or ask people to step aside. They just listened.

But now she looked at his back and felt nothing but a sickening apprehension. What she felt was only a harbinger of a potential future, she knew. It wasn't the whole story. There might be things she could do to stave it off for him. But until she had the vision that explained everything, she wouldn't know.

And even then, it might still happen anyway.

They took the elevator up to the chief's floor, and in the brief interlude of whirring machinery and tinned music, Laura flinched back against the wall. She didn't want Nate to accidentally touch her. Not now she knew how it would feel.

She knew if she didn't get over it, he would notice. He was an FBI agent. He wasn't known for being oblivious to the details. Even with their casual relationship, he would notice if she couldn't bear to have him hand her anything or step too close.

The doors slid open to welcome relief. Nate gestured forward and allowed her to step out of the elevator first, and Laura found herself walking fast along the hall to keep out of his range of touch.

"You in a hurry?" he asked, sounding amused from behind her.

"I just want to get the bad news out of the way," Laura shot over her shoulder. "We've had less than a day. If he's sending us somewhere, I'm guessing it must be bad."

"It's always bad," Nate said. "That's why they call in the FBI."

"Right," Laura sighed.

"Talking of," Nate said, his tone carefully conversational, "how, uh… how did you know about the girl? I mean, everyone's been asking, and I don't really have an answer for them."

"Just tell them it was luck," Laura said. "Luck, and thoroughness. No one else stopped to go back and check the house again, did they? Consistency and hard work. That's what solves cases."

"That much is true," Nate agreed, easily enough. Laura felt another jolt of gratitude for the way he always took her at face value; another jolt of grief that he wasn't going to be around forever.

Nate's long stride caught up with her right before the chief's door, but Laura paused for a moment before going in. She straightened her jacket and her shirt collar before reaching out to knock, making sure to give three forceful raps. No more, no less.

At the sound of a call from behind the door, Laura opened it and stepped through, leaving Nate to follow in her wake. She was being too obvious, she thought. She needed to tone it down. Try to relax. Try to act like she hadn't just found out he was going to die.

"Sir," Laura said, at almost the exact same time that Nate said it too.

"Agents." Division Chief Chuck Rondelle looked up at them from behind his desk, which always looked a little too big for him. The chief was in his late fifties, small and wiry, and for every dark hair he had left on his head he had another two gray. "I heard good things about your assistance with the kidnapping yesterday."

"We did our jobs, sir," Nate said, his voice loud in the small space. Rondelle was known for valuing a humble nature in his agents. As a result, even the most braggartly wouldn't go up before him and swell out their chests. Not if they wanted a promotion at any point in their career.

“Yes. Well, nice work.” Rondelle picked up a folder in front of him and gestured toward them with it. “We’ve got a new case. I need you two on it right away.”

“Where are we headed, sir?” Laura asked, feeling her heart plummet into her stomach. It wasn’t as though she hadn’t been expecting it. Still, it was disheartening to hear. She’d hoped for a couple of nights to rest, at least. Some time to decompress, and, more importantly, to do something about Amy.

“Upstate New York—Albany,” Rondelle said. “We’ve got two victims in as many nights. Looks like the same guy.”

“What’s the methodology?” Laura asked, stepping forward to take the folder. Rondelle gave her a hard look as she did so. He was sharply inquisitive, and she diverted her gaze down at the paper so he wouldn’t have the chance to read too deeply within her eyes. He might ask questions about her mental well-being, and she didn’t want that.

Rondelle shook his head as she stepped back. “I’m putting you on a plane within a few hours,” he said. “All the information you need is in the brief. You’ve got about enough time to get your things together and get to the airport, so you’d best get moving.”

Nate made a face beside her. “But Chief, we’ve only just got back from the kidnapping case. We need time to rest, debrief—”

“No,” Rondelle said, holding up a strict finger. “We need you two on this one. You were the only ones who could make headway on that Texas co-ed spree, and this has a similar feel to it already. I’m not wasting time like we did then, letting more people die because we don’t have our best on the job. It’s you two, and it’s now. Go on, get.”

“Yes, sir,” Nate said, hanging his head but smiling, in that way he had that always got him out of trouble. Even Rondelle seemed to let the comment go.

“Don’t miss your plane, Agents,” he said instead, as they turned to file out the door. “I mean it. Lives are literally hanging in the balance.”

Laura waited until the door was closed firmly behind them and they were halfway to the elevator before she said anything. There were two satellites orbiting her head, and neither of them would stop. She had to do something.

Amy, or Nate. She could stay here for Amy. Or she could go, and try to save Nate.

She could only take one of those right now.

Her heart broke for the little girl. She couldn’t bear to make the decision. And yet…

"You should stay," Laura said, trying to keep her tone casual. "Get some time off. I can take Jones, maybe. I'll talk to Rondelle."

"What?" Nate looked at her sideways as he pressed the elevator call button. The doors swished open immediately. "You don't want me with you for some reason?"

"Of course I want my partner with me," Laura said, and sighed as they stepped inside. "But we have so much paperwork to do. If this is like Texas, then I know what I'm doing. I can get it finished nice and quick. And Jones was there, too. Rondelle won't mind. You do the paperwork and get some time at home. You've got someone waiting for you."

Nate barked a short laugh. "No, I don't," he said. "She moved out. Six months ago."

Laura felt the pain of that cutting through her chest like a knife. Nate reached out and patted her shoulder, making her flinch; the wave of coldness came over her again, but no vision. She relaxed only when he let go.

"It's all right," he said, evidently reacting to the stricken look on her face. "I don't have any need to stay. Actually, I'm looking forward to getting stuck right in again. But *I* can take Jones, if you want to stay."

"No," Laura said immediately, so fast he looked at her with a squint to his eyes. "No, it's… fine. I don't have much to stay for either. Not without visitation rights with Lacey."

Sickness squirmed in her stomach as the elevator dropped. She couldn't let him go alone. Whatever shadow was hanging over him, if it happened because she stayed behind, she would never forgive herself.

She needed to stay at his side—and figure out what was going to kill him before it had a chance to take hold.

# CHAPTER NINE

Laura flipped her tray down as soon as the plane had finished ascending, grabbing the case briefing out of her carry-on bag. "Ready to hear about the case?" she asked.

"What have we got?" Nate asked, settling back in his chair. His broad shoulders filled the seat easily, which made it uncomfortably difficult for Laura to avoid an accidental brush against him. Several times during the check-in and boarding they'd gotten close enough to trigger that shadow of death again, sending a shiver of ice down her back every time. They had only just left the ground, and her nerves were already frazzled.

At least the shadow didn't bring headaches with it. That was one small blessing.

It had been a frantic couple of hours to get home, grab her overnight bag, get to the airport, meet Nate, and get through check-in. All that time, she had been itching to get at the notes and find out what they were up against.

"So, the first victim was killed two nights ago," Laura said, lifting the first sheet of paper to read it out loud. Nate preferred it when she read to him, rather than the two of them having to trade pages to get through it all separately. "Laura Carlisle. She lived in an apartment in Albany, with one female roommate. The roommate came back from working a late shift to find Laura dead in her bedroom. She had been strangled with a scarf."

"Laura." Nate grunted. "That's going to get confusing."

"Not unless you intend to refer to the ligature marks around my neck," Laura said, concentrating on the pages. "Next up we have Caroline Birchtree, murdered last night in her apartment. She lived alone, and there was a fairly obvious point of entry—a smashed bedroom window."

"What floor?" Nate asked.

Laura checked the notes. "Second floor," she said. "But by a fire escape."

"All right. Strangled?"

"Yes, this time with a phone cord. So it looks as though whoever this is, he's using items within the home—not bringing his own weapons with him."

"That we know of," Nate said, lifting a finger. "Let's not make any assumptions this early."

"Right, right." Laura sighed, flicking back and forth between the two pages as she compared the women. "I can't see any obvious link. Local PD say they haven't yet found a connection between them either."

"So it's a random opportunity killer," Nate said heavily, rocking his head back against the seat. "Great. My favorite. Always so easy to solve."

"Let's not make any assumptions this early," Laura teased him. "Might be something that ties them together yet. We don't have the full picture. Besides, they're both in the same area, so that's one connection already."

"Same block?" Nate asked hopefully, raising an eyebrow.

Laura studied the two maps that had been provided, grayscale printouts showing the pinned locations of the two crime scenes. "No," she said. "They're both in Albany, though."

"That'll narrow it down." Nate shook his head. "So, why are they struggling with this one so much?"

"Looks like the killer is meticulous," Laura replied, scanning the last page of the report. "There's no witnesses as of yet, although local appeals are still ongoing. They think he goes in at night when no one else can see. Probably wears gloves—there's no preliminary indication of any forensics evidence. He's using things from within the home, which speaks both to a lack of a planning and yet very clear forethought. He doesn't want to leave a trace behind."

"Still seems quick for them to call us in. Was this their shout, or are we unwelcome?"

Laura tapped the page which had their landing instructions. "It says here we'll be met by the sheriff himself, if that tells you anything."

"It tells me they're freaking out about this. Great. Well, at least we're not going to be given the cold shoulder when we ask for assistance." Nate closed his eyes, his head still tilted back. "I wish this was a longer flight. I could do with a nap."

"Then have one," Laura suggested. "They call it a power nap when it's short, right? Maybe you'll wake up more powerful."

"You're saying I'm not powerful enough?" Nate asked, flexing his muscles with a grin.

Any other time, Laura thought, she would have patted him on the arm and said something condescending. She drew back from touching him again. "You're not funny when you're tired," she said instead, looking out her window dismissively.

She probably would have been satisfied to sit there, staring right out her window and not seeing a thing, if Nate hadn't spoken again.

"Hey, you know, I've been thinking about that little girl," he said. "Amy."

There was something wrong with his voice. It was just a little too casual. Like he'd been thinking about what to say and how to say it.

"Oh yeah?" Laura asked, looking back around. She reached for the in-flight magazine for something to keep her hands and face busy. Not that there was ever anything interesting in these things.

"You knew exactly where to look for her, didn't you?" Nate said, his head still tilted back. His hands were resting on his own legs. Very still. As if he was making a study out of not moving.

"I just guessed," Laura said, shaking her head. Fear tasted bitter in her mouth. It was a familiar feeling by now, but still an unwelcome one. The thought that someone would guess—and the fact that it was someone close enough to really blow up her life—only made it worse. Silently, she begged him to just trust her like he always did. "If I'd have known exactly where she was, there's no way I would have left her for that long. I'd have gone right to her, believe me."

"No, I get that," Nate said. "It's just, you knew she was underground. You said that to me."

Laura shrugged. "Did I? It was just a feeling. I thought I saw dirt on his hands and the knees of his jeans when he was walking over to me. I thought he looked like he'd been digging."

"That's it?" Nate asked. "The special agent in charge thought you'd gotten some kind of tip from him. Like he'd told you a clue before everyone else caught up."

Laura glanced up at him sharply. "You know I wouldn't hold that back," she said. "I don't want glory."

"Right, no, I know," Nate said slowly.

Laura cursed herself internally. She should have owned up to it. Told him that, yes, she'd heard something the kidnapper said. Hadn't been able to interpret it right away, but on reflection, she'd realized he was talking about the girl. If she had passed it off like that, there wouldn't have been any further questions. At least, not any that she couldn't answer.

"It's just," Nate continued, clearly not letting it go, "I mean, we've worked together—what? Three years now?"

"A little over that," Laura conceded.

"And you're always lucky. I mean, I don't know if it's luck, or you just got a real strong intuition, or what." Nate hesitated. From the corner of her eye, Laura caught him turning his face slightly toward her. His sharply chiseled black goatee framed a mouth that was hesitant, a straight line that kept opening and closing without a word. "It's just—that was some kind of luck. I mean, impossible, really."

Laura shrugged again. "I don't know. Call it divine inspiration. Whatever it was, we got seriously lucky. Part of that probably has something to do with the fact we were the only damn agents who thought to give the house a second look, like I said."

"They would have gotten to it," Nate said fairly.

"She would have been dead."

At those words, they both drifted into silence.

"Well," Nate said, finally. "If that's all it was."

"It was," Laura confirmed, flicking to a new page in the magazine even though she hadn't read a word on the previous one. She felt tension rising up the back of her neck. If he asked again, she wasn't sure she had anything to convince him. What would she say?

Wouldn't it be so much easier just to tell him? Just to let it all out? Like the relief that came with no longer resisting a drink: just stop fighting, let it pour down your throat and ease everything away. Wouldn't it be better if she just stopped fighting?

But it wouldn't end there. She'd have to tell him everything. Her father. His death. Nate's own death, hanging over him like a shroud even now. And she didn't want to tell him that—not when she hadn't even come to terms with it herself.

If he pushed again, she didn't know what she could possibly say to make him stop.

But after that, Nate tucked his head back against the seat again and settled more comfortably, falling into a light sleep. Laura was free to sit in silence and stop pretending to be interested in other things, relief washing over her. She stared out the foggy window, seeing the scratches on the glass more than the view beyond it.

The relief was short-lived. She could only think of one thing: Nate was going to die. She couldn't stop thinking it, over and over again. He was going to die.

She could only hope that whatever they were about to walk into wouldn't be the thing to trigger it.

# CHAPTER TEN

Laura spotted the sheriff easily: a tall, older man in a tan uniform, awkwardly holding a sign with FROST/LAVOIE printed on it in block capitals. He stood out from the crowd, both because of his appearance and because of the way he was nervously checking his watch—like he couldn't spare a single moment more before they got started on the case.

"I'm glad you folks are here," he said, walking them toward the exit after the necessary introductions. He swept his formal uniform cap off his head to reveal a bushy crop of gray hair. He'd called himself Sheriff Lonsdale—no first name. Of course, he'd already known both of theirs. "We're a little on edge, as you might imagine. Seems a high possibility that we'll see another one tonight. We're much in need of the help."

"We'll do whatever we can," Nate assured him, keeping up easily with his long strides as the sheriff rushed them out to the parking lot. Still feeling a little dazed and distracted, Laura forced herself to walk faster to catch up with them.

"You've had two bodies in two nights, is that right?" Laura asked. It was always good to check the information provided in the briefing. Everything could have already changed while they were in the air.

"That's right." The sheriff gestured to a parking space not far away, where a black vehicle marked with a gold flash and the word "SHERIFF" across the side waited.

"Then let's try and prevent another from happening," Laura said grimly. "I don't think we should waste any time, given that it's getting to be late in the afternoon already. Can we head straight to the latest crime scene?"

"Absolutely," the sheriff said, unlocking the car and opening the trunk. "We can put your bags in here; I'll have someone come and take them to a motel for you."

Laura climbed into the back while Nate joined the sheriff in the front. It was less a comment on who was superior to who, and more about space; Nate being a good seven inches taller than her meant he needed the leg room. She didn't begrudge him it, either. It was better to stay back and avoid the worst of the small talk.

"Have there been any developments in the last couple of hours?" Nate asked, as the sheriff put the car into gear and backed out of the lot.

"Nothing special," the sheriff said, sighing. "We've been doing our best. Still waiting on forensics reports for the second victim, but the first one came back. Preliminary, at least."

"Any evidence we can work with?"

"Not yet." From her position in the backseat, Laura could see the sheriff's mouth reflected in the rearview mirror; when he wasn't speaking, it settled into a thin, hard line. "They'll run further tests, but we're not seeing anything usable. No fingerprints other than the victim's and her roommate's. No unidentified hair follicles or bits of fabric or skin under the fingernails—nothing we'd want to see in a case like this."

"Like this?" Laura asked, her ears perking up. Understanding how the police on the ground were seeing the case was essential. Not only would it possibly help inform their own impression of it, but there was also the factor of internal bias. If they'd decided already the case was going one way, Laura and Nate needed to make sure that it was the right decision. Otherwise, they could all end up blind to other facts that didn't support their working theory.

"Strangers," the sheriff said, glancing at her in the mirror. Laura caught a glimpse of his eyes as he moved his head. They were flintlike, gray, just like the straggling remains of hair on his head. "As far as we can see, there's no link between the two women. So our working theory is this was done by strangers."

Laura made a mental note of that, but said nothing. It had been the same conclusion they'd drawn on the plane, but that didn't mean it was true. After all, there were countless ways that people could interact—particularly in this internet age. The two women might have commented on the same thread on a forum and the killer was in there too. It could be as tenuous as that. Really, properly checking for connections wasn't a simple job that could be completed in less than twenty-four hours.

Right now, it was looking *likely* that the murders were committed by a stranger. That didn't make it definite.

The cruiser wound down wide streets that looked as though they could have been almost anywhere in the US. Standard block formations, trees at intersections, Starbucks and McDonald's and mom-and-pop stores that were few and far between. The buildings were tall and stately, solid rectangles that had been around for long enough to witness boom and bust over and over. City life was going on all around them as they drove. People walking to and from work, kids coming home from school, moms with strollers running errands.

It always struck Laura how removed they were from normal life. How odd it was that normal life was bustling around these crime scenes, which always had a kind of pallor over them. Like there was one tiny point in the world where time had stopped, and everything was slow and somber, but the rest was unaffected.

When you spent years interacting with others only at these places, these other worlds, you started to forget what it was like to go back to reality. Adding in her visions, Laura hadn't felt like she was anywhere close to touching normal for a long time. The drink had been the only thing that helped with that.

Until it had robbed her of everything else she'd still had, and left her only with that isolated feeling, that morbid existence of lurching from murder scene to murder scene.

"This is it," Sheriff Lonsdale said, snapping Laura's attention to the windows on the other side of the car. They were coming up on a small apartment block, a converted home with three stories and a small porch. It looked boxed in, next to two much larger blocks that dwarfed it, leaving it constantly in the shade.

There was a section of police tape across the entrance, and a deputy standing guard to the side of the building to ensure no one could creep around the back. Laura was already taking off her seatbelt as the car pulled up to the curb, ready to jump out and hit the ground running on the investigation.

Two hours in a plane and then the car journey meant that standing up and breathing fresh air felt good. Well, as fresh as you could get in a city. Laura stretched her arms above her head on the sidewalk, shaking out the kinks.

"The body's been taken to the morgue, I presume?" Nate said, sliding on a pair of sunglasses against the bright sun. Laura had been wearing hers since they got off the plane. It was a habit of hers, so that when she needed to wear them because of her headaches it wasn't so obvious.

"It has," the sheriff confirmed. "But we've preserved the rest of the scene for you to examine."

As they followed him up the short steps onto the porch, Laura felt a prickling feeling on the back of her neck. It only seemed to intensify as they walked inside the building and to another interior door, presumably leading to the first-floor apartment.

What was that?

It dawned on her as the sheriff led them upstairs and through a second-floor door into the victim's home. It was déjà vu. She felt as though she'd been here before.

She felt that way, but she couldn't have been. She'd never even been to Albany until now. How could she know this place? How could she have known to look for the peeled-back edge of the wallpaper by the kitchen door if she hadn't already known it was there?

Laura was silent as she stepped through the apartment, slipping on a pair of gloves so she would be free to touch anything she saw. The kitchen was ahead, she knew that. There was a fridge just a little too close to the cupboards. She stepped through and there it was: just how she had expected.

How was it that she knew all of this?

It was like she had seen it on TV, though of course that wasn't the case.

"This is where she was found," Sheriff Lonsdale said, startling her as he appeared right behind her. "She was lying right there, beside the table. Looks like the phone was just long enough to reach.

Laura nodded, looking down at the cord. The handset was still lying on the floor where it had been extricated from the victim's neck. There was no blood, not much sign of a struggle. The only free-standing furniture in the whole kitchen was the fridge and the table, and they didn't appear to have been affected.

There was a microwaveable tray of congealed mac and cheese sitting on the table, a dirty fork lying beside it. Yes, Laura thought. The mac and cheese was familiar too.

"Do you have the pictures?" Laura asked. There hadn't been any included with the briefing. She'd assumed that was because the local police photographer hadn't been able to finish his images in time for the printout.

"Here." The sheriff pulled out a folder from under his arm and extricated several printed shots, handing them to her. Laura held one of them, a full-body shot, up in the air until it aligned with the view in front of her.

"She was holding the phone," Laura said, loud for Nate's benefit. He had come back into the hall behind them, but there was nowhere near enough room for all three of them to look through the doorway.

"Yes, she actually managed to make a call to nine-one-one before she was killed," the sheriff said. "Unfortunately, he strangled her with the phone cord while she was still on the line. We do have the recording. Would you like to hear that?"

Laura considered it. "Does he say anything? Make any identifiable noises?"

"No."

"Anything relevant from her?"

"No, she barely makes a noise at all, apart from the choking. Just says that someone's broken in, and that's all we got."

Laura shook her head. "Then I don't want to hear it until I have to. We hit a dead end, then we'll listen. But it doesn't sound like it's going to be much use, and this case is dark enough already without audio of the moment of her death." She glanced back at Nate to check he was on board with it, but his expression was open and it didn't change. Laura was no sadist, and no masochist either. She didn't think it would be good for either of them, hearing that. Not until it was necessary.

She just hoped it wasn't going to become necessary.

"All right, what else?" Nate asked. "She had the cord around her neck still?"

"Yes, it's as though he just dropped her to the ground and left her there," the sheriff said. He leaned over Laura's shoulder to point at several areas on the image; she tried not to be too obvious as she flinched back away from his touch. She'd seen enough hovering death today. If she was going to be having visions, she needed them to be focused on the case—not on whether the sheriff was likely to stub his toe on his way to bed tonight. "We think he strangled her from behind, possibly as she was trying to get away from him. He would have used the cord to bring her up short, then used her own body weight and his to keep the cord tight. Medical examiner is telling us that he probably lifted her off her feet, into the air, judging by the impressions on her throat."

"The act of killing is enough," Laura mused. "He kills her, then drops her. She's no longer any use to him."

"So, we're not looking at a sexually motived crime," Nate said. "Anything taken?"

"Not a robbery either," the sheriff confirmed. "Other than the smashed bedroom window, and this phone off the hook in here, it's like no one ever came in. Come and look at this."

They turned as a unit, Nate and Laura both following the sheriff into the bedroom. The space was no less cramped in here; there was only just enough room for one person to walk around all three sides of the bed, with the headboard close to the window. One wall of the room was packed with a dresser, a small table holding an alarm clock, and a makeshift wardrobe rack hanging free.

The sheriff pointed carefully at the alarm clock, making sure they were watching before he lifted it up. Around the clock, a ring of grime and discoloration made the cleaner patch underneath it stand out starkly.

"That's how you know nothing else is missing," Laura said, nodding. She glanced around the rest of the space. The gaping hole where the window had once been and the debris of the shards all over the bed seemed to tell the rest of the story eloquently enough. She leaned over, her eyes scanning the covers, the windowsill. There was no sign of any kind of shoe print.

"He got in over the fire escape?" Nate asked, nodding at the window.

"Oh, yes." The sheriff nodded. He leaned toward the hole, pointing outward. "It's fixed to the side of the building, just here. Not a direct route, but all he would need to do would be to swing out from the fire escape and smash through the glass feet first. Or using something to smash it—a stone or anything, really—and then swing himself through. We believe he left the same way, as the front door was still locked."

"I suppose a witness statement is too much to hope for?" Nate said.

The sheriff grinned at that. "Unfortunately," he said. "It was late in the evening, and the back of the property has no external lighting. Anyway, from what forensics are saying, it's likely he wore a hat or a mask. So an eyewitness report wouldn't necessarily do us much good at this stage."

Laura nodded, glancing around one last time. She stepped back without saying anything, heading back to the kitchen. She need to get some idea of what had happened here. A vision, maybe. Something that would give her another piece of the puzzle. She couldn't see the past, but she might be able to see a clue, something that they would otherwise miss. A new homeowner finding an ID card that had slipped underneath the carpet years later, during renovation. That kind of thing could happen.

She glanced behind to check that the sheriff and Nate were still occupied in looking over the bedroom, and quickly slipped her hand out of one of her gloves. She laid it on the wall by the doorframe, a spot that the killer was unlikely to have touched. Something that wouldn't compromise future evidence. Then she tried to concentrate, to focus in. She smelled the tang of the mac and cheese, sitting and spoiling out on the counter. She heard the low murmur of Nate's and the sheriff's voices, but also the hum of the fridge, the rush of traffic on the street outside. She felt the smooth surface of the plastered wall, cool under her fingers.

The pulse of pressure between her eyes was light this time, not a full-blown headache. That was something of a bad sign; the harsher the pain, the more urgent the vision, Laura knew. This was sometime in the future. She felt it building up and willed it to come quicker, to pour over her like a wave—

*Laura was viewing the scene from the same doorway, but above, hovering somewhere near the ceiling. The door had been removed at some point. The table and fridge were gone, and the stove had been stripped out. The other cupboards hung rotten.*

*There was graffiti on the walls, and a strong smell rising to her nose. Urine, smoke. Laura wrinkled her eyes and tried to squint. The picture was so unclear, like she was watching through dirty water. It swirled around her, leaving her unable to see the whole scene at once.*

*She listened but heard nothing, only the traffic on the street outside. Then something: yes! She found herself drawn closer to it, the vision taking her just where she had wanted to go, down, down to the floor level, to a pile of trash heaped in a corner—*

*And a rat shot out of it, running toward her with some morsel clamped in its jaws, a bit of old vegetable matter that was long past decay, right at her...*

Laura blinked and opened her eyes on the kitchen again, whole and still a crime scene. She took a breath against the flash of the headache that sent her roiling, then slipped her glove back on. The pain wasn't bad at all; she could handle it. That must have been years from now.

No one wanted to live in an apartment where someone was murdered after a break-in, she figured. All too easy for it to happen to the next tenant as well. This place would fall into disrepair in the future, and if there were any lingering clues, there would be no one to find them.

It didn't tell her anything useful. Sometimes the visions were like that. She couldn't control them, except by creating the optimal conditions for them to come. That meant putting herself more into the path of the killer. If she got connected to him strongly enough, she might be able to see his next move—like she had with the scumbag who kidnapped Amy.

Once she was close enough to crossing his path, touching anything could trigger it—her gun, Nate's gun, her own arm if they were going to end up directly linked. But for now, she was getting nothing. Even the sense of déjà vu she'd felt was gone. Maybe it had her imagination, or some lingering shadow of the vision of the broken apartment that she'd been about to have. It wasn't as though she always understood why her visions came, or how they worked. Maybe she was starting to feel them before they came now, too.

Either way, one thing was clear. They needed to get closer. She wasn't going to get any useful visions until they did.

"We should talk to the victim's relatives next," Laura said, turning to join Nate again. "What was her name? Caroline?"

"Good plan," Nate said, looking to the sheriff. "You good to drive us over there?"

"Sure thing." The sheriff nodded. "We've got one of our boys down there right now, sitting with them and providing some comfort, you know the drill. I'll give him a call to expect us and we'll be on our way."

Laura glanced around one more time and then nodded firmly, gesturing for Nate to head to the door first. They were done here, and the quicker they moved on, the better. There was, after all, the possibility that someone else could die tonight.

And going to talk to Caroline's family would be the first step toward a vision that might help her stop that from happening.

# CHAPTER ELEVEN

Laura stood by as Nate knocked loudly on the door, staring up and waiting for it to open. There was always that awkward moment between knocking and being answered. When you weren't sure if you were just waiting outside an empty house. When you tried to rearrange your face to something that would be friendly and open, and then hold it until someone got there.

Laura hated this part of the job sometimes. Having to talk to people who'd lost family members. Sometimes having to be the one to break the news. It was just another layer of separation: always turning up at the worst point in people's lives.

"Hello?" The woman who answered the door was easily recognizable from the photograph of Caroline that she'd seen. There was no mistaking the family resemblance between them: the same thin-lipped mouth, the same long nose.

"Hi, Mrs. Howard? I'm Agent Nathaniel Lavoie, and this is Agent Laura Frost. I'm sorry to have to do this at such a sad time for you and your family, but do you mind if we come in and ask you a few questions?" Nate had the polite voice down pat, along with his polite smile and his politely relaxed body posture. As a six-two Black man who spent a lot of time at the gym, Nate knew he had to keep the intimidation levels down as low as possible when dealing with grieving white people. They'd even spoken about it, back when they were first partners. It was another level that Laura didn't have to deal with, and she was grateful for that privilege.

"Please," Caroline's sister said, stepping aside to allow them in her home. She was pale and her eyes were red; as they passed by her, Laura noticed how she pulled her thin cardigan closer around herself.

Caroline's apartment had been small and cramped, and almost entirely without personality. Like it was a temporary home, even though she had been there for years. Here, though, there were signs of life. The sister had framed photographs on the walls of herself with a man and a few small children—her family. There were toys scattered around as they walking into a cozy living room, where the same man from the pictures was seated on a worn sofa cradling a cup of something steaming.

"Take a seat," Mrs. Howard said, gesturing with a jerky and awkward movement to the dining chairs that had been brought into the room from elsewhere before sitting next to her husband.

"Would you like something to drink?" he offered, his eyes flicking between their faces and their FBI-approved suits. "Tea, coffee, water?"

"I'll take a coffee, thanks," Nate said. He glanced at Laura as he sat down, prompting her to take his cue.

"Same for me, thanks," she said. "Just black, for both of them."

"Got it." The husband stood, squeezing his wife's hand and mouthing something to her—Laura guessed it was something like "you okay?"—before disappearing back into the hall.

"I'll help with that." That was a voice from the sole armchair: the young deputy who had been sitting with the family. He stood and nodded to both Nate and Laura before leaving, allowing the sheriff to sit down in his place.

"So, Mrs. Howard," Nate said, his tone light and gentle.

"Oh—Tara, please," she said, tucking a strand of dirty-blonde hair quickly behind her ear.

"Tara," Nate resumed. "We're very sorry for your loss. You were the older sister, is that right?"

"Yes." Tara had a birdlike way about her, from her rapid movements to her thinness. Caroline had been a little bigger, which on balance made her look healthier. Ironic, considering the only time Laura had seen her so far, she'd been dead. "Oh, god. I'm sorry. I just still can't believe it. I only spoke to her the night before. It doesn't seem real."

"When you spoke to her, did she seem any different than usual?" Laura asked, wanting to get a picture of her mental state. "Was she upset, tired, anxious, angry?"

"Nothing like that," Tara said, with a less frantic tone, a more relaxed sag of her shoulders. Laura saw Nate close his mouth, leaning back against the chair, out of the corner of her eye. If Tara was more responsive to Laura's questions, then he was obviously happy to let Laura do all of the asking. "She was normal. A bit annoyed, but not with anything that would make me think something was going on."

"What was she annoyed about, then?" Laura asked.

"Oh, life." Tara shrugged, then drew a tissue out of her sleeve and dabbed it against her eyes. "She was always complaining about that stupid little apartment. I can't believe she… that that was the last place she saw."

"Why did she have such a small place?" Laura said, her tone gentle enough that she hoped it didn't sound like a rude question. "You seem to be doing better here, and Caroline lived alone. Was she single?"

"It wasn't her fault," Tara said quickly, shaking her head. "She got divorced a few years ago. Carrie and David just weren't compatible in the end. But it left her without any savings, and so she had to start again from scratch. She was working her way up. Not much longer, and I think she'd have been on the path to getting out of there, getting somewhere nicer. Maybe finding love again."

This seemed to set off a fresh round of tears, and Tara held the tissue against her eyes for a long moment, her shoulders shaking up and down. Laura glanced at the sheriff, giving her a moment to herself.

"David?" Nate asked, his voice low.

The sheriff shook his head. "We've already looked into him. He's now happily settled with a new partner, and he has an alibi for last night. Absolutely solid. He was nowhere near the apartment when it happened."

"Any children?" Nate continued, still keeping his head turned toward the sheriff. Tara was getting herself under control, sniffling and looking up from her tissue.

"No," the sheriff said. "Both the parents are deceased, too, isn't that right?"

"Yes, they passed away years ago," Tara said. She had a weary look; she must have been up most of the night, crying and mourning her sister the whole time. She probably needed some rest. "That's why there wasn't anyone to give her any support. I would have if I could, but the kids…"

"She knew you loved her, darling," the husband said, coming back into the room with two full mugs. He put one of them in Laura's hand and the other in his wife's before taking his seat again. Behind him, the deputy entered, handing a third mug to Nate while keeping a fourth for himself. "She knew you would have helped more if you could."

Laura cradled the coffee in her hands, warming them on the surface of the mug. It wasn't cold out, but sometimes the warmth of a cup of coffee was exactly what you needed when you had to sit and watch someone mourn the loss of a family member. It was hard to stay professional, and this little drop of comfort helped.

"I know…" Tara paused, sighing deeply. "I just… if we could have helped her get a bigger place sooner, she wouldn't have been there…"

"It's best not to dwell on what-ifs," Laura said, not unkindly. She would know; that was part of why she'd spiraled over years past, how she'd struggled with alcohol and losing her partner and daughter. "Do you have any idea if there was anyone who might want to hurt your sister? Anyone at all?"

"No," Tara said, looking down into her mug miserably. "No, I don't know why anyone would. She was a good person. She was just living her life."

"Anyone at all?" Laura prompted. "I know it can feel like you don't want to get anyone in trouble, but it's better that we investigate and clear someone from our inquiry than to have no leads to work on."

"So you don't have any leads?" the husband asked, his head snapping up.

"We have a working theory at this time, but any information we can get will always help," Nate said, deliberately taking over as if he didn't want them getting angry with Laura. He was always her rock. A wall between her and the very worst of people. Laura felt grief hit her like a knife to the gut. Who was going to do that when he was gone? "Not just for the arrest, but for help with a conviction, too."

"There's really no one," Tara said, sounding a little distant. "Sorry. I wish I could help."

"You've helped a lot," Laura said softly. "You've given us a bit more of a picture of who Caroline was, and that's really important. We want to catch the person who did this just as much as you do."

The husband looked doubtful, but he nodded. Laura turned her head slightly in Nate's direction, catching his eye to form a question in her look. It seemed he had nothing more to add, taking a long sip of the coffee and then placing it down on the table.

"Well, thank you both for your time," Nate said, making to stand. Laura did the same What a shame it was to waste the coffee. But that was law enforcement. They had things to do, and this killer was probably not going to wait around for them to refuel. "We'll be in touch if we have any more questions."

"If anything comes to mind, please do give us a call," Laura added, dropping her card onto the table.

They left the grieving couple behind, and Nate stayed silent until the door of the house was closed behind them out of respect. "Back to the precinct?" he said then, raising an eyebrow to both the sheriff and Laura.

"Back to the precinct," Laura agreed, with a weary note to her voice.

This had all the hallmarks of one of those cases that could really put them through the wringer—especially if the killer struck again tonight. Because that would mean they were dealing with a serial killer, and then all the normal rules would be off the table.

Unpredictable attacks, constant pressure, and opportunistic crimes added together to make serial killers some of the hardest criminals to catch. And this one hadn't made any mistakes yet. Laura prayed they would find him before they needed him to mess up—because if it got to that stage, there was no telling how many lives might be lost.

***

Laura had a bad feeling as she cautiously sank down into the chair they had pulled into the room for her, hearing it squeak as old springs protested. At least it had cushioning. This case, though, was starting to feel anything but comfortable. "All right, what do we have?" she asked, spreading the pages of the file indiscriminately across the desk.

Next to her, Nate scratched his chin through his beard. "Well, I think the sheriff might be right about there being no link between the women. This is looking more and more like crimes of opportunity."

Laura groaned. "I was hoping you weren't going to say that," she said. She didn't need to worry about insulting the sheriff by not agreeing with him—he'd left them to it. They'd requisitioned an empty meeting room and turned it into their makeshift headquarters, setting up a board ready to stick up images and start making notes.

"Well, I don't see anything between them," Nate said, pointing at the files as he grabbed two printed images. The women as they were when they were alive, newly provided for them by the sheriff's team. He stuck them up on the board as he talked. "Let's make a list of what we know about them. That might help."

Laura rubbed her eyes to clear them and lifted up the first page of information with a heavy sigh. "All right. Caroline Birchtree. Lived alone, no boyfriend, divorced but the husband has an alibi. Thirty-one years old, working as a waitress at a restaurant downtown. No car, so she took the bus to work every day. Lived here her whole life, didn't go to college."

Nate's marker pen squeaked against the board as he jotted down everything she was saying in fast, sharp-angled capital letters. "Okay. And Laura Carlisle?"

"Lived with a roommate, but she was alone at the time of the murder. Dating a guy around her age, but he also has an alibi. She was twenty-two, worked as a nurse, and had her own car. She moved here right after graduating college in the area, but she's originally from Michigan."

Nate tapped the board. "So, all I'm seeing is that we have two women who were alone in their homes at the time of their death, and they were killed right there."

Laura groaned out loud again. "You're right," she said. "Unless something comes up that links them down the line, we're looking at unrelated victims. Damn it."

"I second that," Nate said. "What about the killer? We've got two strangulations, two women alone at home in the evening. All in the Albany area, so we've got that going for us. We just have to figure out if there is a motive, or if it's a crime of opportunity from someone with the urge to kill."

That was an unwelcome thought. Laura hated these random cases. They were always so hard to work on. If the killer was making sudden decisions or acting out of passion, then he hadn't made any plans. That meant there was no determined future in place, nothing for her to see. She might not be able to get any clear visions about him at all, if it went that way.

But then there had been the déjà vu. Whatever that meant. There was something going on here that she couldn't put her finger on. She had to hope that meant visions would come.

"We're at a dead end already," Laura said, frowning. "There's hardly anything to go on."

"Well, we can hope for something in the more conclusive forensics report, once they've had a few days," Nate said. "Although that won't be much help if he strikes again tonight."

"Yeah." Laura paused, thinking. There was only one thing they hadn't done yet—aside from going over the same ground the police had already trodden on with the other crime scene and the other Laura's family. Which didn't seem like a good use of their time, given that Laura had seen with her own eyes that nothing was missed in Caroline's case. "We need to listen to that nine-one-one call."

"I'll get the sheriff's tapes," Nate said, getting up and heading for the door.

Laura nodded as he went, trying to steel herself. Listening to 911 calls was never easy, especially not when the killing happened during the call. It was always a traumatic experience. But she had to do it, because if she got close enough to the killer, she might be able to see him.

And there wasn't much closer you could get than hearing him breathe right into your ear.

# CHAPTER TWELVE

"Miss? Can you hear me? Can you respond? I need you to stay on the line. Miss, are you there?"

Laura closed her eyes for a long moment, trying to keep down the lunch they'd eaten on the plane. The computer speakers in front of them continued mercilessly, playing the sounds of a woman losing her battle to breathe.

Caroline Birchtree gasped and choked on the recording captured by the 911 dispatcher. There were occasional loud bangs and thuds; having seen the place now, Laura could picture her kicking out, hitting the cupboards, connecting with the counter. It sounded as though she was fighting hard.

The recording was heartbreaking. Laura clenched the side of the table until her knuckles popped. Slowly, the sounds of choking petered out. The dispatcher kept asking over and over again if Caroline could hear her, if she was all right, telling her to hold on and to stay on the line.

Finally, there was silence.

There was a clunk of the handset hitting the floor, and then footsteps walking away. A tinkling of glass, only just audible, as he went back to the bedroom and presumably exited the house. Then nothing.

Sheriff Lonsdale cleared his throat, a gruff sound that broke the heavy hush. "It goes on like that for about four or five minutes, before our first responders arrive and you can hear them break down the door," he said. "No more noise from her, and he's long gone."

"Play it again," Laura said, gesturing toward the screen.

"Are you sure?" the sheriff asked, hesitating. "It's a hard listen."

"Exactly." Laura took a breath. "I need to be sure I didn't miss anything. It will be easier the second time."

That was barely true. Sometimes repeat listens could make it worse, because you knew what was coming. But she had to keep listening. Maybe if she heard him enough times, if she learned to distinguish the sounds that he made from the other noises on the call, if she could get down deep enough to know him a little more…

Maybe a vision would come.

"Well, I'll leave you with the computer, if you don't mind," the sheriff said. He cleared his throat gruffly again. Laura did a quick calculation in her head. If he had children, she realized, they would probably be about the same age as Caroline. "I don't need to hear that again."

Laura nodded, waiting until he had moved out of the room and stopped making noise before pressing play. Her thoughts strayed to Lacey in the interim. One day, Lacey was going to grow up to be a young woman too. She'd be just as at risk as anyone. But Laura couldn't think about that right now. It wasn't exactly easier for her to listen to a woman dying, but she had to do this. She had to—so that it didn't happen again.

And there it all was again. Caroline's frantic plea for help. The 911 dispatcher trying to talk to her, to ask questions, to find a way to help. The sound of the cord being pulled tight around her neck, an intake of breath, a—

Laura's mind raced back. Wait—that intake of breath. It couldn't have been Caroline. Not if she was already choking. Laura marked the point in her head, trying to listen hard to the rest of the tape. To Caroline gagging and trying desperately to get free. It must have been hard to hold her while she fought. He must have been breathing hard. There would be more sounds, more traces of him. Laura was sure of it.

"All right, I don't think we're going to get anything out of this," Nate said, as the tinkling glass signaled the killer's exit again. "Let's move on. What's next?"

"No," Laura said, turning and looking at him. He met her eyes with a raised brow. "I'm not done yet. I need to listen to it again."

"Again?" Nate frowned, then shook his head. "Laura, it's horrible. Don't force yourself to keep listening. We're not going to find out anything from it, not on our own anyway. If you want it analyzed, let's send it to the tech geeks and have them try to isolate anything they can, turn up the volume. We're better used elsewhere."

"I nearly have it," Laura snapped, turning back to the screen. "I heard something. Just let me do this."

She instantly regretted snapping at him. Nate was only ever trusting and patient with her, whether she deserved it or not. He didn't deserve to be snapped at. More than that, he was the one who let her get away with all of her quirks, never asking why she did things the way she did.

If she annoyed him enough to start throwing his own weight around, that could quickly change—and it would be her own fault, too.

Maybe she wouldn't need to snap if she could get her hands on a drink. Something to relieve the tension, make everything easier. But she knew she couldn't do that.

"Fine," Nate said, his voice sharp enough that she knew he wanted her to hear he was put out. "If it's that important to you, keep listening. I'll work on my notes."

Laura's hand hovered over the mouse, ready to press play, but she hesitated. "Thank you," she said first, hoping her tone conveyed that she was contrite.

She shuffled her chair closer to the speakers as she pressed play. She considered even putting her ear flat against them, but that probably wouldn't help. Laura concentrated hard, waiting for the spot where she knew she had heard it.

There! An intake of breath, unmistakable.

She had him, now. His signature. The sound of breathing wasn't exactly like a voice. It wasn't completely unique. It wasn't even identifiable in a lot of cases. But if you had a recording of two people breathing, especially if they were straining, often you could tell them apart. That was something Laura had picked up over years of surveillance jobs, listening to bugs, waiting to burst in as part of a raid.

In this case, it was easy to tell them apart. Caroline was choking. That left only two people breathing on the line: the dispatcher, whose microphone was much closer to her mouth, and who besides kept muting the call while she spoke with the first responders. And there was him. The killer. Distant from the handset, overpowered often by Caroline's choking or the dispatcher's voice. But he was there.

At the end of the call he wasn't breathing too heavily. Not panting for breath like he might have been. He wasn't panicked or rushing to get away. He let Caroline drop and then walked calmly back the way he came in. Laura would have given anything for a microphone close by the window—to hear if he made a grunt of effort as he swung back to the fire escape, to listen to him moving further away. The weight of his footsteps on the metal. But this was all they had.

"All right, satisfied now?" Nate asked. He was leaning back in his chair, looking at his notes with exasperation. He thought she was being foolish. Laura could take that. She needed to know.

"Not yet," Laura said. "I've almost got something."

“What are you hearing that I’m not?” Nate asked, dropping his pen back on his notebook and looking at her with frustration. Even so, there was softness behind his gaze. He wanted to take care of her, she realized. Wanted to protect her from listening to this nightmare. But he didn’t know why she had to.

“I can hear him breathing,” Laura said, opting to at least go with the truth. Even if it wasn’t the whole truth. “Just let me go again. I’m figuring something out. You… you can leave the room, if you have to.”

“Okay,” Nate sighed, shaking his head. “But I’m not going anywhere. We’re partners. If you’re listening to this, I’ll stay as well. I’ll just… distract myself.” He looked down at his phone and started tapping the screen. Laura couldn’t tell if he was reading messages, researching something, or just playing a mobile game, but it didn’t matter. So long as he was quiet, Laura could work with that.

She played the recording again. She could feel Nate looking at her every time she reset it to the beginning and pressed play again, but she ignored him. She closed her eyes, trying to block out everything else. Rather than focusing on where she was—on going through her senses one by one—she lost herself in the recording. She blocked out everything else. Now that she was used to the sounds that Caroline made, to the voice of the dispatcher, she could ignore them. She focused hard, trying to drown herself in the sound of his breathing.

Laura pressed play for the eighth time and closed her eyes again. Slowly and carefully, hoping that Nate’s view would be blocked by her body, she reached out and pressed her fingers to the speaker on one side of the computer monitor.

A stabbing pain shot through her forehead, and Laura tried to breathe through it. She kept still, listening hard—there it was, that one loud intake of breath she’d first heard—

*Laura was above her, looking down. The woman—she was definitely a woman, that much Laura could sense as much as see. But her face was obscured by black wisps like smoke, like ink flowing through water. Everything was dark and dim, like an old photograph shot in sepia, scratched and unclear. She fought to see through it, to get past…*

*The woman. There was something around her neck. Just for a moment Laura made it out, just for a moment she heard a desperate cry. A female voice cut off by a choking sound. Laura grasped for more, but everything was too dim. She couldn’t smell or taste or hear or feel a thing. It was all dark ink around her, and the woman was getting further away. Smaller.*

*The woman was dying.*

Laura's eyes snapped open and she snatched her fingers away from the speaker, pressing them against her forehead instead. The headache rolled through her like a wave, pushing every single thought out of her head until she got a grip on it. Then she deliberately unclenched her jaw, relaxed her clenched fist, breathed out.

She was so close. The fact that the vision had come at all meant that she was on the right track. It was closely linked to her own future, her near future, and she would be close enough to stop it. If only she knew where the woman was—who she was—when it would happen. Who was standing behind her, wrapping *something* around her neck. Every single useful detail had been obscured, too far out of her reach.

Except for one. The fact that she was right. The killer was going to strike again.

If she could just get more information, the vision would be more complete. But she didn't have anything else to go on. The killer had left no evidence, no scrap of himself. She couldn't find anything that pointed to his motive, any trace of his DNA, any sign he had left behind. She only had his breath—and that wasn't enough.

She resisted the urge to slam the keyboard against the desk in frustration. She had been so close. Why couldn't he have spoken on the recording? Why couldn't he have left her at least a grunt to work with?

It was like the shadow she felt over Nate. Too vague. Too dim to allow her to actually take any action. It wasn't fair. Why did she have to put up with these headaches and all the inconvenience of keeping the secret if it wasn't going to actually *help* her to save a life?

"You finally given up?" Nate asked, making Laura exhale and turn to look at him. "You look like crap."

"Thanks," Laura said darkly, shaking her head. "Listening to the last moments of a dead woman over and over again will do that to you."

"Did you at least get anything out of it?" Nate asked. He set his notebook aside and leaned forward in his chair, resting his elbows on his knees. His large hands clasped loosely together below his chin as he studied her.

"He's not out of breath," Laura said. "At least, not too much. He strains a little to pull the cord, but I think he's strong. And he's very calm—controlled."

"Meaning he's going to be a bitch to find," Nate said, scrubbing one of his hands back over his tightly coiled hair. "I hate the calm ones."

"I'm sure their victims feel the same," Laura said, with a light twist to the sides of her mouth. "I don't know. It's not much to go on. But I'm confident we're looking for a man, at least."

"You know, I've been thinking," Nate said, reaching for his notebook again. "This was a recording from her landline, right?"

"Yeah," Laura said, frowning. "That's why it was all picked up. He was using the cord from it to strangle her." Had Nate not realized that all along?

"Well, my point is, who uses a landline these days? Didn't she have a cell?"

Laura thought back. "Yeah, I think I read something about this in the notes from the first responders. Her cell phone was left on the bed. She couldn't go back for it, if that's where he came from."

"Yeah, but the landline was out in the hall, right?" Nate sketched out a quick plan of the apartment on a page of his notepad. "Here. So the killer would have walked out of this doorway—right between the kitchen door and the landline itself."

Laura paused, studying his diagram. "Huh."

"Right. So maybe she was already using the landline. I think we should pull the phone records. We might get lucky. Maybe there's a recording of this guy breaking in on someone's voicemail. Maybe we get to hear his voice—or she recognizes him and says his name."

"That's a good thought," Laura said, and grinned. "God, I hope we get something."

"You're welcome," Nate teased. "Since you're so into recordings right now and all."

"I'll call the boss," Laura said, grabbing her cell out of her pocket. "If they put it through on a rush, we might be able to get them right away."

"Fingers crossed," Nate said, leaning back again with the easy grace of a man who worked out enough to know his own body well. He wore a small smile, self-satisfaction for coming up with a potential lead.

If he was right, it could be another piece of the puzzle. It seemed a long shot, but right now they needed something—anything. Laura waited for the line to connect, ignoring the way the dial tone seemed to pulse at the same rate as the throbbing in her head.

If she could hear his voice, maybe the vision would clear up and she would be able to identify his next victim.

It wasn't too late to stop that murky vision from becoming reality. There were a few hours left until nightfall.

It wasn't too late to save a life—but if she didn't hurry, it would be.

# CHAPTER THIRTEEN

"I've got it," Laura said, tapping impatiently on her phone screen to open the email. "Hold on—here we go."

"What does it say?" Nate asked, dragging his wheeled office chair across to her. Laura pulled back quickly before their heads could bump, shifting in her seat to provide an excuse for the sudden movement.

"There's a number that called her right before she called nine-one-one," Laura said, swiping across the file to zoom in. "It looks as though it connected. That's a shame, I guess. No answering machine message."

"It's still a lead, though. Let me see," Nate said, reaching to take the phone out of her hands.

Laura didn't have time to react. His hand brushed against hers before she could stop it, and the veil of death fell over her again, dampening everything for a moment. She shivered and tried to remember how to breathe. As quickly as it happened, it was gone, Nate holding the phone up as he typed out the number into a search bar on the computer.

Laura swallowed on her dry throat, watching him work. He was focused on the screen, frowning as he pulled up the results. He was so—big. So full of life. So vibrant. How could he be under the shadow of death?

"No listed results online," Nate said, shrugging. "Doesn't mean it doesn't belong to anyone."

"Try and give it a trace," Laura said. "I'm just going to call back to HQ. I can't help but wonder whether the first victim had a call as well, you know?"

"It's worth a look." Nate nodded. "Hey, if we don't do it now, we'll only have to do it in a few days when we're trying to trace every single person either of them ever talked to."

Laura groaned as the line began to ring. "Don't say that," she said. "I don't want to still be at a dead end with this in a few days."

Nate only chuckled, returning his attention to his computer. He brought up an FBI portal and logged in, his fingers running easily over the familiar keys of his password, and began inputting the data.

Laura's attention was taken away when the call was answered, and she spoke directly to the team back in DC who would be able to request the phone records.

"Did you find anything?" Laura asked as she ended the call, looking back over at Nate.

He nodded, tapping his fingers against the desk. "Sort of. It's not good news. As far as we can trace, the number belongs to a burner phone."

Laura sighed. She wished burner phones weren't a thing. Cheap, no-contract handsets you could buy at any convenience store and load with a calling card instead of having to sign your name to something. Virtually untraceable, unless you got really lucky. "I've got the other phone records coming shortly. The phone company didn't put up a fight, for once."

Nate smirked. "Well, there's one silver lining. Let me think about this phone thing. Maybe there's a way…"

Laura didn't press him as he trailed off into silence, his head cocked to one side. Nate was good with technology. Just like he didn't question her so-called intuition, she knew better than to interfere when it came to tech.

A buzz in her hand drew her attention to her phone, and the incoming email. She opened it hurriedly, checking the attachment. It was a report from the same phone company—given that the two victims lived in the same area, that wasn't a surprise.

Laura spun around to look at their investigation board, to what Nate had written about the estimated time of death of the first victim. Then she checked the report again. And she checked it a third time, just because it was almost too good to be true.

"Nate," she said. "There's another call. To Laura Carlisle, right around the time of her death."

Nate's head snapped up. "Tell me the number."

She rattled it off as he typed, leaning forward over his keyboard as the details came up.

"Same deal," he said. "Burner phone. Same model, different phone. Both of them were activated on the day of the killing and have now been marked as inactive."

"So, they were bought just for this one call," Laura said. "That together with them being untraceable—it's got to be the killer, right?"

"Yeah," Nate said, though he still sounded thoughtful. Like he had something else on his mind.

"What?" Laura prompted, seeing that he didn't seem to be getting anywhere.

"Well, this type of phone," he said, slowly. "I've come across it before. I'm sure I saw it in a case before you and I partnered up. This model needs to be activated with a unique serial number before it can make calls out."

"So… does that mean it's traceable?" Laura asked, hope springing to life.

"Maybe," Nate said, nodding. "Yeah, probably. We can see which store it was bought from. The manufacturer will have records of which identifiers went to which customers. Then we can talk to the store—maybe they have detailed enough sales records that we can see who bought them."

"Unless he paid in cash," Laura said. "But still. This is great, right?"

"It's a start," Nate said, jumping to action. "I'll call it in, see if the Chief can get a warrant for us, just in case. Then I'll jump on the line with the manufacturer."

"It could take a few hours," Laura said, and then shrugged. "But it's all we've got to go on right now."

Nate nodded, putting the phone to his ear as he waited for it to connect.

Laura tuned out his conversation, rubbing her face as she looked over at their investigation board. The faces of the two women who had died stared back at her. Laura and Caroline. No one had moved fast enough to save them. If they didn't get this information before the end of the night, there could be another face going up on the board.

Laura reached for her purse while Nate was distracted, and quickly pulled out a blister pack of painkillers. She took one straight down, without water. When you were on the move a lot and suffered with near-constant headaches, you got used to being able to take whatever pain relief you needed without waiting for convenient facilities.

She sat back in her chair then, waiting for the painkiller to take hold. Having the throbbing in her temple out of the way would certainly make investigating a bit easier. But right now, she wasn't sure there was anywhere else they could go. The phones were a good lead. If they were really lucky, this would clear the whole thing up. They'd be able to get a name, go arrest the guy, and it would be over.

But it was getting late, and Laura couldn't help but feel they were racing against time. The vision she had seen—the pain had been bad, which meant it was probably happening in the next few hours at most. If they didn't get the information before then—or if they got it when the killer had already left home to go after his next victim…

Laura didn't want to think about the girl she had seen, or half-seen, in her vision. That girl was on the cusp of death. She probably didn't even know it yet, but her life was in grave danger. And what was Laura doing? Kicking her heels at the local precinct, resting in a chair and waiting for her painkillers to kick in.

She picked up her cell phone, needing to do something to distract herself. Something to keep her mind away from the urgency. Sitting on her hands had never been her favorite thing to do, and right now, it amounted to torture. Besides, she needed to check whether she had any messages or updates from home. An invitation to go visit Lacey would be nice, though she didn't hold out hope for that anymore.

She just braced herself in case one day she would receive word from Lacey's father that there was an emergency.

Laura checked her emails online, skimming through a load of junk mails from Nigerian princes and supposed purveyors of magic pills. Down below them, though, there was at least one message she actually wanted to read: a reply from a forum she was signed up to about psychics.

She'd joined as a bit of a last-ditch effort to find someone who was like her. After years of just reading the forums and remaining a passive bystander, Laura had come to realize that she wasn't getting anywhere at all. And she figured it was possible that anyone who was like her, might be just like her. Meaning that they, too, would hang silently around on the outside, watching and waiting.

And if they all did that, well, they would never find one another at all.

So, she'd taken the plunge. Signed up with a fake email address and a fake name, initially from a library computer so that it wouldn't even register the account to her IP address. She was fairly certain there was no way the account would be connected back to her or the FBI. She wasn't as good with the tech stuff as Nate was, but she'd learned a thing or two from him over their time working together. VPNs, for example.

She'd created a post a while back on a few of the various sites that existed for discussion of the psychic gift, and she'd had a few replies over time, too. She'd asked for people who genuinely had psychic gifts, and who saw snatches of the future, to contact her. She'd only found charlatans so far. The same story as any other method she tried to figure out if she was not alone in this.

This post intrigued her. It was from a user who had only just created a brand new account, presumably just to be able to reply to her thread. And it was free of the usual bragging or links to websites where she could "test" their skills for a price.

It read: "*Hi AnnaSmith8932. I think we may share the same gift. I don't talk about it a lot, but I see things happening around me all the time. To my friends and family. And after I see it, I get the chance to try to fix it or stop it from happening.*

*I would love to know if we are experiencing the same thing. I'm living in Virginia, so I don't think we're too far apart. We should meet up and compare notes.*"

Laura bit her lip, reading it through again. Did they seem genuine? It was altogether possible this was one of the frighteningly lonely people who seemed to stalk these kinds of sites and try to get dates out of them. But then again, the message hadn't seemed flirtatious. In fact, the tone of it was serious enough that it gave Laura real pause.

She shot a glance behind her. Nate was still on the phone, on hold. Laura guessed he was waiting to be patched in on a call, or else to be transferred to another department. She couldn't hear the hold music, but she could see him bobbing his head just slightly from side to side, almost unconsciously. She smiled in spite of herself and turned back before he could feel her watching him and look up.

She took a single deep breath before typing out her reply.

*Hi, VirginiaMan383. Nice username! I would like to meet up. I'm not in DC right now, but I'll contact you when I get back.*

And that was that. Laura figured she didn't need to really meet him. If she looked into him a little more and changed her mind when she was home, she just didn't need to contact him again. But if he was the real thing, if there was even a chance of him being the real thing, she needed to know.

Laura tried not to let it happen, but it did, every time. She felt a flare of hope in her chest, the same place where it had blossomed with regards to the case a few minutes before. What if this was real? What if she'd finally found someone just like her?

She had so many questions. For the person who had made her like this. For the universe, if it wasn't a person. Maybe someone who was just like her would be as clueless as she was. But maybe he would have some pieces of the puzzle, and she had her own, and together they could figure it out more. Find a way to make it stop. To give her peace.

Peace was a little thin on the ground right now, and Laura would have given a lot to get some.

She got up from her chair, lifting her coffee cup and gesturing at Nate. He nodded silently in response and passed his own over. Laura walked out into the hallway, down a couple of turns to the coffee machine, which was one of the only things she could navigate to effortlessly in the building. A few hours into the job, and she knew where the coffee machine was. You had to get your priorities in order.

She was filling up Nate's mug, her own already waiting for her on top of the machine, when one of the sheriff's deputies came and stood by her, waiting with an empty cup in his own hand.

"How's it going?" he asked, obviously trying too hard to be casual. He was young. Laura guessed he'd never dealt with an FBI agent before.

"Would be going a lot better if this stuff was stronger," she said, giving him a bland smile over her shoulder.

He chuckled. "You can say that again. Oh, if you push this button over here, it'll give you an extra shot."

He reached out and pushed it for her. He didn't even touch her. He didn't need to. Because now they were intertwined, the lines of their fates running together for just one moment. And when Laura took the cup from under the machine with a grateful nod, she felt the stab of pain in the center of her forehead.

It took her by surprise—a vision coming out of nowhere. What was happening now? Was this officer in danger?

There was nothing for it. She grabbed hold of the other cup and turned away from the deputy, so that at least he wouldn't be able to see her face when the stab of p—

# CHAPTER FOURTEEN

*Laura was in a bullpen, looking over the desks of the assembled men and women of the sheriff's department. Some of them were talking, others sitting behind computers and staring at the screens. A couple were on the phone. One was just slowly eating an oatmeal and raisin cookie.*

*Laura looked around, saw the deputy she had been speaking to coming back into the room. He had a cup of coffee in his hand. He looked a little cocky, a swagger in his step. Like he'd just met his first FBI agent and was feeling like a real cop.*

*"Hey, man." He nodded to one of the others in the room as he passed by, walking like he thought he was cool. He was very young, Laura thought. He put his coffee to his mouth and sipped at it as he walked.*

*By one of the desks, a round-shaped woman was half-sitting on a low filing cabinet, her back right up against a potted plant that was rocking precariously. She must have felt it beginning to give, because she lunged for it suddenly, shooting to her feet and grabbing hold of the pot.*

*She jumped right into the deputy and knocked his arm. The coffee flew into the air, drenching down the front of his uniform. It splattered onto case files on the nearby desk, and Laura heard someone yelling, "Hey—"*

Laura blinked, unable to prevent a gentle sway as the pain of the vision receded slightly. At least she had already taken the painkiller. Maybe it would take care of this headache as well as the earlier one, whenever it finally kicked in.

Relief flooded over her, some of the tension easing out of her shoulder. Not a death. Just a spilled coffee.

She hesitated, hearing the sound of the coffee machine whirring to life behind her. The deputy was right there. She could delay things. Speak to him. Say something. Then he wouldn't be walking past the lady right as she stood up. He wouldn't spill the coffee.

Laura sighed and started walking back to the office. It wasn't her job to save the whole world. All her life she'd warned people when she knew she shouldn't. Tried to give them advice, which often got thrown back in her face. Given them hints of what to avoid, which only got her accused of setting them up or knowing that they were being set up. A few times, it had been her warning that had directly led to the person being in the wrong place at the wrong time, because they were trying to see if she was right.

And then there were the ones where something even worse had happened. You stopped a waitress in a diner from getting coffee on her apron, and maybe it was a six-year-old child walking by when the hot water fell instead.

Laura didn't like taking those kinds of risks. Not when there wasn't already a life at stake. You tried to fix everything little thing around you, and you'd end up with an even bigger headache—and who knew if any of it would actually help?

Behind her, she heard the deputy shout, followed by a general uproar as the coffee splattered over everything in sight. She didn't turn around.

"I've got it," Nate said, as she reentered the room, already on his feet. He was reaching for his jacket. "Both phones were purchased at the same store, right here in Albany."

Laura took one hurried mouthful of her useless coffee and set it on the desk, grabbing her own jacket and shrugging it on. At last—a lead. Maybe this would give them the name of the killer.

Maybe this would allow them to stop him before he killed again.

"I've got this," Laura said. "Why don't you stay behind?" Surely it was safer for Nate here, inside the precinct, than out there in the world.

"No way," Nate said, putting his jacket on and reaching for his phone. "I've been all cooped up in here. I need to get some action. Let's make some progress."

So much for that. There wasn't anything else she could say that wouldn't come across as suspicious; she was already pushing it.

"All right. Let's go," Laura said, striding out of the room before Nate had the chance to.

***

"This is it," Laura said, leaning forward in her seat as she pulled the car into the parking lot. "Can you see anyone?"

Nate leaned his long frame forward as well, straining to see in the dark. "Not yet. Guess we'll get out and head for the doors, see if anyone's inside."

The store was not as dark as the parking lot, though the blazing yellow lights did not seem to illuminate any customers. There were still a couple of cars parked here and there, but that didn't indicate much. There were other businesses around the same lot, no doubt sharing it. It was late, and most people had gone home for the night. Laura parked near the entrance and got out of the car, feeling the cool evening air flow over the skin of her face like a welcome balm.

Nate stepped out away from the car, looking around, squinting into the distance. "I can't see anyone at all," he said. "Are you sure they're open? Maybe if we—"

Laura only had a split second to grab hold of the back of his jacket and pull, making him stumble back into her. A moment later, the car that had pulled into the parking lot at a reckless speed rushed past the spot he had been about to step right out into.

"Jesus," Nate panted, one hand going to his chest. "That was close. Thanks."

Laura gasped in a breath, relief washing over her. It was short-lived. Her heart was hammering in her chest with the stress of pulling him back, of seeing what could have been his impending doom. The car had come out of nowhere, and she almost hadn't seen it in time.

She wanted to think that she had just saved him from the shadow of death that she had seen hanging around him. But she knew she hadn't. For one thing, the feeling would have been much stronger if the danger was that close.

For another, she could still feel the lingering chill of its touch as she let go of the back of his jacket. It was hanging over him still, and she still had no idea what it meant.

"You should be more careful," she scolded him, as she got her voice back. "I might not be here to pull you back next time."

"Yes, ma'am," Nate said, with enough sincerity and earnestness that Laura didn't shoot him an elbow in the ribs for being cheeky. Even if she had wanted to, she didn't want to feel that again. She couldn't. Not when she needed to concentrate on what they still had to do.

They walked the short distance toward the entrance of the store together without further incident. As they stepped in through a blast of air conditioning—still turned on despite the fact that the outside temperature had cooled—Laura blinked to adjust her eyes to the harsh light. They were in a store that looked much like any other she had been in: several aisles of racks containing items for sale lined up all in a row, more items around three and a half walls. On the remaining half, a counter area was currently manned by an employee in his early twenties.

"Oh, hello!" That was an older man, in perhaps his forties or early fifties, approaching from the left. Laura's gaze snapped to him, then back to the younger man behind the counter. A quick analysis of their features showed a familial resemblance. Same messy brown hair, same dark eyes, same angular nose. Laura guessed the server was his son. "You're the FBI agents I'm supposed to be meeting?"

"Yes," Nate said, flipping open his badge to show the man. "I'm Agent Lavoie, and this is Agent Frost. You recently sold a couple of items that we need to trace. If possible, we want the customer's identity."

"Right, yes," he said, gesturing them over to the counter. "I'm the owner—my name is Fred. I've pulled up some of our records on the computer to show you."

The young man stepped aside as the three of them all bundled behind the counter, taking up almost the whole space. He waited nervously by the side of the gate that let them in, holding one of his arms across his body. He looked nervous, his eyes constantly tracking over Laura and Nate, from one to the other, from one to the other. What did he have to be nervous about? Laura wondered.

"We log all of our sales through an electronic system," Fred was explaining, something which Laura wasn't particularly interested in. It was a standard modern system, and she just wanted him to get to the point. "If you have the item code, I can bring it up easily. Or I can search by name, too."

Nate took his notebook out of his pocket. "Here," he said, pointing to a scrawled note on one of the pages. "This is the type of item we're looking for. It's a cell phone."

"Oh, yes, we don't sell a lot of those," Fred said, quickly typing in the identifier. "Should be easy to find them… Do you have the serial number for the particular phones?"

"I do," Nate said, flipping back a page. "Can you isolate the exact sale?"

"Yes, we can," Fred said, his eyes scanning the list of results as his finger hovered over the entry in Nate's notebook.

Laura glanced over at the son again. He was looking even more shifty, now that the topic of the phones had come up. He had shoved his hands into his pockets and was rocking back on his heels slightly, looking at the floor. Like a naughty kid.

"Hmm," Fred said. "That's odd."

"What is it?" Nate asked, instantly on high alert. For her part, Laura looked at the kid, not at Fred or the screen. Yes. He was biting his lip now. He knew something about what Fred was about to say, no question about it.

"Well, both of these are listed as shrink." Fred checked the screen one more time, then shook his head. "They weren't sold at all."

"What does shrink mean?" Nate asked.

Laura had once worked a part-time job in a store while she was a student. "It means they aren't accounted for in the stock take. Either they went missing somehow, or they were stolen. Right?" she said.

"Yes, that's right," Fred replied. He gave an apologetic shrug. "This happens from time to time. We review the cameras on a regular basis for thefts, but unfortunately, we don't always catch things. These ones aren't listed alongside a crime identification number, which means we couldn't find any evidence of the theft on the tapes."

"Do you at least know when they went missing?" Nate asked.

"To the nearest week, yes," Fred said. "We only do stock take on Sundays. They could have gone missing any time within the past week."

"So we can't narrow it down to a day?" Nate sighed. "Then there's not a lot of hope in going over the security camera footage again."

"Afraid not," Fred said. "We've got seven cameras running twenty-four hours a day, so it would be hours of footage to look through for little reward. As I say, my son and I do check all of the footage as much as we can, and there's nothing that was flagged within the timeframe of these phones going missing."

Laura was barely listening. She had a good idea of what was going on here. The son was tall and lanky, not as well-built as she would have expected. But he might have had hidden depths. It was altogether possible, she thought while looking at him, that he was capable of strangling someone to death.

"Hey," she said, getting his attention. "Could you pass me that pen over there? I want to make a note of something." She gestured to a pen lying on the far end of the counter, next to where he was standing.

"Sure," he said, his voice coming out high and cracked; he cleared his throat as he picked up the pen and walked the two steps closer to her.

Their fingers brushed as she took it from his hand, and Laura felt a pulse of pain in the middle of her forehead, mild but distinct. She lowered her gaze to the pen, feeling the vision take hold of her—

*Laura was standing in the same store, behind the same counter. It was later at night, and the place was deserted. Except for Fred's son, leaning on the counter with a bored expression.*

*He stood up and ambled out from behind the counter, heading toward a nearby display rack. It held various electronic items, phone accessories like headphones and wireless ear buds. He rearranged a few of the cases, putting them back into the correct places. He glanced up at the security camera in the corner of the room, and as he straightened up, his hand brushed over one of the packets.*

*He continued rearranging the shelves, moving down the whole of the rack to the center of the room. Laura watched, hearing only the gentle buzz overhead of the lights, as he casually slipped the box he had picked up into his pocket, below the range of the camera.*

*He turned and drummed a brief pattern on top of one of the packets of cereal at the end of the rack, as if he had run out of things to do. He wandered around for a few more minutes, the time agonizingly long; Laura couldn't help but wonder when the vision would end. It was beginning to feel excruciating.*

*And then he turned and walked toward the back room, out of range of the cameras, and Laura saw him slip the box out of his pocket and into his backpack.*

Laura blinked, finding herself resurfaced back in the real world. It had been minutes in there, but for the others around her, only a second or two had passed. There was a moment of sharp, crushing pain in her head that subsided to a dull ache and lingered. She guessed from the intensity of the vision that this little setback would put him off for a while. The pain wasn't strong enough, despite the repeated visions of the day, to suggest that it was going to happen any time soon. He would be too scared to take another phone, in case the FBI came back. But eventually, he would get bold again.

Because he was the one who had been skimming stock out of the store. He was the one who had taken the phones.

Laura didn't have any time to mess around. If he was the killer, then he could be going off and finding his next victim as soon as his shift ended. She needed to move things along, right now. If anyone asked how she guessed it, she could just say that his nervous behavior had made her suspicious and she'd taken a gamble.

"You took the phones, didn't you?" she said, looking him directly in the eye as she said it.

Behind her, she heard Nate and Fred turning to look. She heard Fred expressing some kind of noise of disbelief, but she didn't turn or look away. She held the kid's gaze, watching as he tried to open his mouth to deny it. As he saw deep in her eyes that she knew, and she wasn't going to be misled. As he realized that he was now in trouble with not just his father, but the FBI.

And she was watching when he turned on his heels and ran.

# CHAPTER FIFTEEN

Laura set out at a run herself, hampered by having to go around the side of the counter first. The kid was already dashing headlong through the store, his sneakers squeaking on the floor as he hurled himself around the corner toward the door. His father gave a single shout, but the kid didn't respond or look back.

Laura swore mentally, hearing Nate react behind her as well. The kid was fast. He was tall and lanky, and that went in his favor. He was already out the door as Laura turned the corner after him, knocking a few bags of chips to the floor as she took it too fast.

She took the force of the door swinging closed on her forearms as she shoved through it, reversing the momentum. The kid was running through the parking lot, in what seemed like a straight line. Laura kept after him, but she could see it was almost pointless. He was opening the distance between them inch by inch. She pushed her straining muscles harder, trying to force them to a faster rhythm.

Behind her, she was aware of Nate's footsteps—but they peeled off, going in a different direction. She hoped he had some idea that would help. She could only stay on the kid, keep him in her sights. She had no hope for anything more than that. If she could just have a vision now—if it would just come—if it would tell her where he was going so that she could cut him off—

But there was nothing she could do. Running like this, focusing all of her attention on catching him, she didn't have the mental space to focus down on each of her senses. And besides, what could she touch? When she had gone after the kidnapper, it had been her hand on the grip of her gun that had triggered it. Now, she had no idea what would set her vision off.

She reached for the gun at her hip, losing a precious second of pace as she twisted to touch it. But there was no tricking the visions. She knew she was never going to pull the gun on this kid, not unless he was armed himself. That wasn't protocol. She had no proof that he was a killer—only a suspicion that he was a petty thief.

The kid vaulted a low wall at the edge of the parking lot and ran between two buildings ahead, a warehouse and what looked like some kind of entertainment center—Laura didn't have enough time to take it in. She saw the thin strip of alleyway between them with diminishing hope. It was dark on the other side. If she didn't catch him here, she would have no way of seeing where he had gone.

She put on one last desperate, hopeless lunge of speed as he reached the end of the alley, knowing as she did that it was pointless. She was going to lose him. He would be out of her reach—they'd have to set up some kind of manhunt—have to track his phone or go to his regular haunts—

And the car screeched around the corner, flashing out in front of the mouth of the alley so quickly that Laura could barely process it.

The kid bounced off the side of the car and hit the concrete, going down hard. The door was flung open even as Laura breathlessly closed the distance down, and Nate got out from behind the wheel—dragging a pair of handcuffs off his belt as he did so.

"Kid, what's your name?" he asked, as Laura panted to a stop beside them. They both looked down at him. He appeared physically fine, though too scared or winded to move.

"Hunter Mason," he said, breathing hard himself.

"Hunter Mason," Nate said, "you're under arrest for theft."

Laura caught her breath as Nate read Hunter his Miranda rights, wondering if that was the only charge they would be adding to his rap sheet this evening.

She could only hope there would be one more: murder.

***

"You okay to go in?"

Laura turned to see Nate coming toward her, a slim file in his hand. It didn't contain much: just the details of the phones that had been taken, including their activation and deactivation dates and times, as well as the printed records from the store. They'd brought the kid back to the precinct, where he was currently sitting under the watchful eye of a deputy in an interview room.

"Yeah." Laura threw back the last of her coffee and dumped the empty cup into the bin. "I'm ready." She had recovered from her earlier exertions, and the coffee had helped her to stave off both the tiredness and the small headache from her vision. It was no substitute for real sleep, but for now, it would have to do. It was getting on toward midnight, but if this was their killer, they would soon be able to get back to a bed somewhere.

"Usual approach?" Nate asked.

"Usual approach," Laura confirmed with a smile. "Go ahead, Bad Cop."

She followed Nate into the room, the heavy door snapping shut behind them with a ring of finality. Hunter was slumped over in his chair, his thin shoulder blades seeming almost to stick out from his body through his thin store uniform shirt. He looked like he hadn't yet finished growing into his lankiness, like he still needed to finish filling out.

He looked up with alarm as they entered, though he didn't change his posture. He didn't say a thing, just swallowed.

"My dad said I should wait until I have a lawyer," he said immediately, his eyes wide and shining as Laura took a seat opposite him. Nate was slower to join her, slapping the file down on the table in front of his chair first.

"Sure, we can wait for a lawyer to get here," she said. "You're entitled to that. Unless you just want to speed things up and tell us why you committed these murders right off the bat."

It would almost have been funny, the way his eyes widened even further, his face turning into a comic book expression of shock. It would have been, except for the two dead women—and the third that Laura had glimpsed in her vision.

"What the fuck?" he burst out, shaking his head rapidly. "Murder? I—I don't have anything to do with any murders. What are you talking about?"

"You want to play innocent?" Nate asked, his voice a deep rumble beside her. He slid into it so easily: the menacing, angry, vengeful man. A perfect foil to her helpful, innocent woman act. "We can do it that way. It will just take longer. You're going to tell us the truth, one way or another."

"No, I'm serious—I thought this was about stolen phones." He looked even more panicked than before, his head snapping from side to side as he looked at the pair of them. His hands were gesturing wide on the table, his face pale and drained. "You never said anything about a murder!"

"Why did you think we might be looking into the phones in the first place, Hunter?" Laura asked. She kept her voice calm and controlled in comparison, with just a hint of accusation. Enough to keep him thinking that she and Nate had all the power—and that they weren't going to believe his lies. Not enough to make it seem like she wasn't trying to help.

"I…" Hunter hesitated. He seemed to search the tabletop for something, before looking up at her again with a pained expression. "I thought it was just about the weed."

Laura exchanged a glance with Nate. He had a cunning curve to his lips, as if he was amused by the story Hunter was giving them. "What weed, Hunter?" Laura asked.

"I…" Hunter struggled, looking down again. The muscles of his jaw clenched and moved as he fought with his inner impulses. "I stole the phones, okay? I did. I just—I don't have anything to do with any murder. I swear!"

"Why did you take the phones?" Laura asked patiently. They were getting somewhere here, she knew. She believed the kid. He was nervous enough, frantic enough. It didn't look like he was acting. But she also didn't like the direction this was going—because she was starting to believe that he was innocent.

"I've been dealing pot on the side," he said, examining his own hands as he said it. His face was flushed beet red, and his eyes were welling up with liquid, but he managed to keep his voice steady. "Just bringing in a little bit of extra cash so I could get a new car. That's all. I used the prepaid phones to talk to buyers. That's why I've been taking them."

Laura shifted in her seat and glanced at the file, a silent signal to Nate.

"If that's the case," he said, taking his cue as he pulled out the phone records they had been able to gather, "then why were these phones turned on, activated, and used to make only one call—both of them right before the murder of a local woman?"

Hunter shook his head from side to side. "I don't know, man," he said. "I took more phones than I needed. I… I keep them with my stash. Maybe I lost one or two of them somewhere. I don't know."

"We're going to need something a lot more convincing than maybe, Hunter," Nate threatened. But Laura knew it was no good. The kid was telling the truth. He really had no idea.

He was probably high at some point and left the phones somewhere. She wouldn't put it past him. Or maybe a wily client had pickpocketed him, only to wind up with phones rather than pot.

Figuring out what exactly had happened to them could turn out to be impossible—and it would take precious time.

Time they didn't have. Because the killer was still out there—and that meant that, even now, he might be going after the woman Laura had seen.

Laura stood up from her chair, nodding silently to Nate as she did so. He returned the nod, with only the slightest twitch to his eyes to indicate that anything was amiss. He was probably itching to ask her where she was going. But he wasn't going to show in front of Hunter that he wasn't in control of the situation. He wasn't going to show a shred of weakness. Always better for the suspect to think that the agents had a whole routine worked out between them, a routine he wasn't privy to.

Laura left the room without saying another word. As she left, she heard Nate asking the question again—for Hunter to back up his story. Telling him to focus.

As soon as the door was closed behind her, Laura broke into a run down the corridor. She was done playing games. They were wasting their time with Hunter. The kid had no idea about anything. And Laura knew the killer was out there tonight. She *knew*. She'd seen it.

The only thing she could do now to save that woman was to see it again—and clearer this time.

# CHAPTER SIXTEEN

Laura barged through the door into their investigation room and shut it firmly behind her, walking over to the computer with determination. Within a few clicks, she brought up the recording file and pressed play, turning the volume up. She pushed her hand flat against the speaker without sitting down, feeling the vibrations through her hand. She breathed deep. She was going to do this. She was going to trigger the vision, if she had to sit here all night and play this damn recording over and over again. Even if she had to contend with Nate trying to get her taken off the case and committed for obsessive behavior. She was going to have a vision, no matter what.

It was, paradoxically, sweet relief when the stabbing pain in her forehead began. It was as sharp as a red-hot blade, branding into her skin. Laura was sure that if she reached up and touched her head, she would feel blood running down. Or at least some kind of—

*She was above them again. The woman, fighting for her life. Yes. Laura knew it was the same scene that she had visited before, but this time it was stronger. Clearer. So much more real, she could almost taste the air.*

*The woman was there, and Laura felt the vision moving in toward her face. She was choking, turning red, her eyes beginning to bulge out with the stress of the strangulation. Her hands were clawing at her neck so viciously that she scratched a line in the skin of her own face on the way down.*

*There was a piece of fabric around her neck. A familiar pattern. A dish towel, Laura thought. Yes—they were in a kitchen. The white, shiny surface next to them was a fridge. The murder would happen in the kitchen.*

*All right, she thought. Now show me more. Show me more!*

*But all she could do was stay frozen in place, right above the woman's face. Everything around her was fuzzy, some of it dark, some of it completely blank. All Laura knew for certain was the woman's face, and the towel around her neck. Her dark eyes were huge with fear, bulging with the strain to breathe. Laura watched as the woman kicked out with her legs, her upper body bucking in reaction, how she reached out and attempted to scratch at the person holding the towel. It made no difference.*

*Laura wanted to reach out, to stop this. She wanted to grapple with the killer for the woman's sake, to save her life. She struggled desperately to do so, even though she had no arms to reach with here. No physical presence to fight with. She was only an observer, floating above it all, not even able to control where she looked.*

*She watched as the woman lost her battle. As she slipped lower and lower toward the floor, unable to lift herself up. As her eyes rolled back in her head. As she convulsed, the last desperate attempt of the body to gain air for use in the lungs. Then she stopped moving at all, and for a long moment the killer continued to hold her, long past the point that the body could still survive.*

Laura opened her eyes, gasping for breath. She tore her hand away from the speaker as if it was burning hot, and closed out the recording before she heard one more moment of it. She sank down into the chair waiting behind her, no longer trusting her legs to keep her standing.

It wasn't just the shock. The pain and terror of seeing that happen in front of her eyes. It was the pain in her head, washing over her now in terrible waves. The vision she had seen—it had been one of the most powerful she'd had in a long while, despite the edges being so fuzzy.

And it had been one of the most terrible for a long while, too. The visceral nature of it, the way it had been so detailed and close. She couldn't stop seeing the woman's eyes, straining and bulging for air, desperate and afraid. Laura closed her own eyes to hold the tears in, trying to keep control.

There had been something else, too. That same déjà vu washing over her. The feeling that she had been there before, and not just in the sense of having seen the same vision in a more fragmented way earlier. No, something about the setting, the woman. Even though most of the room was obscured from her, Laura felt as though it was somewhere she had been before.

But they were still in Albany. And Laura still hadn't been to this city in her life until now. None of it made any sense.

And when it came down to it, what had she seen? Laura knew the woman by sight now, but that wasn't useful at all. The power of the headache told her that what she had seen was happening imminently. It could be happening right at this moment. That meant there was no time to save the woman. It would have been difficult even if Laura knew who she was, where she lived. And she hadn't seen the killer. Not even his hands, which were behind the woman's neck as he pulled the dish towel tight. Her own dish towel, no doubt.

It gave her nothing to go on. She'd gone through all of that, forced herself to watch, triggered this horrible pain, and for nothing.

Her eyes flew open when the door did, jolting her out of her own thoughts as she attempted to plaster on a blank expression. It was pointless. Even the motion of lifting her head like that sent dizzy waves of pain through her.

"What was that?" Nate demanded, entering the room and walking right up to her. "You just walked out on me."

"I'm sorry," Laura said, nursing her head. "I… I just. I don't know. I just had this migraine or something come on."

"Are you all right?" Nate asked, squinting at her. A look of concern fell over his face, transforming him from the man who could easily come across as the Bad Cop to a worried friend. He squatted down beside her chair so he could look up into her face. "You're very pale. And you're sweating. Are you coming down with the flu or something?"

"I, um." Laura shook her head. The pain that flowed through her immediately took away her reasoning for a moment. "I don't know. I just got… ha. I don't know. Maybe it's an overnight thing."

"You've been peaky the whole day," Nate said, worry creasing a deep frown between his eyes. "At the kidnapping, too. I thought you were just exhausted from the chase, but—you haven't been well for a while."

"No, no, it's just been tiredness, like you said," Laura replied, waving her hand. She forced herself to smile and to hold her head upright, even though the throbbing was making her feel sick. "Honestly. I'll be fine after a good night's sleep."

"We going to the motel?" Nate asked. "I know I'd do good on a couple hours' more sleep, at least."

"Yeah, good idea," Laura said. But even as she agreed and stood up, reaching for her jacket, she had no faith that she would be getting her head down tonight.

She only had a short while to wait before someone found the body of the dead woman and called it in. Enough time to dose up on painkillers, and not much more, she would bet. Neither of them would be getting much rest.

And with the face of the dying woman replaying behind her eyelids at every step she took, Laura knew she wasn't going to be able to rest properly at all until she caught this killer.

# CHAPTER SEVENTEEN

Laura shoved her hands into the pockets of her jacket as she walked, trying to keep the pace brisk. The longer she lingered in any one spot, the higher the possibility that she would wind up leading herself right into a vision, and she couldn't afford to see anything that didn't affect the case right now.

Of course, there was also the possibility that walking this fast would put her into the path of someone else and trigger a vision anyway, but Laura could hope.

She didn't know where she was going and barely remembered how far she had walked already, but she was stuck in a cycle in her mind that she couldn't seem to break. First, she would try not to think of anything at all. To clear her mind. Instead, she would end up seeing the face of the poor dying woman from her vision, the woman she knew would be killed tonight.

And she would think about that woman, helpless and alone right now, maybe even dying right now. Or lying already dead, waiting for someone to find her. And Laura would feel sick to her stomach, and powerless, and she would clench her fists to stop herself from crying.

And then the rest of it would pile in afterward: the knowledge that she couldn't save anyone right now. The shadow of death hanging over Nate, which hadn't given her a vision. Which might not give her a vision for months.

And from there, onward to Amy, little Amy trapped with her father and in need of help. Maybe in need of help even now. Laura would remember what she had seen and the sickness would roil in her stomach again, and she would wonder what the hell she was doing here in Albany instead of back in DC trying to make sure none of it ever happened.

Because no matter which way she turned, Laura was needed. She had to do something to stop all of these awful things from happening, because she was the only one who knew that they would. But she couldn't keep all of these plates spinning in the air. She couldn't report crimes that hadn't yet happened, and she couldn't be everywhere at once.

She had to choose who to help, and when.

Laura felt something at the bottom of her pocket and pulled it out. She hadn't worn the jacket during the warm days of summer, and it was only in flying out here that she'd pulled it out of the closet; she couldn't even remember when the last time she wore it would have been. Looking at the disc between her fingers, Laura realized what it was: a sixty-day chip.

She'd only ever made it to the full sixty days once, so it wasn't hard to recall when she'd put it there. And then, like every other time, she'd fallen off the wagon.

She could do with falling off the wagon right now.

How else was she supposed to cope with this awful knowledge, these terribly images that kept flashing behind her eyelids, than having a drink? If she went to a bar right now, she could order something cheap and strong and feel the burn as it slid down her throat. Before long, she would forget about the visions, forget about the people who needed her. She didn't get visions at all when she was drunk either. It drowned everything out. She needed to drown everything out.

But Laura only spurred herself to walk faster as she dug her cell phone out of the other pocket. She hit the speed dial—the one number she would need the most in emergency situations—and waited for it to connect.

"Laura," he said, answering the call. "This is late, even for you. It's past midnight already."

Laura took a deep breath. "I know," she said. "I'm sorry, Garth. I just needed you to talk me down."

He chuckled. "Well, that's what I'm here for."

It was true. Garth Rupertson was Laura's AA sponsor; they'd met when she first starting going to meetings and hit it off, although it wasn't as though Laura had been to a lot of them lately. She vacillated between being too ashamed to show her face and admit she'd been drinking again, too busy with a case, and too overconfident that this time she was going to stay sober without help. Garth was always there for her in the moments between, when she was able to accept she still needed a hand—and to reach out for one.

"I've been out walking for half an hour," she said, partly to explain why she was breathing a little faster than normal. "I can't stop thinking about how much easier everything would be if I just went out and had a drink."

"Would it?" Garth asked. He had a hint of amusement in his voice. "Will it be easier to deal with everything you're doing right now, as well as a hangover? Will it be easier to work if you can't walk in a straight line or remember anything you did for the past twenty-four hours?"

"No," Laura admitted, but Garth wasn't even done.

"Will you find things easier to deal with when you've lost your job because you were drunk on duty? You are on duty, right?"

"I'm working a case in Albany," Laura admitted. She wrapped her free arm around herself against the night's chill. "No, it wouldn't make things easier. Not in the long run. I know."

"What are you dealing with right now?" Garth asked, then continued before she could interrupt to fob him off. "Now, I know you can't tell me the details of an active case. Just in general, Laura. Are you feeling overwhelmed?"

"Yes," she said. "There's so much pressure. Right now, I'm the only one who can do anything about this—this danger. If I don't stop the person we're chasing down, then people will die."

"Now, that's not quite right," Garth said. "I know it isn't. You've told me before you have that wonderful partner of yours. The one who doesn't judge you for your past mistakes, isn't that him? And he's a good agent, too, the way you tell it. You're saying he doesn't share any responsibility at all for doing this work?"

"Of course he does," Laura said, closing her eyes for a moment before refocusing on the sidewalk. There were so many times in her life when it would be so much easier if people understood where she was coming from. Saw that she really was the only person who could do what she could do. "It's just—the pressure is still on. We have different leads to follow, and if I don't get mine right, this guy ends up walking free for longer."

That, at least, was close enough to the truth.

"So, you've got to do your job right, and you will," Garth replied, his voice steady and reasonable. "But stop discounting your partner. He's got his part to play as well. And if you make a mistake, that's what he's there for—to catch it."

"I get it," Laura said, and sighed. In spite of the fact that she wanted to argue, Garth was right. Nate was a good agent. If she didn't get a lucky break with a vision, that didn't mean they would never solve the case. He was just as capable at chasing down a lead as she was.

Now, anyway. While he was still here. Laura shuddered, remembering that aura of death that surrounded him and hugging herself tighter.

"You don't sound convinced, Laura," Garth said. "Talk to me."

"I just want a drink," she said, her voice cracking. "I know there are so many reasons not to. But it's not…"

"Not logical. I know." Garth paused, and when he began to speak again, his voice had a cadence that Laura recognized as him settling into one of his Life Lesson Moments. "I've been sober for twenty-one years, Laura. Since I was around your age. Do you know what I think, every time something bad happens?"

"No," Laura said, prompting him impatiently when he didn't go on.

"I think, I could really do with a drink." Garth paused to let that sink in. "Twenty-one years. But, see, here's the thing. You've got to build yourself a wall of reasons. Not just one thing, or two things. You need this giant wall of reasons that stands between you and that bottle. So that if any of those reasons get taken away, the wall still stands. Do you understand me?"

"I think so," Laura said. Her pace had started to slow down. She kicked a loose stone and made herself jump as it skittered away from her, out into the road.

"Right now, you're trying to get sober for your daughter, and that's great. It's amazing. Kids—they're one of the best reasons in the world to fight those inner demons." Garth paused again. Laura rankled at these long pauses of his. If she didn't appreciate his guidance so much, she would be telling him to hurry the hell up. "But, Laura, one reason won't keep you sober. It won't. It can crumble so easily. You mess up by showing up late to a court appointment, you realize you've let your little girl down, and there you are—you might as well have a drink and really finish the job off. You know? I know you've been there."

Laura sighed, pinching the bridge of her nose. He was right. She had.

"So, you've got to work on this. Come to meetings when you're home. Build yourself up a wall of reasons. And every time you think about having a drink, instead of going out for one, start building up that wall. Think about all of the reasons you can't have a drink right now."

Laura nodded, even though Garth couldn't see her. "Okay," she said, at length, realizing that he was done and not just leaving one of his long pauses.

“All right.” Garth took a breath. “Now, you go ahead and work on that. You call me again if it’s not working. And, Laura? For goodness’ sake, go to your motel or wherever it is you’re staying. It must be freezing out there.”

Laura half-laughed. “Yeah, it is,” she said, stopping in the middle of the sidewalk. She turned her steps back in the direction she’d come, trying to remember the way back. “All right. Thanks, Garth.”

She ended the call, slipping the phone back into her pocket as she took a deep breath and thought about the walk she had ahead of her. A pang of homesickness hit her: being at home in her own bed would be fabulous right about now. And hearing her daughter’s voice. Maybe tomorrow she could try Marcus again, see if he would let her talk to Lacey. Even for a moment. Even to hear her voice in the background of the call.

She must have pressed a button on the side of her cell phone as she put it away, because it buzzed in her hand.

But then it buzzed a second time—and a third.

Laura grabbed it back out of her pocket, realizing that it was ringing. She checked the caller ID and began to walk back to the motel faster even as she answered. “Nate?”

“Why aren’t you in your motel room?” It was him, all right, and he sounded irritated. Laura didn’t doubt that he had been woken up from what would have been a pretty short nap. “It doesn’t matter. Get back here now. We’ve got another body.”

# CHAPTER EIGHTEEN

Laura leaned her head, looking out of the car window at the building as they pulled up outside it. There was no need to ask which building they were looking for. The sheriff's cars and the deputies milling around gave it away, as did the ambulance.

"This is different," she said, as Nate put the car into park. "A house, not an apartment."

"Let's go see what else he's changed," Nate said grimly, getting out and walking around to her side as they crossed the sidewalk together. "Third time proves the rules, after all."

Laura nodded, her head heavy. Nate was right; this was an opportunity to see which elements were truly tells of their killer's MO, and which were coincidence. But Laura already knew what they were going to see when they went in there—or at least who.

She couldn't recognize the building from the outside. It looked like any normal family home: a short driveway with enough room for one car, three windows on the front side, one solid-looking door. She didn't know the bearded man who was standing to the left of the entrance with his arms folded across his chest, a look of faded and strained grief frozen on his face. But she knew that she was going to recognize the victim.

Nate flashed a badge and then followed one of the sheriff's men into the house, down a hall to the kitchen. This was where the majority of the activity was taking place: a crime scene photographer was flashing images of the body, and white-suited forensics professionals were taking samples from the rest of the room before starting in on the victim herself.

Laura felt no joy at the fact that the woman lying on the floor next to her fridge was the same one from her vision. That feeling of déjà vu lingered, though this time she wasn't concerned by it: she'd seen this vision twice, after all. This was her third visit to the home. Of course she would feel like she'd seen it all before.

Perhaps she should at least have felt glad. It meant that she was getting closer to the killer: the vision had been much more clear, given her so much more detail. And it had been accurate.

But Laura would have given away all of that progress in a heartbeat if it meant that this woman didn't have to die.

"There you are," Sheriff Lonsdale said, turning his gray eyes on them as they stepped inside the room. Nate took up most of the doorway until he moved to one side, allowing Laura to stand by the sheriff and look down on the grisly scene. The woman's neck was marked by ugly red marks where the dish towel had slipped away. "This is the work of the same guy, no doubt. The lady here is Nadia. Her son was sleeping upstairs while she was strangled to death."

Laura's heart clenched desperately at his words. They were said so casually as to sound bitter; Sheriff Lonsdale, too, seemed to find the situation deplorable. But Laura's pain hit twice as hard, then three times. Once, for Lacey. Twice, for the other little girl she hadn't yet been able to rescue: Amy. Laura thought of either of them dealing with the loss of a parent and it made her blink back tears. Mostly because Lacey effectively had—and Amy was going to.

"Is he okay?" she asked, one hand going up to her chest.

"Oh, yes," Lonsdale said, his voice softening as he looked her over, realizing he had caused unnecessary worry with his words. "Yes, the little lad is fine. His father came home and found the body, and the boy was still sound asleep up there, none the wiser. He's been taken to a neighbor."

"It looks to have all the usual hallmarks," Nate commented, seemingly unaffected by their conversation. He didn't have children, Laura thought, uncharitably. A moment later she reprimanded herself. The boy was fine. Nate was getting on with the job of getting justice for his mother. "I can't see anything that stands out as different."

"Me either," Laura said, swallowing hard and fighting to come back to a professional standard. Of course, she knew firsthand that nothing was different. She'd seen it.

"Well, shall we go talk to the husband?" Nate asked. "Get his statement before he collapses?"

"Good idea," the sheriff said, gesturing toward the door. "He's right outside. Name's Paul."

"We saw him on the way in, I believe," Laura said, nodding. She nodded one more time to Nate, an unspoken communication. "Thanks, Sheriff. We'll wait to hear the preliminary forensic report—I guess, tomorrow morning?"

"Right," he agreed, as Laura turned and led Nate back outside.

She headed right for the bearded man she had seen earlier. He was easy to spot: the only one not in a uniform, the only one standing around idly, the only one who looked like he still had no idea what was going on. He was tall and broad, his arms folded across his chest with the air of a linebacker, but he couldn't have looked more lost. Laura felt terrible for him. He'd had the shock of his life, coming home and finding his wife like that. If she had been able to get here quicker and save him that, Laura would have.

"Excuse me," she said, feeling the cold air of the night on her face again. It was welcome right now. It kept her awake and alert, soothed off the sickness in her stomach at the thought of Nadia's eyes as she died. "You're the victim's husband?"

He nodded. "Yeah. I…" He stopped, seemingly at a loss as for what to say.

Laura gave him a sad, sympathetic smile. "We'd like to talk to you for a moment, if you can. I'm FBI Agent Laura Frost, and this is my partner, Agent Nathaniel Lavoie."

Paul looked at her sharply for a moment, and gave a bark of unhumorous laughter. She thought he was probably thinking that he didn't know if he could do anything right now. "Okay," he said, though, and so she took the opportunity to press on.

"Do you know if there is any reason why someone would want to harm your wife? Or hurt you?" she asked. It wasn't as though she thought he was going to come up with anything. Nothing had come up with the other two women. But there was always the possibility that this one was going to be the one that cracked the whole case wide open.

"No, no one," Paul said. He was distracted, looking back toward the house often. His eyes had a glazed look to them. He still hadn't processed things properly. "Why would they?"

"Well, it's entirely possible this was a more random crime," Laura said, trying to keep her voice even and calm despite the fact that it made her so angry. To think of this woman cut down in her prime, her son left without a mother—just because this killer wanted a victim, and anyone would do? "Have you noticed anything unusual over the past few days? Anyone in the neighborhood that you didn't recognize?"

"No, nothing like that either," Paul said, running his hand over his hair. He turned and froze; Laura followed his gaze and saw that he was looking at a half-deflated ball on the lawn, obviously one of his son's toys. "Ashton. My—my son. I should go and check…"

"Of course," Laura said quickly. She could see that he wasn't in his right mind right now. Her questions were barely getting through to him at all. She glanced up at Nate, checking whether he wanted to say anything before they let him go.

"Just let us know your contact details, sir, if you would," Nate added, his voice low yet brisk. "So that we can get in touch with you if we have any more questions later."

"Sure." Paul reached into his back pocket and pulled out a wallet, extricating a business card from it. He handed it to Nate, who responded in kind with one of his own. With the exchange complete, Paul slipped away, moving through the stream of law enforcement professionals and heading next door.

"Huh," Nate said.

Laura looked around at him; he was studying the business card with a raised eyebrow. It looked tiny in his large hands. "What?"

He turned it without a word, allowing her to read it for herself. *Paul Frost, Realtor.*

Paul Frost.

"Hey," Laura said, reaching out to snag the sleeve of a deputy that was just passing by. "What's the victim's full name?"

He stared at her like she'd asked him to name the seventy-nine moons of Jupiter. "Uh… Nadia Frost?"

Laura let him go, reeling.

Frost.

She had a terrible, terrible feeling that she finally understood what was happening here.

# CHAPTER NINETEEN

Laura turned and strode forward, marching right off the property and out into the road. Behind her, she heard Nate call her name and then run to catch up.

"Hey, where are you going?" he asked, getting level with her again just as she reached the car.

"Back to the precinct," she said. "Come on. Get in."

Nate made a confused noise. "Why? We haven't had a good look at the rest of the house yet."

"We don't need to. Get in, Nate!" These last words were shouted as she ducked her head, already climbing into the driver's seat.

"Wh…" Nate gave up arguing and opened the passenger's side door, to her relief, taking a seat beside her. He hadn't even closed his door yet when she started the engine, prompting him to throw up his hands in alarm. "Whoa, whoa, whoa. Just where is the fire right now?"

"For god's sake, Nate," Laura said, turning to him. "The first victim's name was Laura. Now Frost? You don't see that?"

"Well, what about Caroline?" Nate said. "I mean, Laura's a common enough name, and so is Frost. This can't be your first time dealing with someone with either of those."

"It's not," Laura said, gesturing impatiently for him to put his seatbelt on. One moment longer, and she was going to reach over and do it for him. "But Caroline's nickname was Carrie."

The second his seatbelt clicked into place, Laura nudged the car forward, heading out into the road again. She checked her mirrors and then peeled out, putting her foot down as much as she dared in this urban setting.

"I'm not getting it," Nate said. "What? Is that your middle name or something?"

"It's my mother's name," Laura said grimly. "Laura, Carrie, and now Frost. There's no way that's just a coincidence. Which is why we need to get back to the precinct—right now."

***

"We have to find out who the next victim is," Laura said, half-running through the precinct to their office. She almost knocked over a hapless deputy who was going back to his desk with a cup of coffee, obviously left behind to man the phones. "We have to figure out the name."

Nate trailed behind her, only just managing to keep up. "Laura, I don't know…"

"Please," Laura said, throwing the word over her shoulder along with a desperate glance. "We need to think about this." She reached their makeshift office and threw the door open, heading right for the board. She grabbed a pen and circled two things: Laura, for Laura Carlisle, and Caroline, for Carrie Birchtree. Underneath, she added Nadia Frost, circling Frost.

"Do you even have any more women in your family?" Nate asked, closing the door behind him with a sigh and folding his arms across his wide chest. "I didn't think you had a sister."

"I don't, except for Lacey. But I don't know if she counts. She's a child, and the other names have been adults. She doesn't live with me. Everyone else has been older. I don't think it fits the pattern." Laura tapped the end of the pen against her chin for a moment, thinking. "It has to be my father. Me, then my mother, then our family name—my dad has to be next."

"What was his name?" Nate asked, sounding as though he was only playing along because he knew what she was like. That she was too far down this rabbit hole to listen to reason—and that sometimes she came out the other side of the hole with an answer that made sense. It was far from the first time she'd worked a whole case on what she told him was just gut instinct—but they always got an arrest.

"Alex," she said, writing it on the board in block capitals. "Alexander, but he went by Alex."

"There are probably hundreds of men called Alex in Albany," Nate said, unfolding his arms and throwing them wide in an exasperated gesture. "That doesn't help us at all, Laura. We don't have any way to use this information."

Laura felt her heart quickening its already rapid pace in her chest. Nate was right. How were they ever going to narrow it down?

They had to figure this out fast. If they didn't…

"Someone's going to die," she said, out loud. She heard her own voice shaking. "We only have twenty-four hours, maybe less. We have to figure this out, or we're not going to be able to save them!"

"All right, whoa," Nate said, holding up his hands and stepping forward. He stopped just shy of touching her as she flinched away. "Laura, I need you to take a breath and slow down a minute."

She dropped her shoulders, closing her eyes for a brief moment. He was right. She was on the verge of some kind of panic attack, and—

She wrenched herself backward with a cry. Nate had reached out and put his hands on her shoulders. The cold feeling of death washed over her in a wave, almost bringing her to her knees with despair.

"Jesus, Laura…" Nate stepped back and gave her space, shaking his head. "Sit down. Please. You need to rest for a minute, get your breath back. You're on edge."

Laura did as she was told, trying to swallow on her dry throat. She was, but he didn't know why. She couldn't tell him all the things that were flying around in her head. The killer. His death. Amy. Her own daughter. The burning need for a drink. The killer. Round and round in a circle, over and over again. All of them needed her attention right now. None of them could wait.

"All right, just take a deep breath in," Nate said, drawing in his own breath with an exaggerated noise as he waved a hand encouragingly in her peripheral vision. "That's it. And now let it out… Good, Laura. Let's breathe in again, nice and slow."

Laura followed his guidance, against her own will. There were tears pricking the backs of her eyelids. She needed this—to calm down, to think, to breathe. But she didn't have the time. She couldn't spare it. People were going to die and get hurt if she slowed down. People she cared about. Strangers, too. It didn't matter. They all deserved to be saved.

But she followed Nate's calm and soothing voice, breathing in when he told her to and breathing out only when he commanded it. Slowly, Laura found herself coming back down to earth.

She blinked and looked up at him, realizing that his face was full of worry and fear. He obviously thought she was losing it. She didn't blame him.

"I'm all right," she said, finding her voice steady and quiet again. "Just… we need to get back to it. Figure out who the next victim is. Alex something, it has to be."

"Just wait a minute," Nate said, shaking his head. "We need to think this through. I get that it's a big coincidence. It's really strange. Laura and Carrie is weird, Frost is even weirder. But I just don't get how the rest of the pieces fit together."

"What pieces?" Laura asked, frowning.

"Well, Albany, for one. Have you ever been to Albany before?" Nate sat up a little straighter, gesturing toward the local map they had pinned up on one wall, red pushpins indicating murder scenes. One more still needed to be added.

"No," Laura admitted.

"So, if someone is targeting you somehow, why would they do it here in upstate New York? Why not closer to home—DC, or where you grew up?"

Nate's voice was reasonable. Too reasonable, actually. If he would scream and shout at her, Laura would at least feel justified in arguing back. "I don't know," she said, blowing out a heavy breath. "I haven't figured that out yet."

"And why would someone want to target you like this?" Nate asked, gentle but relentless. "Laura, if someone had a grudge against you, wouldn't they just want to kill you? To hurt your family directly? Going after random strangers like this—does that make sense to you?"

"No." Laura paused, then shook her head fiercely. "But, Nate, I've made dozens of arrests. And each of them had family members, people who might bear a grudge for taking them away. There are even family members of victims I didn't manage to save in time, murders none of us were able to solve. There are probably hundreds of people who have a reason to dislike me."

"We're not talking about dislike," Nate said, half-laughing on the word, but there was no humor in it. "Laura—killing three strangers. That's not dislike. The only thing that could motivate that would be pure and unrestrained hatred. Do you really think someone out there feels that strongly about you? I mean, just you. Not a partner of yours or a judge or a local cop who did the groundwork before you arrived. Why would there be anyone out there who would hate just you, and you alone, that much?"

Laura paused, studying her hands. Everything he was saying made total sense. She couldn't think of an answer.

"Look, it's late," Nate said. "Or early, maybe. I'm too tired to work it out. And you didn't even get any rest at all. We need to head back to the motel, get some sleep."

Laura opened her mouth to object. "But—"

"No, please. We aren't going to get any further on this tonight—especially not sleep-deprived." Nate only paused for a moment before continuing, not leaving her enough room to argue again. "We have to wait until morning for the forensic report, anyway. What else could we possibly be doing right now? We've spoken to the husband, and we can ask the sheriff to carry out all the background checks to make sure there's no link between the three women. Forcing yourself to stay awake now doesn't make any sense."

"I could be going through my old cases," Laura said stubbornly. "I could check through all of them and try to see if there's someone who would hold that kind of grudge. That would be worthwhile."

Nate sighed, buried his head in his hand for a moment, and then looked at her again. "Okay, fine. I had a couple of hours' sleep earlier, so I'll make a deal with you. You go get some rest, and I'll start going through your previous case files. I'll go through them with a fine-toothed comb, look for anyone who had any reason at all to be mad at you and crosscheck it against recent prison releases, see if we can make a shortlist of candidates who it could be."

"I'm not going all the way back to the motel," Laura said immediately. "I want to be here in case something happens."

Nate growled under his breath. "Goddammit, woman. *Fine*. We'll find you a room with a sofa somewhere, okay? But you are going to go to sleep."

Laura hesitated, but at the look on his face, she finally nodded her head. "All right. Just for a few hours." She didn't want to agree to it at all, but she knew two things.

One, that he wasn't going to take her theory seriously while he thought she was so tired she wasn't thinking straight. Especially if she refused to take the reasonable course of action and get some rest.

And two, that she was so exhausted she really did feel like she was going to fall over on the spot. Which meant she was in no real condition to be helping anyone.

"Just for a few hours," Laura repeated to herself under her breath, already trying to calculate whether there was some way she could reduce the time even further before she could come back to it and figure out who this killer with a grudge was.

# CHAPTER TWENTY

*Laura was sitting outside the office, holding onto her favorite doll. The seats were wide and covered in a soft gray fabric that she liked running her hands over, but she had stopped doing that. Her mommy and daddy looked sad and angry and she didn't know why. She didn't understand why they were here.*

*Daddy had said a big long word, something like say—no, not say. Sy. Sy-ky-a-tist? Laura hadn't heard it before, and she didn't know what it meant, and everything was so quiet in this room. Like you weren't supposed to talk here at all. Even though there was only Laura, her mom and dad, and a woman behind a big shiny desk near the door, she felt like she'd be told off if she said anything.*

*"Laura Frost?" A big door at the other side of the room opened soundlessly, and Laura stared up at the woman who had opened it. She was beautiful, with long shining dark hair like a princess, and she knew Laura's name.*

*"... Yes?" Laura said, at length, her voice small and quiet, not sure what she was supposed to do. Her mother's elbow landed in her side, trying to push her forward.*

*"Come on in," the princess said, and Laura got down off the chair, following her with wide eyes.*

*Halfway there, she stopped and turned and looked at her parents. They were still sitting on the chairs. Neither of them had moved. Weren't they coming, too? Her mother nodded encouragingly, but both of them still sat blank-faced, like she had done something wrong.*

*They had yelled at her when she told them about the dog. Was that why she was here?*

*Laura turned and walked after the woman, into the big office room, unsure what was going to happen to her now.*

Laura gasped, her eyes flying open as she surfaced from the dream. No, a memory, she thought. That had all really happened, when she was just a little girl. No bigger than Amy was now, really. Or Lacey.

She sighed to herself, sitting up and trying to chase those old ghosts out of her head. After the first time she made predictions that had come true, therapy had become a habit. That was, until she learned to never talk about her visions, to never tell people what she saw. The therapist had declared that there was nothing wrong with her, and deep inside, Laura had known there was.

She shook her head at her own self, at these memories surfacing just now when she could do without them. She needed to concentrate, not get stuck in the past.

She stretched her arms above her head, feeling the cricks in her muscles from the tiny sofa she'd managed to find in an abandoned office. It was still dark out, which was lucky. No one had come in to wake her up—or to find an FBI agent unexpectedly curled up on their sofa, which might have been an unpleasant surprise for both of them.

Why had that memory come up now? It had been five or six years after that when Laura first felt the shadow of death around her father. When she first had a vision of his death, of his body propped up and shrinking in a hospital bed, bald and prickled with wires and tubes all over. She'd been too afraid to say something then. The therapy was still too recent a memory. She hadn't wanted to cause trouble again, so she'd kept what she saw to herself.

When he'd been diagnosed at long last, Laura had a vivid memory of the moment the specialist had delivered the news that it wasn't going to be possible for him to make it out alive. He'd said it in a soft and gentle way, aware of the fact that he was talking to a wife and a teenage daughter. But Laura had never been able to forget the way he had delivered it: the exact words he had said.

"If we had caught this sooner, we might have been able to do something—but I'm afraid it's too late."

It had been too late because she'd kept it to herself. Stayed silent. She had watched him die a slow and painful death, losing his dignity, every single element of life that might give him pleasure. Swapping it all for just a few more months of chemo-ridden life, with his family forced to sit at his bedside and watch. And now it was happening to Nate, and she still couldn't say a word. If she did, she risked losing her job, being committed, losing the only people she cared about. Being pushed even further back from the possibility of getting visitation rights with Lacey.

How many times in her life had Laura been forced to stay silent and watch things unfold, even when she already knew how they would go? How many times had she said nothing?

Yes, there were times she had stepped in. So many times she'd managed to find a way to make an impact. But there were so many other times, too, when she had tried yet failed to change fate.

Too many failures on both sides. Too many silences. And now it was happening all over again. Nate. Amy. The killer.

What would she do, Laura wondered, if anything ever happened to Lacey—because she was no longer close enough to her daughter to see it and stop it?

Laura grabbed her phone and dialed Marcus's number, needing to hear her daughter. *Needing* it, with everything she was. Every fiber, every bone. The line rang and rang, until finally Marcus's voice kicked in, telling her to leave a message.

Voicemail. Laura ended the call, taking a breath. Of course he wouldn't be awake yet. That would be too much to expect.

She only had to wait a moment, lingering in the disappointment, before the phone buzzed. A wild flare of hope spoiled to sickness as she read the text Marcus had sent her.

*What the hell, Laura. It's five in the morning. Leave us alone.*

Laura bit her lip hard. She'd probably made things worse now. Why was she only ever capable of making mistakes when it came to the people she loved?

She wiped her hands over her face, rubbing her eyes and trying to force herself out of this funk she was in. The dreams and the text had done nothing for her mood, even if she did feel physically a little better thanks to the sleep. She had to get up, get moving, get back to the case.

But first, there was someone else whose fate she needed to check up on.

She dialed another number, seeing dawn just beginning to arrive through the windows and knowing that it was early. Maybe too early. But it was always worth a try.

"Hello, Fallow residence." It only took Laura a moment to place the voice: it was Amy's mother. So she was awake at this time of day, after all.

"Hello, Mrs. Fallow," Laura said, trying to keep her voice smoothly respectful. "I hope it's not too early to call. This is FBI Agent Laura Frost. We met when your daughter was in the hospital."

"Oh—yes," Mrs. Fallow said, her voice uncertain. "You were the one who went in and spoke with Amy directly?"

"That's right," Laura said. "I'm just doing a quick follow-up to check on you all. How are things? How is Amy coping?"

“Um,” Mrs. Fallow said. She sounded as though she was distracted, almost as if she couldn’t focus on the question. “She’s—I mean, she’s quite fine—yes, I…”

Her voice trailed off, and Laura heard something in the background. She strained to hear, but there was no need; the noise was getting louder, presumably closer to the phone. She recognized what it was. It was a man’s voice, asking who she was talking to.

“Sorry, it’s not a good time,” Mrs. Fallow said, and immediately ended the call.

Laura remained still for a long moment after the call had ended, hearing the flat tone beeping in her ear. A man. It had to be him. Governor Fallow.

His wife was obviously already petrified of him. There was no telling how long it might be before he would start to lay his hands on little Amy.

Laura bit her lip. There was nothing she could do from all the way over here. Shouting in the background of a call wasn’t a good enough reason to send somebody over there to check on the family. Even if she did make that call, it wasn’t Laura’s first time dealing with an abusive spouse. She already knew how immensely likely it was that Mrs. Fallow would just make up some excuse that delivered her husband from all guilt, put the minds of the agents or cops that were sent out at ease, and mark Laura down as interfering and paranoid.

No, she couldn’t do anything right now. But she didn’t want to just wait for it to happen either. There had to be a way to spare Amy from what would happen to her. Maybe if there was an FBI agent visiting regularly, the governor would think twice about using his fists…

She vowed to herself that as soon as she was back in DC, she was going to pay them a visit in person. She would see Amy with her own eyes, check that she was still okay.

First, she had a killer to catch—and she wasn’t going to achieve that sitting around in here. Laura stood and strode back to their office, ready to get back to it.

# CHAPTER TWENTY ONE

"Find anything?" Laura asked, grabbing a chair to pull up beside Nate where he was working.

"Well," Nate said, dropping his pen for a moment and rubbing his eyes. He looked as though they were on the verge of going square from staring at the screen for so long. "I started with your most recent cases and worked my way back, through the central database. I haven't found anything just yet. A lot of these guys are still in prison. The ones that aren't, I was able to check in with their parole officers. Every single one of them is far enough from here that there's no way they could be involved."

"Hmm." Laura leaned over, looking at his notebook. Nate leaned back in his chair to give her an easier view. "What about earlier than this?"

"This is as far back as I've gotten," Nate said, with a touch of grumpiness. Laura glanced at his face, saw how deep the bags under his eyes were, and knew he was just tired. "Do you know how long it took me to work through all of these?"

Laura checked her watch and opened her mouth.

"*No*, that was not a literal question." Nate sighed and shook his head. "How far back do you want me to go?"

"A lot further," Laura said, frowning. "If we're looking for a criminal who has been released, then we'll probably get more luck with the cases from earlier in my career, surely? They'll have done some time already."

"All right, fine," Nate said, taking his cursor and scrolling right to the bottom of a long list of Laura's arrest records. "Let's see, this is your first…"

"No, not that one," Laura said, recognizing the name immediately. "I was only assisting. That was my first case. Not him, either. And that one wasn't even a big deal. Keep going…"

"Are you doing this the thorough and logical way, or are we just going to start checking records at random now?" Nate asked, sounding peeved. "I have a system in place, and it's very—"

"This one," Laura said, tapping the screen impatiently. "This one was really angry. Brent Dockhand. Check him out."

Nate sighed and did as he was told, clicking on the entry and bringing up the details. "All right, so what was this? A sex offender case?"

"He was targeting random women in their homes," Laura said, thoughtfully. "Breaking in to assault them, or worse. I could see that as an escalation, don't you think? Assault graduating to murder?"

"I thought we agreed there didn't seem to be a sexual element to these murders?" Nate frowned. He was typing anyway as he spoke, looking up the man's details. With him on the sex offenders' list, it was going to be even easier to track down his current whereabouts.

"It could have changed for some reason," Laura said. "We can figure out the whys and wherefores later. Is he still inside?"

Nate held his breath while the page loaded, and then blew it out sharply. "No. He's been released—about six months ago. And his registered address is about forty-five minutes from here."

Laura swore in surprise. "That's him," she said. "Right? It has to be."

She almost expected a vision to come there and then. It was so close to the mark. This had to be the guy, and that meant they were right on his tail now. Close enough to stop him.

"I…" Nate paused, then shook his head. "I can't believe I'm saying this, but yes. It looks like this might actually be our guy."

"I told you," Laura said, for a moment almost feeling pleased. But then the reality hit her: she was right. This was all about her. These women had been targeted directly because their names just happened to have a connection to Laura.

The guilt hit her like a ton of bricks.

It was her fault that they had lost their lives. Her fault that they weren't going home to their families, or kissing their loved ones, or going to work. She was the one to blame.

"Coming?" Nate asked, wrenching her attention back to him. He was by the door already, hesitating with his hand on the handle, no doubt wondering why she hadn't yet gotten up.

"Right," Laura agreed, grabbing her jacket and following him out of the precinct.

She brought up the information again on her phone as Nate started the car, pulling out and typing in the address on the GPS at the same time. Laura found the information she was looking for and copied the number of Brent Dockhand's parole officer, dialing it right away.

"Hello, Albany co—"

Laura cut the woman off before she had the time to finish her official greeting. "Hello, am I speaking to the parole officer for Brent Dockhand?"

There was a moment's pause. "Ah, yes. Who is this?"

"This is FBI Agent Laura Frost. I'm looking for some up-to-date information on your parolee."

"Right, okay." There was another short pause, as if the parole officer was still mentally catching up. Laura impatiently ground her teeth, needing her to get it together faster. "What is it you need to know?"

"When was his last check-in?"

"Two days ago."

"And that was with you at his registered office, yes?"

"Yes, of course—if he moves, we have to update his details on the system, so everything should be completely up to date."

"And just to confirm, that's what address?"

The woman read it out from her system after a moment of typing, and Laura compared it with the address Nate had entered into the GPS. It was a match.

"All right, thank you for your help." Laura ended the call, cutting off the parole officer's request for her to wait and tell her more about why she needed the information.

"We're on the right track?" Nate asked, reaching up to pull down his sun visor. The first golden rays of light were breaking across the road, shining right into their eyes.

"He's here," Laura confirmed grimly. She still couldn't feel the pulse of pain that signaled an oncoming vision. She reached her hand up to her holster, glancing over the grip of her gun, to see if that would trigger something. There wasn't a thing.

That she wasn't having a vision was not necessarily a bad sign. It could mean that there was no altercation coming, that the man would go without a fight. It was possible that Laura wouldn't ever see another vision about this case, because it was about to be closed—and any other possible futures were dwindling rapidly as she and Nate converged on the man's house to arrest him.

She could only hope. And given that the GPS was still showing a time of at least thirty minutes before they arrived at the address, Laura had a lot of time to carry on worrying about it before she would get her answers.

## CHAPTER TWENTY TWO

Laura jumped out of the car before it came fully to a stop, checking her gun was in its place one last time before she rushed toward the house. It was a tiny terraced building, shabby and dirty, the windows caked with grime—though the other homes in the terrace looked clean and well-kept. She heard the car door slam and knew that Nate was right on her heels, backing her up. She didn't want to give this guy any warning that the FBI was at his door.

She reached the door and banged on it with her whole forearm, rattling it in its frame and making a loud enough noise that she had no doubt would be audible anywhere in the house. The sun had risen completely now, the day just beginning to warm. The rest of the street was almost silent. He'd managed to find himself in a nice enough neighborhood, for a scumbag.

There was no answer within the first few seconds of her knock, so Laura banged on the door again. One more time, she thought, and she would add the standard yell that it was the FBI waiting for him. That usually made them hurry up—though sometimes to the back door of the property, not the front. She was just about to turn and look at Nate, hinting with her eyes for him to go around back, when the door opened.

"What?" the man who opened the door asked, his voice groggy. He was wiping his sleeve over his eyes and squinting at the light as if he had just woken up. Of course he would be tired—if he had been out all night killing women. When he dropped the sleeve, though, Laura recognized him easily. It was him—Brent Dockhand, the creep she had arrested once already. His greasy black hair was longer now, and he had a new tattoo of a roaring tiger on his neck, but it was him. The same sallow skin, the same sunken dark eyes.

"Mr. Dockhand," she said, giving him far more respect than he deserved. "Do you remember who I am?"

He looked at her and blinked, and then a dawning realization came over his face. Laura felt some gratification to see that it also included a kind of horror. He knew exactly who she was. "You're that FBI agent," he said, then looked up several inches to Nate's face and blinked. "What do you want with me?"

“I’m here to arrest you on suspicion of murder,” Laura said grimly, bracing herself; she expected him to run now as she reached out toward him. “Put your hands in front of you, slowly.”

“What?” he said, but he put his hands out all the same, obediently and quietly.

Laura was watching closely for the trick, for the moment when he would snap his hands back or go for a weapon. But he didn’t. Not as she pulled the handcuffs from her belt. Not as she snapped them onto his wrists. Not as she read him his rights.

He just stood there, looking bemused. He didn’t say another word. Didn’t confess. Didn’t resist.

What the hell was he playing at?

“Let’s get him into the car,” she told Nate, leading Dockhand out by his cuffed wrists. He stumbled a little as he crossed the step out of his house, and then looked back.

“Hey, uh, would you lock up for me?” he asked, looking at Nate instead of Laura. “My keys are on the side, just by the door. I don’t want anyone taking my stuff while I’m gone.”

“Sure,” Nate said. By his narrowed eyes and the set of his jaw, Laura knew that he was also puzzled by the lack of reaction. Instead of moving right away to find the keys, he walked with Laura back to the car until she had Dockhand seated inside and buckled in. She waited by the car while he turned back, ensuring that there was no opportunity for Dockhand to dive for the door and try to run.

But he didn’t even try. He just sat there in the back of the car, calm and quiet. Even though he didn’t look happy about the arrest, he also didn’t look particularly concerned. Laura couldn’t help a feeling of prickling unease swarming over her skin as she got into the front seat, timing her moment with Nate’s return.

They drove back to the precinct in silence, only the sound of cars passing them by on the busy roads to keep them company. Laura kept watching Dockhand in the rearview mirror, in the mirror inside her sun visor, the side mirror on the outside of the car, any angle she could get on him. For the whole thirty-minute ride, he didn’t so much as raise an eyebrow. Something wasn’t right. Why was he so calm and cool? She remembered the last time she had arrested him, the way he had fought all the way to the nearest station. How he’d hissed and cursed at her in court.

Several times she thought about opening her mouth, but he was so quiet and still that she didn’t want to risk it. She wanted to get any confession he made on tape when they were back at the precinct. The last thing they needed was for him to admit to it all, but then refuse to repeat it once they were in a position to record his statement as evidence.

By the time they pulled up in the precinct's parking lot and Nate hauled Dockhand out of the car to take him to questioning, Laura was feeling worse and worse about it all. Something definitely wasn't right. She just couldn't put her finger on what.

And when you were dealing with a vicious killer, the last thing that you wanted was something intangibly wrong. Because you might just turn around and realize that someone else's life had been at risk, and you didn't see it in time to stop it.

Nate took him through the booking process as Laura moved away silently, stealing through the corridors to find their little office. She grabbed them a couple of coffees from the machine in the hall, then sat staring at the board they'd put together. The faces of the women, their names. Their crime scene photographs.

What was she missing?

"You ready?" Nate asked, pushing in through the door and reaching to pick up his coffee.

Laura looked around, feeling as though he'd just woken her up. "Yeah, I'm ready. This guy is acting weird, right?"

"Very weird," Nate agreed with a frown. "He was quiet as a mouse while we went through the process. The sheriff's guys took him to an interview room for us. He's waiting now. You want to let him stew?"

Laura shook her head. "The way he is, I don't think it would work. It's almost like he has no problem being here at all. That worries me."

"Me, too," Nate admitted, furrowing his brow. He passed a hand over his neatly trimmed beard, which remained neat despite the fact neither of them had had enough sleep or time for beauty routines, and shrugged. "Can't let him see it, though. All right, let's go."

Laura silently agreed, getting up and walking with him a short distance to another room. It was set up for the interview already. Looking through a small window in the door, Laura saw Dockhand sitting at a table, with two chairs facing him. He was quiet, his hands laced on top of the table.

Laura doused her hesitation by grabbing hold of the handle and stepping inside, placing her coffee down on the table alongside the file which contained all of the information they had on the case so far. It also contained a number of blank pieces of paper, a technique which bulked it out and made it look as though they knew far more than they did.

"Brent Dockhand," Laura said, then hesitated, looking at the empty space next to him. Beside her, Nate was taking his place, folding his large frame into the uncomfortable metal chair. "You are entitled to a lawyer. You're waiving your right to representation?"

Brent nodded calmly. "For now," he said, looking up at her and then across to Nate. "I may change my mind, but I'm hoping that I don't have to."

Laura narrowed her eyes and folded her arms across her chest. She wasn't going to play this guy's game. If he was going to act like this was all fine and easy for him, she was going to call him on it. "You're very calm, for someone who has been accused of murder," she pointed out.

Brent shrugged. "I wouldn't have been if it was anyone else," he said. "But it's you. So it all makes sense."

Laura frowned at him. "What makes sense?" Given that she was looking for someone that she knew was directly targeting her, his words made the hairs on the back of her neck stand up. Was this his plan all along? To get her to arrest him again, for some sick reason?

"Well, I heard about the murders," Dockhand said. His tone was humble and quiet, his eyes landing somewhere on the table rather than meeting hers. "I knew they would be looking into offenders. That's what happens whenever there's something like this. They come knocking on your door."

"Sex offenders," Laura pointed out. "That's what you mean, isn't it, Brock? Men who have been violent towards women."

"Yeah." He cast his eyes further down for a moment, as if ashamed. Laura wasn't buying it.

"But why does my involvement have anything to do with you being calm?" Laura asked. She wanted to needle him, to goad him into saying something he shouldn't. "I've taken you down once before. You don't believe I can do it again?"

"Oh, I believe it," Dockhand said, with a wry smile that quickly faded. "But I didn't do anything this time. And it makes sense. You hear about these murders, you see that I'm here—I don't blame you. I would bring me in for questioning, too."

"So you admit that you look guilty?" Laura asked. She was determined not to give in to him. She was rolling with what he was saying, trying to find a way to twist it against him. She needed to, if she was going to get a confession out of him.

"Well, I guess." Dockhand shrugged. "I'm not, though. Like I said. I'm not… like that anymore. I don't do things to other people."

"You don't?" Laura asked, giving him a look that told him he wasn't believed. "How convenient that is. And we're expected to, what? Just go by your word?"

"I know it's a big ask, but I'm really not that way," Dockhand said. Even as his tone became pleading, his body language stayed quiet. His shoulders were slumped, his hands loose on the table. He hadn't formed them into fists or taken on any tension. "I'm just trying to live this quiet, peaceful life now. Not getting into any trouble. Keeping to myself. Really. I want to be a better person than I was."

Laura stared at him for a long moment, assessing. His face was open. He didn't glance up at her slyly to see if she was buying it. He just kept his eyes on the table. Sad eyes. Not afraid or angry or defensive. Just sad.

Sad that he'd been caught?

"Where were you last night?" Laura asked, switching tactics. They could get to the bottom of this easily. Either he had an alibi, or he was guilty.

"I was at home." Dockhand paused, looking at his own hands. He moved them slightly, picking at a bit of loose skin on his thumb. Was that a tell? "On my own."

"Not really an alibi, is it?" Nate spoke up for the first time, grunting.

"Not an alibi at all," Laura said, her voice hard. "And the night before last?"

"I was watching TV on my own, at home, every night this week," Dockhand said, taking care of her next question as well. "I know. It's not proof. But I live alone and I'm not going out after work. I'm sober and I don't want to get into anything again. I just… ask me about what I've been watching. Go on. I can tell you anything you need to know. Or—you can access my viewing records, right? See what I've streamed?"

"It doesn't mean anything," Nate told him. "You could have set it up to run and then left home, and got back before you ever needed to press another button."

Dockhand sighed. Miserable, not impatient or angry. "All right. But that's where I was and what I was doing. I swear."

"Do you hate me?" Laura snapped. "Is that what this is? I put you away for years. You must have missed so much. Do you want to hurt me with this?"

Dockhand blinked at her. "No," he said. "I haven't even thought about you for years."

Laura sat back in her chair, studying him. He didn't look up at her. He looked, strangely, contrite. But that could easily be an act. She'd come across psychos before now that were able to pretend convincingly enough.

But this one… she wasn't so sure. He was totally different from how she remembered. He had been hot-headed back then, always ready to scream abuse and insults at anyone who crossed him. But a coward, otherwise. And now he was so meek, so quiet, just sitting there and accepting the accusations as if they didn't matter.

The only reason Laura could think of for a man to act that way would be if he truly was innocent. Even if he was supremely confident that he wouldn't be caught, Laura would have expected arrogance, flippancy, not calm and quiet.

She wanted it to be him. She wanted it badly. If it was him, then their work was done. They'd caught the killer, brought him off the streets, prevented any more women from being murdered. But just because she wanted a thing to be true didn't make it so. One of the key tenets of being a good FBI agent was to keep your mind open, to avoid hemming yourself in to one theory. If you blinded yourself, you wouldn't be able to see the truth.

Was that what was happening here? Laura knew she hadn't had any new visions, even when she'd touched him to put the cuffs on. Sitting here opposite him now, she felt nothing. Did that mean that he wasn't the killer? That she was touching the wrong things, putting herself in the path of the wrong people?

Of course, it could just have meant that they did have the right guy. No more visions because there were no more killings to come. It was over.

On the other hand, it could mean that she was now so far off base with her guess at who the killer was, that she had undone all of her earlier work and put herself at too much of a distance for a vision to come.

There was only one thing Laura knew for certain. They couldn't let him go until they were sure he was innocent. Which meant that they were only just getting started with the mind games.

# CHAPTER TWENTY THREE

He loitered in the doorway of a store, pretending to look at the window display, waiting for his next victim to pass him by on their way to lunch.

A man, this time. He'd thought, back when he planned all of this, that it was the right time to vary the pattern. Let them get absolutely sure it was only women who were at risk, and then take a man instead. That would put them all at a loss. He'd thought, back then, that it would be just a random agent keeping track of his misdoings. By the time this one was done, though, they would surely have made the connection and sent for her.

How lucky that she had been the one to come right away. That he had been able to savor every moment of her failure to catch him.

He had spent weeks preparing for this, and now he knew every moment of these people's schedules. He even had reminders on his phone. It was noon, and that meant that his next target was heading to the same bakery that he always stopped at, picking up one of his favorite sandwiches for lunch before moving on to the park.

Did he vary his routine when winter came? The watcher could only wonder. He hadn't been following them for that long. And it wouldn't matter now, anyway. After tonight, this man would be dead, and he would never be going anywhere for lunch again.

The reminders on his phone were thinning out rather nicely now. It was so rewarding to delete them all one by one, to think about that FBI agent tearing her hair out as she tried to find the link between all of it. He liked to think of her, despairing, no idea who was going to be next. It was all rather fun.

The only unfortunate thing was that he couldn't see her reaction in person. He had no idea whether Frost had yet worked out that it was all linked to her. He would have loved to have seen the fear on her face when she made the realization. Maybe she already had. Maybe it wouldn't happen until much later. Until the number of dead bodies piled up in her name made her collapse with despair.

Yes, that would be sweet. How he would love to see her life ruined, the way his had been. How he would love to get his revenge.

The watcher caught a glimpse of a reflection passing by him, and he turned casually as if he was done with looking into the window. He stepped out into the street, shielding his eyes against the midday sun for a moment, and then strolled along behind his target, keeping easy pace a good distance from him. Just enough to keep him in sight, to be sure that there was no deviation from the norm.

Tonight, of all nights, it was important that everything went as normal. Because tonight was the night that this man was going to drive another nail into the coffin of Agent Frost's career. Not just her career, but everything else. He was going to take this one last victim, and then she was the last. Number five.

Was she quaking with fear already? he wondered. Did she realize she was in danger? Even if she did, it wouldn't matter. That was why he'd brought her out here. Somewhere she wasn't familiar. Doing it in her home would have been so much harder, but here, she came into contact with new people all the time. Deputies, room service, servers, members of the public.

And, of course, when she did go back to the motel, she would be totally on her own.

He took a deep breath of the city air, tilting his head up to enjoy the late summer sun on his face. Yes, today was a good day.

But tomorrow was going to be even better.

# CHAPTER TWENTY FOUR

"Aren't you going to say anything at all?" Laura asked. "You're not even going to defend yourself?"

Dockhand stared back at her mutinously. His arms were folded across his chest, and he quickly returned his gaze to the table, returning to the status quo. Not a single word.

Laura shoved her chair back with a frustrated scrape. Nate looked up at her, and though no one else would have been able to interpret it, his expression gave her permission: *Go take a break. Get a bite to eat. Come back when you've got your second wind. I'll handle this.*

Laura stormed out through the door, and Nate announced her departure for the tape.

Laura sipped at her coffee as she stared at the recording on the computer in their makeshift office. An hour ago, Dockhand had finally lost his cool and stopped being so reasonable and calm. But that didn't mean that he had snapped and confessed to anything. Quite the opposite. He had started refusing to say anything at all. She had fast-forwarded through most of it, playing back a few moments that she'd wanted to analyze deeper, but he was giving nothing away.

Laura blew out a deep breath and rolled the greasy packaging of her lunch sandwich up into a ball, then threw it into the trash can on the other side of the room. It hit the inside with a satisfying slap, then rattled down on top of the other trash. If only this case would be such an easy slam dunk.

Laura cast around for the small evidence bag she'd requisitioned. It contained the contents of Dockhand's pockets when he came in. She reached in and touched the loose change he'd had, wishing it would trigger some kind of vision. Anything, really. It didn't have to be his next intended murder. It could have been a sight of him inside a cell. Anything to tell her that she had the right guy, that his future was behind bars.

Nothing.

She sighed and put the bag to one side, rubbing her hands over her face. There was no evidence either way. The hard fact of the matter was that if they couldn't get him to talk, they were going to have to let him go anyway. They had nothing on him. Only circumstance and the lack of an alibi.

That was what was so annoying about this case. If there was one shred of forensic evidence that they could use, they might be able to get somewhere. But the killer seemed always to wear gloves, and that meant that there was no evidence they could use to compare to Dockhand's DNA. They had him right where they needed him to be, but they couldn't prove a damn thing.

Not unless Nate managed to get him to admit everything, but given their progress over the last few hours, Laura wasn't hopeful.

She needed an outside perspective, someone who could tell her what they thought of the case without any bias. Not that she was allowed to reveal the whole details of the case, but she could say enough to get a second opinion. Someone who wasn't in law enforcement. Who didn't have the trained perspectives that she and Nate did. Someone who could see things differently.

She picked up her phone and dialed, hoping that twice in twenty-four hours wasn't too much to ask.

"Hello, Laura? Are you all right?"

Laura bit her lip at the sound of Garth's concern. She hadn't meant to worry him quite so much—but given that their last call had been about her sobriety, maybe she shouldn't have been surprised.

"Yes, I'm fine. Sorry," she said, quickly. "I actually just wanted to pick your brain about something. Get a second opinion."

"Oh," Garth said, breathing a literal sigh of relief. "Well, shoot then."

Laura smiled to herself. He always came through, even when she didn't really deserve it. He was probably on his own lunch break, and he didn't care about letting her use his time. "It's this case. It's… targeted at me."

"What do you mean, at you?"

"The victims." Laura took a deep breath. "He's choosing the victims in order to send me a personal message."

"You're sure about that?"

"Absolutely sure. The third one last night confirmed it." Laura bit her fingernail as she waited for his response. She didn't want to mention the fact that Nate had had his doubts. Even if he did, she didn't entertain them herself.

"Well, damn." Garth paused. "There's no wonder you're feeling like you're teetering on the edge. Now is the time when you have to stay more committed to your sobriety than ever. It's these moments that catch us out. Stay strong, Laura. Don't let it drag you to the bottle."

"It's not that," Laura said, waving a dismissive hand even though Garth couldn't see it. "We've arrested someone. I just don't know if we have the right guy. All the signs seem to fit, and yet… I don't know. I can't put my finger on it, but something doesn't seem right. But then again, it all fits. And I just keep going round and round in circles in my head."

Garth digested her words for a long moment. Just when she was about to speak up to prompt him to say something, he did. "Well," he said, taking his time over the words. "You know you're looking for someone who wanted to send you a message. But now you're not sure if you have the right guy. Is that it?"

"That's it," Laura said, impatiently.

"Do you remember step number nine?"

There was no question as to which step he was referring to. It wasn't as though there were any other steps that really mattered in an alcoholic's life. He was talking about the steps of AA, how addicts were supposed to progress toward healing.

"Of course," Laura said, mildly annoyed that he would question her memory. "That we have to make direct amends with those we have wronged."

"So?"

Laura thought for a moment, trying to dig into what Garth was trying to say. "You're talking about the killings—that whoever is doing this was wronged by me. But that doesn't make any sense, Garth. They all deserved to be put away. They were criminals. They broke the law. I've never put away a single suspect that I didn't feel absolutely sure was guilty."

Of course, he couldn't know why she was so sure. That she had seen each of them with her own eyes, breaking the law, red-handed. Sometimes she'd seen things she really wished she hadn't, and she included Dockhand in that. He deserved to be in prison. The fact that he'd been released was concerning, frankly; she wished he could have been inside for longer.

"That's not the point," Garth told her. "You're not the one doing the killings. What *you* feel doesn't make a lick of difference."

What he was trying to say slowly dawned on her. "You're saying that the killer—he feels that I wronged him."

"Right. Nobody goes ahead and takes revenge on someone they don't think did them wrong. It's not like antagonizing you would take away the past. It's pure hate that drives something like this. They want you to suffer. That's not the actions of a man who knows he was caught dead to rights."

"It would be someone who doesn't think they deserved to be put away," Laura thought out loud. "Someone who feels that I interrupted their grand plan, maybe, or that they weren't to blame for their actions. Or even that they did nothing wrong."

"Does your suspect seem to feel that way?" Garth asked.

Laura sighed. "No," she admitted. "If anything, it's the opposite. He told us that he's been trying to be a better person, that he knows he did wrong in the past. He wasn't even angry when we arrested him. He said he totally understood. And I believe him. I've been on the job long enough that I can usually tell when someone's trying to play me, but I don't get that impression from him."

"That doesn't sound like the right guy to me," Garth said, with confidence. "So, you've got to take a real look at yourself now. Look at your past. You've got to find someone who would feel that you wronged them, from their perspective—not from your own."

"I get it," Laura said, closing her eyes and pressing her fingers against her forehead for a moment. She was going to have to start again, and it was going to be a lot. "Thanks, Garth."

"No problemo, Laur. You just give me a call again if you waver, okay?"

"Okay," she promised, before hanging up the phone and staring off into the distance, not seeing a thing.

Someone who had been wronged.

There had to be someone like that in her past.

If she needed to, she would go through every single file she had ever worked on until she found them. But she was going to have to do it fast—because if the man in that room with Nate wasn't the real killer, then he was still out there, and he was still going to strike again tonight.

# CHAPTER TWENTY FIVE

Laura stared at her own record on the screen, and tried not to let utter despair completely take over.

How had Nate faced down this list before and not just given up? It was immense. The cases built up quickly when you were working one a week, maybe more. There were cases that she had had only secondary involvement in, such as providing backup to a larger team. Cases where she'd been a junior agent assisting someone else. Cases she'd covered on her own. Cases with Nate.

So many crimes, and so many criminals. Any one of them could have the potential to be a killer. Even the ones who were arrested for less violent crimes—as much as Laura hated to admit it, the justice system didn't always put out reformed citizens back into the world. Sometimes they were hardened, more ruthless. Sometimes they got their first kill on the inside.

She pushed herself back from the computer screen, holding her hands to either side of her temples. Nate had been checking through everything one by one, and he'd only gotten through a few years before she intervened. She wasn't about to waste time in the same way.

She had to think about this logically. This wasn't just a random selection of an agent who happened to be helping on the case. This was someone whose life she had impacted in a very direct way.

So, who would be angry with her for her actions against them? Angry enough to trigger a rampage of killing?

She recalled a particular case. A guy who had battered his wife to death, then staged it to look like a break-in. The FBI had been called in after the local PD made no headway at all on the case. It was Laura, with her outsider's perspective, who had managed to see that the man was guilty as hell. He'd gone to prison for life.

He could have been one of the potential suspects on her list, if it wasn't for the fact that she knew he was still locked away. Maybe it was someone like that, someone who could directly point to her as the one single person responsible for their incarceration. But a few years in jail wasn't really enough to justify murder, was it? And those who had gone to jail for life, well, they were still there.

A family member? She'd had that idea early on. She remembered one woman who had killed her own husband, shooting him right in the face. She had tried to use the battered woman defense, although there had not been enough evidence for it to stick. Laura had felt bad for her, partly believing her and partly not. She'd ultimately been convicted. Laura remembered how the woman's teenage son had screamed in the courtroom, until he was taken out and forcibly restrained. Could it be him? Did he hate Laura enough to try to get his revenge in this way?

No. She couldn't believe it. Grief and fear for a parent were not the same thing as killing intent. The tears that had streamed down his face told her that he was at least empathetic. These killings—they were cold. Ruthless. They weren't the actions of someone who could feel that emotional pain.

A thought struck her. A memory from a courtroom, of a man who seemed to feel no remorse whatsoever for what he had done. In fact, he had tried to pretend that he was insane at the time of the kidnapping he was eventually sent down for. But that had all been a story.

Laura had been a junior agent then, nowhere near as experienced as she was now. She hadn't been able to distinguish the truth in his eyes when he said he didn't remember anything that had happened, that he had been in some kind of fugue state.

That was back in Brooklyn. Years ago. It was a missing persons case when she was brought in as an extra body to help with the hunt. She remembered long nights searching through the city, accompanied by police dogs and even local volunteers, all of them combing through abandoned buildings and back streets and looking for some kind of sign that would tell them where the young woman had gone.

She'd had a vision. One of the first times that a vision had actually led her to solve a case. She'd followed it right to where the woman was being held, passing it off as pure luck, and found them. The man who had kidnapped her, and his victim. He had been standing over her with a knife, ready to end it all. But Laura had pulled her gun, stopped him with the threat of death, and arrested him. She had saved the woman's life.

In fact, it was the first time that she had earned the reputation of having such a lucky touch on these cases. The start of her lucky streak, something that was infamous enough within the agency for Nate to have known about it before they were partnered up. That was where it all began.

Laura had gone to court to see the kidnapper enter a plea of insanity, and that night at home she had had a terrible vision. She had seen this same man going on to murder several women, strangling the life out of them and then abandoning them in their own homes for their families to find. She had seen the vivid colors, felt the last exhalation of the women's breath on her cheek, watched their eyes as the life drained out of them. She had awoken shaking, terrified that he was going to get away with it.

It was simple. If he was judged to be insane, he would be sent for mental treatment. Then, once he proved himself to be sane—which the physicians would think was a result of their treatment—he would be released. He would be free to kill again.

Laura couldn't let that happen.

So she had gone into the courtroom and presented herself as an expert witness. She had spoken to the killer's state of mind when she arrested him. She had embellished it a little here and there, just enough to make him sound absolutely sane and rational, to show that he had had every intention of killing the woman before she interrupted. That had put paid to his insanity plea. Even so, the fact that he had only kidnapped and tried to kill someone, rather than actually doing it, gave him a lighter sentence.

Attempted homicide. It didn't exactly carry a short sentence. But he must have gotten out early, probably on good behavior. Some kind of reform program.

Laura didn't have to look it up. There was no point. She knew now. She knew why the feeling of déjà vu had been so strong when she walked around the apartment in which Caroline Birchtree lost her life. She knew why she had looked at the body in the kitchen of Nadia and Paul Frost's house, and felt that same tingling feeling. She knew now.

She had seen all of these victims before. Years ago, she had seen them in another vision. She had watched them die the first time. She just hadn't been able to put it together until now, because of all of the awful things she had seen between now and then, both in person and in her mind. She had managed to partly block them out, believing that she had seen a future which no longer existed.

But it did exist. It was real. It was happening now. What she had seen wasn't what would happen if the killer was released early because of an insanity plea. She had seen what was going to happen all along.

No, that wasn't quite right, she realized. Horror shot through her veins, making her hair stand up on the back of her neck. No, if she had let him enter his insanity plea, he would never have needed to kill these women. He would probably not even have remembered Laura's name, because she would not have personally testified against him. She would have just been the anonymous agent who caught him. It wasn't as though they'd had time to introduce themselves to one another while she was arresting him.

She had been right all along. Her vision had been correct. But her actions taken to prevent it had actually been what caused it to come to pass. She wasn't the hero who had saved a woman's life.

She was the woman who had damned several more to death.

And they had the wrong guy in custody. Brent Dockhand had nothing to do with this. The killer was still out there.

He was going to kill in her name again.

# CHAPTER TWENTY SIX

Laura looked up as Nate walked in, almost jumping out of her skin. Just for a single moment, she was so scared she almost reached for her gun. Her nerves were going haywire, so many terrible thoughts about the revelation she'd just had going around and around in her head.

"I'm not getting anything out of him… whoa, are you okay?" He paused halfway to the board, frowning at her. "You look like you've seen a ghost."

"You're not going to get anything," Laura said grimly. "He's innocent."

Nate turned fully to face her, his arms crossing over his chest. "I take it this means you've come across some new evidence?"

"Better than that," Laura told him. "I've worked out who the killer is."

Nate blinked. "Are you going to let me in on it?"

Laura scrubbed a hand across her face. "Sorry. I only just worked it out. I remembered the case. This was years ago, back in Brooklyn. He was put away directly because of my expert testimony about his mental state. I stopped him from getting away with a cushy psychiatric sentence. It's got to be him."

Nate was already moving to the computer. Perhaps seeing she was still reeling and in no state to navigate the complex and outdated database system, he leaned over the keyboard, nudging her wheeled chair out of the way. "Name?"

"Ed Bronston," Laura told him. "Edward, maybe. I know he went by Ed during the trial."

Nate's fingers sped across the keys, clacking out the name. "Here we go. Wait, you said he didn't go to a psych ward?"

"No," Laura said, looking up and frowning. "He went to jail. Why?"

"Well, his last release is recorded as being from Albany State Hospital." Nate shook his head, scanning quickly through the results on the screen. "Ah, here: he was jailed for a year first. That's why he didn't come up when I was scanning for recent prison releases."

"What does it say?" Laura asked, bending her neck to see the screen while he stood in front of it. "Why wasn't he kept in jail?"

"Uh…" Nate clicked to open up the record, waiting for what seemed like an age for the page to load. "Looks like he started exhibiting abnormal behavior which was referred to the prison's psychiatrist. Then he was referred on to a psych ward for evaluation, where he bit a fellow inmate."

"Bit?" Laura wrinkled her nose. "He should have been restrained, surely?"

"Hmm," Nate agreed, scrolling through another page of a scanned-in handwritten report. "I don't know. Sounds like the other prisoner was doing work in the wards, maybe. Earning some good behavior points by serving food. Then he got too close to Bronston, who bit the inside of his wrist so deeply the guy nearly bled out."

For just a brief second, Laura had a vivid image of a vein spurting blood into an open mouth, and she swallowed down nausea. Had she seen that before? Or was it just her imagination working overtime at the gruesome story? "And that didn't get him thrown into solitary?"

"Apparently, it was deemed that he was suffering from a severe mental break and delusions, and hearing voices." Nate clicked onto another report before continuing. "His release record shows that he was given a clean bill of health after several years of ongoing treatment which showed gradual improvements. He was then released back to live with relatives—here, in Albany."

"He's from here?" Laura asked, searching for the information on the screen.

"You didn't know that?" Nate's voice held a note of surprise.

"No," Laura said, sighing and shaking her head. "I thought he was from Brooklyn. But it makes sense. That's why he's killing here. Because this is where he lives, not because it has any particular significance to me."

"Well, then how did you figure out it could be him?" Nate asked, frowning. "I mean, it does make sense. It looks like this is our guy. I just don't get how you made the leap."

"Call it divine inspiration," Laura said, getting up from her chair and gesturing to the screen. "Whatever it was, we've got to go. Do you have his current details?"

Nate nodded, grabbing a piece of loose paper from beside the monitor and scrawling down the address he had on the screen. "I have his parole address. Nothing else is registered to him—no car, no cell phone number, no employment record. I guess we better hope he's at home."

"If he's not there, we'll have the sheriff track him down," Laura said, already rushing for the door. "Come on. We haven't got any time to waste. There's only a few hours left until evening starts to draw in—and we need to find him before he kills again."

Nate followed her as she marched as quickly as she could through the halls of the precinct, out to their waiting car. This was it. Laura knew they were on the right track, knew it in her bones—and they weren't going to miss him this time.

# CHAPTER TWENTY SEVEN

Laura glanced up at the sky as she got out of the car, noticing just how low the sun was. They had the benefit of it being late summer on their side, because darkness wasn't happening until later in the day. But it was still coming. It was happening inexorably, and there was nothing they could do to stop it.

The only thing they could do was to stop Ed Bronston before he struck again.

The building they had pulled up in front of was an apartment block, shabby and faded. Paint was peeling on the window frames of the ground floor, and someone had tagged spray paint by the entrance. Their path to the door was littered with a punctured football, empty chip packages, and a broken down old children's stroller with no wheels.

It wasn't the nicest place to live. Bronston had gotten out of a psych ward, and before that prison, so there was a good chance that he was unemployed now. If this was even his home. Most parolees had to live with a family member, someone who would take them in and vouch for them. If time wasn't so much of the essence, Laura would have stopped to talk to the parole officer first, find out what Bronston was doing now. What his situation was.

But the parole officer had not answered the call when Laura had tried in the car, and there was no time to wait. They had to go in now, even if that meant not having all of the information on hand. It made her itchy, made her hands twitch back toward her gun in fear, but what else could they do? If they waited, another death was certain.

But even that thought pulled her up short as they approached the intercom that controlled the front door. Death—she had been thinking all the while about the death of the next victim. But what about Nate?

His death was coming soon, too, and Laura hadn't allowed him to get close enough to potentially trigger another vision. She had been too focused on the case. She hadn't wanted to see his death coming. She just wanted to save as many lives as possible, and then worry about him afterward. She had assumed that his death was a long way off.

But maybe that wasn't the case. She had seen the shadow over her father not long before the cancer first appeared. Death had been on the way for him even then. It had been many years coming, but it had started when she saw the shadow.

So, what if the events of this evening would set Nate's death in motion? What if he was about to get shot, or receive some other kind of injury, that would limit his life? What if it would eventually become infected, or he would need some kind of transplant that failed, or a hundred other million possibilities that she could think of that could lead to his death further down the line?

He should not even have been there. It was too dangerous. But Laura could not say that to him now—could not expect him to go back to the precinct meekly just because she told him to.

So, instead, she took control.

Laura walked right up to the intercom, first testing the door to see if it was broken, and then hit all of the numbers she could see except for the one she actually wanted. She didn't want to alert Ed that she was coming, and that included telling someone out loud why they were there. She waited, and sure enough someone was lazy; they unlocked the door without bothering to see who it was that was down there, no doubt assuming she was delivering something.

Without waiting to check that Nate was following her, because she really didn't want him to, Laura turned and pushed the door open, running inside. She took the stairs two at a time, racing up as fast as she could, her gun drawn. She held it in front of her as she hit the third floor, only a little out of breath, and surged down the hall.

She counted off the doors as she passed. Apartment thirty-one, apartment thirty-two, apartment thirty-three. And there! Thirty-four, his address. This was where Ed Bronston lived. This was where they were going to find him.

Laura paused only for a moment by the door, leaning her head against it and listening. There was no back way out here. If Ed wanted to run from them, he was going to have to jump out of the window. She didn't much rate his chances of survival if he tried that. Still, there was a chance that he could destroy evidence if he knew they were coming. She only had a short time to make this work.

She hammered on the door, shouting loudly, announcing that the FBI was present and Ed needed to open up. She waited for just a few moments, then hammered again, repeating the same routine. Nate had caught up to her, much to her chagrin; he slammed his forearm against the door as well, joining her voice with his before nodding to her and gesturing for her to step back.

"Nate, no," she began, afraid that this was the thing that would get him into trouble—but before she could say or do anything else, he had stepped back and launched a powerful kick right at the door lock. On the second try, it splintered away, exploding backward in a shower of broken shards of wood, and Laura was ready.

She stepped right in front of Nate while he was still recovering his balance, before he had the chance to go in first.

"FBI! Come out with your hands above your head!" Laura shouted one last time, before moving rapidly into the cramped hallway. Shoes littered the space near the door, and she had to step over them, all the while keeping her eyes on three spots: a door up ahead, a door to the right, and a bend around the corridor to the left.

"Show yourself!" Nate bellowed from behind her, making Laura wince. He was too close. Why couldn't he just wait? Why did he have to come in right behind her?

*Because he always has your back*, a traitorous voice in the back of her head reminded her. And it was true. She was always able to count on him.

She just wished that wasn't the case right now.

She nervously drew level with the first door on her right, then in one swift motion reached out with one hand to push it open while the other pointed the gun right inside. It turned out to be a bathroom, stained and with a chipped and discolored toilet and basin, but utterly empty otherwise. A quick glance told her everything she needed to know, and Laura continued onward.

She swung around the corner, putting her back against the wall and pointing the gun straight ahead. The view opened up, and she could see that ahead was a combination living room and kitchen, all of the kitchen cupboards visible from here and all filthy. She hedged along hesitantly, knowing that Ed Bronston could be behind any door, could be waiting for her just around the corner where the room opened out. But there was nothing else she could do. She had to press on—had to be the first in line. She couldn't let Nate take her position.

Laura steadied her gun with both hands, then rushed forward. She slammed her back against the wall again as she swept the kitchen and living room area, seeing that it was empty. As soon as she was sure that there were no other doors from this part of the apartment and that there was no one in sight, she reached for the door handle of the final room and wrenched it open. Inside was a bedroom, equipped with only a mattress directly on the floor, but again it was empty.

Laura felt her whole body sag with relief as she realized the truth. Ed Bronston was not there. He was not going to be shooting Nate today.

But it was followed by a renewed wave of fear, hot on its heels. He wasn't here. Which meant that he could be out there right now, already stalking his next victim. And they had no idea who that might be.

"Christ," Laura gasped, holstering her gun and glancing back at Nate. "It's empty."

He was already digging his phone out of his pocket. "I'm calling the sheriff for backup," he said. "We need to leave someone here, to guard the place in case he comes back."

"He's not coming back," Laura said, shaking her head. "Not now. He's too smart. He would have to expect that we'd find out who he is, and besides, with the noise we made, the neighbors will be talking. He won't get within sight of the building without figuring out what's going on and turning the other way."

"I'm calling them anyway," Nate told her. "We need the guards plus an APB with his photo. You try and find some clue about where he's going next."

Laura nodded. What Nate said made sense. It was likely that the killer would have left some kind of clue behind. Some trace of his intentions. He might have written something down somewhere, and if it wasn't on his person, she would be able to find it.

There was too much planning that went into this for it to be all in the guy's head. Or maybe that was just what she was telling herself to keep her hopes up. To keep the faith. She knew who it was, she knew his name and his face. She was a whisker away from getting proof.

So why did Laura feel as though the fourth victim was slipping out of her hands?

She started in the kitchen, rifling through drawers, checking every cupboard, every surface. There was a single battered cookbook, the pages stained and even charred in one place. She picked it up and shook it upside down, looking for anything loose that might fall out. That done, she turned her attention to the living room. She could hear Nate talking in the hall, hear him requesting all of the backup they might need to help run Ed Bronston down.

There was nothing on the coffee table, nothing on the floor around it. Laura turned up the seats of the sofa, and only found a giant slash across the bottom of one of them. She slipped her hands into the gap, trying to feel whether there was something shoved between the cushion and the case. When it turned up empty, she retreated and regrouped, heading for the bedroom.

The closet revealed only a few shabby items of clothing, most of them looking as though they had been through the wash a few too many times, faded and thin. The bed was unmade, the sheets rumpled. Laura grimaced to herself before lifting up each of the pillows and even searching under the mattress, grateful that she was wearing gloves to prevent herself from contaminating the evidence.

There was a wonky dresser by the bed, missing one foot. In all of the drawers Laura only found a few more items of clothing, several books, a comb, and a couple of other items of personal grooming. She rifled through each of the books one by one, making sure that there was nothing written in the margins or slipped inside.

Nothing.

By the time Nate was done with his call, she was still looking through the bathroom. There was nothing of any note whatsoever in the cramped space, and she backed out before the flickering light bulb overhead gave her a headache.

"Nothing," she said, with a sigh. "It's like he barely even lives here. He has nothing."

"Came out of the psych ward, got dumped into this place, couldn't afford to keep going." Nate made a tsking sound with his tongue. "Makes sense he would get bitter about it. Angry, even. I wonder how long he's been stewing on all of this."

"Long enough to find out everything about me." Laura wrapped her arms around herself, staring at the space where Ed Bronston made his home. There was nothing homely about it. She tried to imagine living here, and couldn't. Not even at her lowest, when the alcohol had taken nearly everything from her. Even her own cramped apartment, filled with secondhand furniture, looked like a palace compared to this.

She had mementos. Belongings. Framed photographs and books and decorations, even if they were simple ones. Bronston had nothing.

She didn't feel sorry for him. Not in the slightest. It was his own violent behavior that had brought him to this point. But she could see where Nate was coming from.

"We're going to get him," Nate said, with a firmness that was reassuring.

"But how? I mean, what now?" Laura asked. "We can't just sit around and wait for the APB to catch him. He could slip past a dozen checkpoints and be out of town. He could be in someone's house waiting for them already. We can't just wait."

"You're right," Nate told her. His hand swept backward over his close-cropped black hair, rubbing it thoughtfully. "We have to be proactive. We've got to try and figure out where he would be going next."

"The next victim," Laura said, nodding.

It seemed like an insurmountable task. But right now, it was the only direction they had left to turn.

They were going to have to try.

# CHAPTER TWENTY EIGHT

Laura sat in front of the computer, trying not to panic. Even the short wait for the deputies to arrive and take over, and then the drive back to the precinct, had been almost unbearable. Now she was starting to appreciate the sheer size of the task that lay ahead of them, and she was about ready to tear out her own hair.

"Well, at least we can be happy the census was taken not too long ago," Nate said. He was tapping a pen against the side of the desk beside her, a noise that was just about driving Laura out of her mind.

"That doesn't help a whole lot," Laura mumbled. She was waiting for the results to finish loading. A search of the residential records of Albany for anyone with the first name Alex was, perhaps predictably, taking a long time.

"We have to narrow it down," Nate said. "He's only killed women before. You really think he's going to go after a guy?"

Laura thought about it, then hesitated. "I guess it's not uncommon for women to be called Alex, too. Maybe he hasn't changed his MO."

"So we can narrow it down to probably half, right?" Nate said, as Laura ticked a box on the screen and reloaded the results. This time they came back far quicker, but there were still pages and pages of them. "What else?"

Laura squeezed her eyes shut, as if she could force thoughts out of her brain. "I don't know… um… they were all attacked alone."

"Right, but they didn't all live alone," Nate said, tapping that pen again. Laura wanted to reach out and yank it out of his hand, but she didn't want to risk their skin touching.

"Nate, please," she said, gesturing to his hand.

Nate gave her a momentary and lopsided smile, dropping it. "Sorry." He took a breath, rubbing his eyes and shaking his head. "Dammit, there's still too many of them. How are we supposed to figure out which women are going to be alone tonight? It doesn't even have to be all night—Paul Frost was on his way home."

"And the child was still in the house," Laura said. She had not forgotten that horrible image: the innocent child lying asleep upstairs while his mother was brutally murdered. If he had come down for a glass of water, what would the killer have done?

Nate let out a frustrated breath. He leaned back in his chair and read from their board. "He calls them first. He finds a woman who is alone and has the right name, and breaks into the house after she answers. Then he strangles her to death before leaving."

"Add in the fact that phone records show the call going to Nadia's cell phone, not her landline, and it doesn't give us anything," she said, but an idea was beginning to take hold. "Nothing except the way he likes to do things. What if we could stop his usual technique from working?"

"I'm listening," Nate said.

"We have to warn them. Let them know that there's someone going around doing this. Tell them not to stay home alone."

"All of them?" Nate gave her a sideways look, his eyes wide. "Laura, there are *hundreds* of people on this list. And that doesn't even include anyone who might have just moved here."

"And we have a whole station of deputies and receptionists and assistants, not to mention the media," Laura said. "We've got to do this. We've got to warn them."

She didn't wait for Nate to agree with her. She knew he would, even if it took him a short while to think it over. They didn't have a short while. They needed to get on this now. She headed for the door, straight down the hall toward the sheriff's office.

Sure enough, he followed. He always had her back.

Except that someday soon, he would be dead. If she couldn't stop it.

Laura pushed the thought away along with the roiling sickness that threatened to bubble out of her stomach. So many things she needed to concentrate on. So many people whom only she could save. She had to stay focused, had to remain on-task. Ed Bronston first.

***

Laura stood at the top of the bullpen ten minutes after she'd had the idea, watching ten members of staff seated at desks with their phones, calling through their own sections of the phone book to every single Alex they could find. Warning them not to go out alone, not to be at home alone, just in case. Telling them to go and stay with family or friends if they needed to. Warning them about not answering the phone if they didn't know the number.

Laura listened anxiously in the bullpen as the first calls were made, making sure the deputies had all the details right. They couldn't afford for this not to reach the people who needed to hear it.

"Hello, is that Alex Allen?"

"Hi, am I speaking with Alex Busch?"

"Yes, hello, I'm looking for Alex Carmine."

She glanced up to the glass window at the back of the room. Sheriff Lonsdale was visible through it in his office, making calls to local news stations about an emergency press conference. Somewhere behind them, in another room, the dispatch team were working hard to recall every member of law enforcement they could from breaks and nights off, trying to get them back in to join in the effort.

"We should join them, at least until we hear anything different," Nate said, casting around for a desk phone. Then he shook his head at himself and pulled out his cell. "Come on. We can start going through some of these batches that haven't been assigned yet."

"Wait," Laura said, calling him back. Something was happening in her head. Not a vision: a thought. A realization. It was right on the tip of her tongue, something that she could almost grasp. "Why does he call them?"

"You know we haven't figured that out yet," Nate said. "Probably just to check that they're home. Maybe he asks for someone else in the household, to make sure that they're alone."

"But Carrie lived alone," Laura said. "And he wouldn't need to make a call like that if he was watching them. Didn't we work out that she was killed pretty soon after she got home from work?"

"Yeah," Nate said, frowning. "I don't know, then. Maybe it's all part of it. Maybe he gets off on talking to them first."

Laura shook her head. "It's too significant," she said, biting her fingernail. She spun in a circle slowly, thinking. She was visualizing the last moments of each of the women, the ritual the killer had to go through. Trying to see it from his side, not theirs. "There must be a reason why he has to talk to them first. He goes to all the trouble of getting the stolen phones, knowing that they might potentially be traced back to him if he isn't careful enough. That's the one piece of evidence we've had that went anywhere. It has to be significant enough to justify the risk."

"Is it a risk?" Nate asked pointedly. "We still got no closer to figuring out who he was, even when we knew how he got the phones."

“He’s right outside,” Laura said, almost to herself at this point. “He knows they’re in there. He waits for them to go in. Maybe… maybe for Nadia Frost, he waited until her son was in bed. He knew. So why call them? What else could he need to be sure of?”

“Their identity?” Nate suggested. “If he’s only seen their names written down, he won’t know what they look like in person. He might want to be sure.”

“Yes!” Laura clicked her fingers. “That’s it—it has to be. So where does he get their names? The first two—the first two, he called them on landlines. Home phone numbers.”

She looked down at the desks across the bullpen. Right now, each of them had a copy of the phone book, open to a new section. Surnames A through J were already in use.

A source that contained both names and phone numbers. A place where you could find anyone with the right name. Even easier if you were going for surnames, like Frost. A listing for everyone in the city, everyone who was registered.

This was it.

“He’s using the phone book, too,” Nate said, his voice echoing and confirming her own thoughts.

“The third victim, Nadia Frost, she was called on her cell,” Laura said, hastily grabbing her own and looking up a page she’d already visited earlier on. “But she had her own online store—yes, here it is! Her personal number is listed on the site, for potential customers to call. He must have found her in the phone book, then looked her up online and seen this.”

“That’s amazing,” Nate said, grinning. “We’re on his trail.” But his smile faltered as he looked out across the room, at the deputies who were only now starting their second calls. They were going to be at it all night. Even if they managed to call all of the women on the list before darkness fell—even if they got a press conference together in time—was it going to be enough?

Laura pushed her hair back from her face, grabbing a scrunchie out of her pocket and sweeping it back into place. “Let’s join them,” she said, decisively. The only thing they could do now was try.

# CHAPTER TWENTY NINE

Laura bit the inside of her cheek as the phone rang and rang. Her fifth call, and just like the last two, it seemed like it was going to go unanswered.

"Hello?"

"Yes, hello!" Laura said, sitting up sharply. She'd all but given up hope of connecting, and for a moment she almost forgot what she had to say. "Is this Alex Vardy?"

"Who is this?"

"My name is Special Agent Laura Frost," she said. "I'm calling to—"

"You can prove that?"

"Excuse me?" Laura stumbled, finding herself cut off in her mentally rehearsed speech.

"You got any way to prove you're FBI?"

"I…" Laura paused. "Not right at this moment. But ma'am, no one is in trouble. I'm actually calling because we think that Alex Vardy could be in danger tonight. If that's you, I just want to keep you safe."

"There's no Alex Vardy at this number," the woman on the other end of the line said. "She moved out. Couple years back. No idea where she went."

Laura opened her mouth for a follow-up question, but the line went dead.

She groaned with the horrifying realization that at least one of them was now out of reach. What if Alex Vardy was the Alex that Ed had chosen? Sure, he couldn't call her at home, but what if he'd found her online like he did with Nadia Frost and discovered her new location?

She looked up to the windows that allowed light into the bullpen, and saw that they were now overpowered by the electric lights overhead. It was getting dark. He would be striking soon.

This Alex, whoever she was, was about to die. And even though several more bodies had joined them on the phones, it wasn't enough. It was never going to be enough. There was no way they could get through all of them, not in time.

Laura thought about the grim reality setting in—the fact that she was probably about to find a fourth body, another woman who bore the name of one of her family members—and it took everything she had not to hurl the phone book at the wall.

The book. That was a thought. Ed was using one of these. She knew him now, knew who she was looking for. She was getting so much closer—she had to be. If there was any time a vision would come, it had to be now. Right?

She glanced up surreptitiously, making sure that Nate was engrossed in a call. All across the bullpen, everyone was involved in their own journey through their section of the phone book, scanning pages or going over a hastily written script. At the far end of the room, the door to the sheriff's private office was ajar, and through the window she could see him making his own calls. No one was paying any attention to her.

Now was her chance. She shut her eyes, flattening the palm of her hand against the phone book, hoping it would look as though she was just saving her place. She took a deep breath, tried to shut everything else out. Focused in on the feel of the book under her pages. The texture of the cheap, rough paper. The slight musty smell coming from it. The sharp tang of coffee in the air, and the generally stale aroma of a room that enclosed working law enforcement professionals for long shifts every day. She let it all filter through, the padding of the chair she was sitting on, the sharp edge of the desk drawers against the side of her leg.

Laura breathed deeply, letting all of her senses in one by one. If she couldn't do this, Alex was going to die. Whoever Alex was. And then Nate. And—

Laura tried to start again, recentering herself. The rough pages. The musty smell. The chair. *Come on, Laura.* The sounds around her of voices, of tapping on phone buttons, of handsets jolted back into receivers. Words. *We need you to stay safe tonight, is there anyone who can come and be with you? Or can you go anywhere?* A clattering sound from somewhere across the room; Laura didn't know what it was. Someone being clumsy. They were wasting time. They needed to concentrate—

Laura gasped, letting her eyes fly open. It was useless. No matter how hard she tried, she was too anxious, too on edge. Those intrusive thoughts kept coming, reminding her that she was responsible. That she was the only one right now who could save Alex, save Nate, save Amy, get better for Lacey. Ironically, it was that same anxiety taking over her mind that was stopping her from having the vision she needed to see this through.

She could have done with a drink. Something to take the edge off. But that was stupid. Apart from all of the other many, many reasons why she couldn't have a drink right now, it would have deadened the vision, too.

Laura's mind drifted to her meetings, to Garth. He was right that she hadn't been back in a long time. The meetings were too much. Having to admit that she had failed yet again, month after month. Feeling judged, even though the whole point of AA was supposed to be that you could get better without judgment. All that religious crap, drilled into you whether you believed in God or not.

Did Laura believe in God? Probably not, she thought. Right now, God was letting an innocent woman die because He couldn't see His way clear to show her another vision. Not even when she'd tried to clear the way for Him.

But then again, where did the visions even come from? And if there was something out there, or someone, then it couldn't hurt, could it? She was desperate, and Laura had no idea how to get through this on her own. She needed help, from any quarter she could get it.

So she allowed her eyes to slide closed again, and she prayed. *Please, God, or whoever,* she thought, imagining her brain waves beaming out into space, penetrating the ether, reaching the ear of someone or something powerful. *Please don't let this woman die because of me. Please help me save her.*

She kept her eyes closed, hanging onto that last thought. It was a little reassuring, she had to admit. The idea that if something all-powerful was out there, it might be looking out for her. It might hear her call and help, after all.

She floated on a thin stream of calm for the first time all day, resting only in the moment. For just that moment, nothing was wrong. It was all going to work out. She was going to sort this out, and—

A sharp stab of pain hit her right in the center of her forehead, so powerful she almost cried out. Her hand flattened sharply on the phone book, gripping onto the center of the page as if it could keep her grounded, her eyes opening blearily on a too-bright room, her head almost ricocheting with the pain—

*She was floating in the air above a room, an empty living room where a comfortable couch rested in front of a television. It was switched on, playing some evening comedy show. She was looking down on the flickering lights, the only illumination in the dark room. They played over the legs and feet of someone sitting in an armchair, facing the television.*

*Laura tried to focus, to see what she was looking at. Who she was looking at. From above, it was hard to know much about them. A slim body, no way to tell their height, only the top of the head carpeted with short-cropped hair.*

*A slim, straight body with no curves—short cropped hair. Laura put the pieces together. It was a man. She was looking down on a man. Was he the killer? After a moment, she heard him laugh at something on the screen and then saw him raise a beer bottle to his mouth, taking a quick swig.*

*Beer. Her mind, her thoughts, zeroed in on that bottle. On the way it would feel to let that liquid pour down her own neck. On the way it would ease off all her cares—*

*Laura's attention snapped back to the room. Something was different. Something subtle, but it sent a chill down her neck. Someone else was there.*

*The vision was infuriating. She could see only what it showed her, unable to cast her view beyond the dark and flickering edges. Like she was looking into a TV screen herself. But she knew that the atmosphere had changed, even if the man in the chair didn't seem to sense it.*

*She focused on him, on what he was doing. His attention was fully on the television, no sign that he had noticed anyone else around him. Then again, perhaps it was simply a housemate of his. But she had a different feeling. A feeling that this person, whoever they were, was not supposed to be there.*

*Her eyes darted across the scene over and over as she waited for something to happen. She was shown this for a reason. Something bad was coming, and she knew it.*

*Without any warning, a pair of hands shot into her view. They were holding something , something she at first could not recognize. Then, as it slipped over and around the neck of the man in the chair, she thought she recognized it. A tie, a simple necktie with a dark blue stripe running across a light blue background. It was pulled tight around the man's throat, yanking him back in the chair, making him tilt his head back and claw at his own neck.*

*Laura looked at his face. He was young. Younger than her. Not even thirty, she thought. His eyes were wide with panic, his mouth contorting as he fought for breath and struggled to get out from under the tie. His eyes were looking right up into those of the killer. If she could just get closer—if she could see the reflection in those eyes—she might see that it was Ed Bronston—*

Laura opened her eyes with a start, wrenched away from the vision too soon. At least she hadn't had to finish watching this one die, she thought.

But there was something that gnawed at her as she replayed what she had seen in her mind, searching for clues. A man. The victim had been a man. She was sure of it. This wasn't just an androgynous woman; he was male, completely.

And he was dying in the same way as the others.

It was definitely their killer. Which meant he was changing his method. Going for a man instead of a woman. Trying to throw them off the scent.

And, like a bucket of ice water down her spine, Laura realized something else.

Everything they were doing right now was a waste of time.

Alex—whoever he was—would never hear their warning.

# CHAPTER THIRTY

Laura didn't have time to think of a clever strategy to tell them how she knew. She didn't have any time at all. She needed to get them to change their tactics now, right now, or the man she had seen—Alex—he was going to be dead before they got to him.

She had no idea who he really was. What his last name was, where in the city he lived. She knew that he was watching a certain show on television, but how would that help her in a city where people were probably all watching that show at the same time? How would they even get that information to track down who was watching?

No, they had to do it with the phone book. It was the only way.

"Nate," Laura hissed urgently, calling his attention before he picked up the phone to dial a new number. He hesitated, his hand hovering over the receiver. "We're doing this wrong. We need to be looking for a man."

"What?" Nate glanced around the room and lowered his voice, trying not to disturb the other officers who were still on calls. "Did you find something?"

"No," Laura said, cursing the fact that she couldn't tell him what she'd seen. "But I'm sure of it. The next victim will be a man, not a woman. Thirty-five or younger, listed in the phone book, and probably living alone. Called Alex. We have to—"

"Wait a second," Nate interrupted, shaking his head. He was leaning out across the desk toward her, stretched out, giving her the impression of a resting panther. "Where is this coming from?"

Laura bit her tongue. What was she supposed to say? "It makes sense," she said. "Alex—my dad was a man. Why would the target not be a man?"

Nate shook his head again, rubbing one hand over his eye. "Laura, we talked about this. We already agreed. The killer has been going after women all this time. Why would he suddenly change his MO and go after a man? It doesn't make sense. We agreed."

"I know we did," Laura said, hesitating. "But… Nate, I just know. This isn't right. We're never going to find him like this. He's going to die. We have to switch over to men."

Nate narrowed his eyes, sighing. "Laura… I know you're anxious about letting another one slip through the cracks. But we're already up against it on time trying to reach all of these women. If we add men into the mix as well, we'll never get through everyone, not with a hundred volunteers. Even if we only focus on men—it's not getting any earlier. We've come this far. We have to push on."

"Not all men," Laura protested. "The parameters are much more precise. We'll be able to get through them quicker. Nate, I can't explain it, but I have this feeling—"

"And what if that feeling is wrong?" Nate paused and cast a glance around the room before continuing, as if to make sure no one had overheard how irrational she was being. "We made this choice based on data. All of the signs we have currently point to the killer going after another woman. We've asked all of these people to work long and hard at these calls, tracking down the next victim, and they're doing it on faith that is already stretched thin. Now you want to change that when we're not even halfway through. I'm sorry, but… unless you can give me evidence or even some kind of hint that a man could be at risk, we have to carry on focusing on women."

Laura stared at him, her mouth hanging open. What was she supposed to say?

She didn't have any evidence. Not even a hint. All she had was her vision, and even if she could come clean about that to Nate and expect him to believe her, it didn't matter. It wasn't exactly admissible in court. Nor would it convince the sheriff—and Nate was right. They were asking him to take a lot of this on faith already.

He had never doubted her before. She'd never given him a reason to. But she knew what he was saying made sense. Without proof, there was no reason to change their methods.

He'd trusted her this far. Gone along with everything she said. It stung deep in her chest that he couldn't do the same now, but she couldn't argue.

He was right.

Laura closed her mouth and turned back to her phone book, as though she was accepting what Nate had said and getting back to work. She heard more than saw him turn away and do the same, starting a new call. But her mind was racing. She couldn't just carry on pretending to make the calls. There was no point. She knew now that they wouldn't reach the one person they needed to. And there was no way she could get through enough names in the phone book on her own to have any shot at warning him herself.

She was going to have to do this alone—and she wasn't going to achieve anything sitting at a desk with a phone in her hand.

She got up, grabbing her coat from the back of her chair, putting her cell into her pocket. "I need a break," she muttered into the general air above Nate's head, making him glance up at her. He couldn't do anything else. He was midway through a call.

He couldn't stop her as she walked right out of the precinct toward the parking lot, car keys in hand.

***

Laura was driving through the streets of Albany, taking random turns and exits, covering whole blocks just to take a corner or two and go right back in the opposite direction. It was a kind of grid search, except without a fully logical plan, letting her foot on the gas and her hands on the wheel lead her by instinct.

Somewhere out there, Ed Bronston was moving closer and closer to his victim. Somewhere, a victim sitting in his house, or maybe still making his way back home. If she could somehow get onto the right track, start moving in the same direction so that she was on a collision course with one of them, maybe she could force a vision to come.

Laura rested her head against her hand, one elbow propped on the side door, as she pulled up toward a red light. She was getting nowhere. On the one night that she desperately needed to get somewhere, she felt like she was just driving around in circles.

She looked up, the red of the traffic light seeming to burn right into her brain. It was so bright. So bright that it seemed to be making her head pulse with pain. No wonder, after she had had so many visions, forced herself to see so many things. But this pain seemed so insistent, so harsh—

*Laura found herself looking down at the same head she had seen before, the same cap of hair. The man, the one who was going to die. It was him. But this time he was not sitting in front of her television. He was walking, heading to a refrigerator , moving across a shabby kitchen. He opened the refrigerator and pulled out a bottle of beer, cold enough that he pressed it to his forehead with an audible sigh of relief. He was still wearing his coat. He must only just have come in from work.*

*A phone rang out, loud and startling. Laura felt the noise ricocheting around inside her skull, reminding her yet again that pain was the price of seeing the future. Even here, she could not avoid it. She watched as Alex, or whoever he was, headed toward the landline, frowning at it as he picked it up. It was on a low table.*

*"Hello?" he said.*

*Laura could not hear what came next on the other end of the line, could only see Alex frowning. The table, she could see, was scattered with envelopes. Unopened mail. One of them was stamped with a red "URGENT."*

*"Yes," he replied. "Why?... What? I just told you, yes. This is he. What are you talking about? Hello? ... Hello?"*

*And then he hung up, putting the phone back on the receiver with an audible sound of disgust.*

*Laura strained to look at the envelopes, to try to read more. There was a set of keys sitting on top of the pile, car keys and house keys. They had landed right on the clear window of the topmost envelope, obscuring almost everything. Almost everything, but she thought she could read the name... Thomas...?*

*The man paused for a moment, looking at the phone as if expecting it to tell him more—but then he shook his head to himself and moved away, back through the same house. Jettisoning his coat as he went, he switched on the television and settled into an armchair with a thump, groaning as he worked his back into a comfortable position against the cushions. He relaxed, flicking through channels until he chose something funny, turning it up loud enough that he wouldn't be able to hear anything else. And then he reached for his beer...*

A car horn behind her startled Laura out of her vision, making her blink her eyes and try to focus. The light was green above her. It must have just been turning when the vision started, and even though she had only been gone for seconds, it was enough to make the driver behind her impatient. She started the car again and pulled forward, trying to think.

She had seen something. She knew she had, even if it didn't make sense to her. Her visions never lied, though there was always the possibility that they showed something that would not actually come to pass. Still, this didn't seem like one of those times. Not if she didn't get there in time to stop the killer.

But how was she going to find the next victim in time, if the killer was going after someone random?

Because that was the only thing she could think of that made sense. The only reason why there might have been the name Thomas on the envelope that she had seen. Thomas was not Alex, and though she had not seen the full last name, she thought she had seen the very edge of a letter. A straight line, not a diagonal. Not an A. This wasn't some clever ruse where the man's name was Thomas Alex.

But if this victim's name was Thomas, then he was categorically not Alex. Not the same name as Laura's father. There was the possibility that he had recently moved, or was getting mail that had come to the wrong address, but that wouldn't help her. She could pass it off as that and move on, but ignoring anything she had seen in a vision was always a massive risk. She had seen it for a reason. She had to cling on to that.

So, Thomas. But what connection could there be between Thomas and Alex? Or, for that matter, between Thomas and herself? There was no one in her family with that name, at least as far as she knew. It didn't ring any bells at all.

Bronston was going after a man now, changing his method. Did that mean he was changing everything? Changing even the reasoning behind picking his victims? Was he done with Laura and now moving on to victimize someone else who he thought was behind his incarceration?

If that was the case, she had literally no hope of tracking him down.

But then, she still really had no idea if this vision had been of the killer she was looking for. The pain throbbing behind her eyes told her it was something that would happen imminently, but the location and the killer were still hidden to her. She hadn't actually seen Ed. He didn't have any kind of marking on his forearms that would give him away. She had noticed his hands in the other visions, of course, but in the one where she'd seen Thomas being killed, the arms had not been clear enough to her. Just out of shot, dark and muddled, hidden behind Thomas's head as it tilted back. His hands covered with gloves to avoid leaving fingerprints, meaning she had nothing to go on there.

She carried on driving in circles, looking in vain for somewhere to pull over. What she really needed now was a dark parking lot where she could stop the car and give in to despair. Maybe one that adjoined a liquor store—that would have been ideal. But the brightness of the streetlights boring into her eyes from above seemed to have her trapped on the city streets like a fly under a magnifying glass.

A link to someone else… who would it be? Laura racked her mind, trying to think back to that case. The DA? The defense attorney who hadn't done a good enough job at getting his client off the hook? She didn't know them well enough to know anything about them that would help.

It was all so long ago, and not that long ago at all in other ways. Laura had been through so many cases since then. How was she supposed to remember tangential details from a case that had been just one of many, in the end? Yes, she had stepped in—but even the visions had faded enough in her memory to avoid triggering an instant revelation when she saw them again. The fact that she'd spent a lot of the intervening years blackout drunk probably had something to do with that.

She remembered how she had been at the time. Her father had already been dead, of course. And her mom—

Her father had been dead. Did that mean something?

Why would Ed Bronston target someone using the name of her father, when he wasn't even around to be threatened? Because that was what this was, wasn't it? Telling her that he knew the names of her family—that was a threat. Something to scare her. And she wasn't particularly scared by someone implying that her dead father might somehow end up more dead.

But then, if it wasn't her father, who was Ed targeting? Whose name would he use?

And, as if a strike of lightning, it hit her. Of course. It had to be. She had no idea why she hadn't thought of it before.

She knew what Thomas's last name was, and with that, she would be able to find him. She just hoped she hadn't made the connection too late.

# CHAPTER THIRTY ONE

Laura pulled over on the side of the road, not caring about whether she was making a legal move or not at that time. She could always use the excuse of being right in the middle of a case, trying to save someone's life. That was the benefit of being an FBI agent. She flicked on her hazard lights and grabbed her phone out of the center console, immediately opening her browser.

She accessed the online phone book quickly, inputting the search details that she knew would find him. Thomas Lacey. Of course—the one person left whom she would care about a threat to. Her own daughter.

The results loaded too slowly, making her bite clean through the top of her fingernail in frustration. When they finally did, her initial surge of adrenaline tapered down quickly.

There were two.

Two Thomas Laceys.

Right now, she had no idea what their connection was. Whether they were related, perhaps, two men in the same family given a traditional family name. Whether they were the same person, updated to a new address but not removed from the old one. It didn't matter. What did matter was that there were two possible locations she could need to go to, and no way she could be in two places at once. They were on opposite sides of the city.

Because, of course they were.

Laura copied and pasted the telephone number attached to the first one, then called it. She knew that the real Thomas Lacey, the one she wanted, wouldn't answer. He was still on his way home. He would only just be getting in when the phone rang to tell him that Ed Bronston was outside, and then it would be too late. But the second man listed might answer, and then she would know—she could go to the other…

"Come on, come on," Laura muttered under her breath, listening to the line ring and ring. She saw a flash behind her eyes of Lacey's face, the way she had looked the last time they were together. Ed knew her daughter's name. She closed her eyes briefly, swallowing down nausea. It didn't matter. Lacey wasn't in danger.

She was going to track Ed down and stop him, and she was going to do it tonight, before he ever got the chance to put his hands on her daughter.

Laura swore under her breath as she ended the call, realizing it was going nowhere. No one was picking up. She navigated back to the record and chose the other number, calling it with a rising sense of desperation. *Pick up*, she silently begged. *Pick up. Tell me I can go to the other one.*

A car screeched by her, honking its horn to show the driver's displeasure at her choice of parking spot. Laura shook her head wordlessly. No one was answering.

She ended the call, feeling doubt like a ball of acid in her throat. She wasn't going to be able to cover both of them.

If she chose the wrong one, the man was going to die.

She had nothing else to go on. No glimpse of an address on the envelope. No idea what the outside of the property looked like. She didn't even know if it was an apartment or a house.

She couldn't cover both of them alone.

Laura made a snap decision, inputting the first address into her GPS and swinging the car back out into traffic. There was another angry blow of a horn, but she ignored it and started to drive. While the GPS routed her, she dialed another number, letting it connect through the car's Bluetooth.

"Laura? Where are you?" Nate asked, not bothering with a hello as the call connected. "I thought you were just stepping out for some air, but the car's gone!"

"I found him," she said, her voice too loud and sharp, the moment too urgent to moderate it. "I know who the victim is. But there's two people with the same name. I can't cover them both, Nate. I need you to go."

"What?" Nate's voice was a shout, but he hushed himself before he spoke again. Laura heard movement in the background, like he was walking out of the bullpen and into privacy. "How did you find her? Where have you been?"

"Him. It's a male. Thomas Lacey."

"Lacey…?" She heard his intake of breath. "You're sure? You were convinced it would be Alex, and—"

"It's Lacey," Laura asserted, cutting him off. "Please, Nate. I'll send you the address. Go and get a car right now. We don't have any time for this. Just trust me."

"I…" Nate hesitated, and for an awful moment she thought that he would refuse. That he would say she was out of her mind, and she had no proof. That she was going to have to somehow do this alone. "All right. Send it to me. I'll see if I can take a deputy's car."

"Thank you," Laura replied, ending the call quickly as she fumbled for her phone. It was dangerous, but she had no choice. There was a red light just ahead, and she pulled up to it quickly enough to still have the time to send the address as a message to Nate before she could drive forward again.

She felt a sick spike of fear hitting her stomach. Nate. Was she sending him to his death? Was this how he died? Killed by a random choice of which address to go to?

She fought for breath as the lights changed, swallowing down bile and putting her foot on the accelerator. No. She couldn't think of it. She couldn't let the fear rule her. If she found out that her address was wrong, all she had to do was go in the other direction as fast as possible. She might get there in time to save him. She wouldn't let Nate die tonight.

She set her hands firmly on the steering wheel, looking ahead with determination. She was feeling good now. Clearer. Even the headache was starting to feel like it was ebbing away. She was…

She was on the wrong track.

The realization washed over her like spilled ink over a white page. The headache was ebbing away because the chance of a vision was. She was moving in the wrong direction.

Laura pulled over sharply to input the other address, her hands shaking as she typed it in. She had to turn around, get back over to the other side of the city. To the same address that she'd sent Nate to.

She just hoped that she'd realized in enough time.

***

Tommy pulled up in his parking spot, turning off the engine and resting for a moment. It was late; another shift that went on past his normal start time. There were getting to be too many of these lately.

He got out of the car, slamming the door shut as he walked past the side of the building and around toward the front door. He passed his mailbox on the way, opening it up and grabbing whatever the mailman had left inside for him. He leafed through it with minimal attention as he moved to unlock the door, realizing quickly that he could toss it all aside. Mostly just bills that he couldn't pay. What was the point in opening them?

He tossed his keys on top of the pile of mail that was growing on the table by the door, shrugged off his jacket and hung it up, and left his shoes on the rack. A good cold beer, that was what he needed right now. Something to take away the stress of the day. He headed for the refrigerator, opening it and barely even glancing inside before he took out the one thing he wanted. Food could come later, when he had gained back enough energy to cook.

The landline phone rang as he was about to go and sit down in front of the television. *Huh, that's odd,* he thought, before reaching to pick up the receiver.

# CHAPTER THIRTY TWO

Laura brought the car screaming to a stop outside the address, looking up as she did so for any sign that she was in the right place. Her head was back to pounding again, and she felt like she was on the verge of triggering another vision. That had to mean she was in the right place.

As she leapt out of the car and ran for the door, she caught a glimpse through a window set into it. A hallway. A table set in the hall. A pile of mail on top of it, crowned with a set of keys.

This was the place.

She was here, and the victim was already home.

There was no time to call for backup, no time to hope that Nate was on the way. She had to go in, and she had to do it now. She didn't even have time to be afraid for herself as she charged for the door, landing a kick squarely underneath the lock, waiting for it to splinter. It took one more try, and she barreled forward with her shoulder braced to hit the frame, relying on the damage that she had already done to yield to her momentum. The old, poorly maintained, and half-rotted door exploded into splinters as she staggered into the house, taking a course straight through to the living room, following in the footsteps of Thomas Lacey as she had seen them in her vision.

And there he was.

Thomas Lacey, his head tilted back against the chair as he kicked and fought for purchase on his neck, the blue striped tie firmly around it, his face reddening with the pressure. Above the neck, with his gloved hands grasping the tie from the other side, was a tall, lanky man wearing a dark mask over his face.

But not dark enough.

The moment she saw his eyes, Laura knew it was him: Ed Bronston. She'd been right. But that was no consolation now.

For a moment they simply stared at one another, both of them in shock. Laura, because she had finally tracked him down, and now she was almost too late, but there he was, and he was just looking at her. He, probably because he had never believed he would be interrupted in the middle of carrying out another kill.

"How—?"

Laura didn't need to let him finish the sentence, didn't need to answer. She hadn't been able to draw her weapon before, while she was hurling herself into the door, but she could now. She reached for the gun in her holster and pulled it out quick, holding it right to the level of Ed's head and freezing still again.

In the time that it had taken her to pull a gun, Ed had gone for his own backup plan. He had pulled a knife from his belt and was now holding it against Thomas Lacey's throat.

He said nothing, but the intention was clear. Lacey had stopped struggling, his body going limp. His eyes were closed, and the motion of going for the knife had loosened Ed's grip on the tie. Most people didn't die immediately after they fell unconscious from strangulation. It was a survival method. Playing dead, quite literally. The body went into shutdown mode to preserve what little oxygen it had left; leave the airways clear, and they could come to. Laura had heard of it happening before. Serial killers getting caught out because their "dead" victim woke up and escaped.

Thomas Lacey still had a chance. Just not if Ed Bronston cut his throat for him before he could wake.

Laura's hand tightened on the trigger. She had a good line of sight. She was staring Bronston right in the eye, and he her. There was nothing between her and his head. One shot—that was all it would take. If she could land the bullet quicker than he could move the knife, it would all be over.

She had to take the chance.

She moved her finger, preparing to squeeze—

The pain came out of nowhere, almost knocking her sideways, so instantaneous she had no time to prepare—

*Laura pulled the trigger, and the bullet flew from the gun toward its target. Like in slow motion, she watched it happen. It moved through the air like it was water, slow, leaving ripples of movement behind. As it moved closer to Ed, he moved, too. He pulled his hand forward and across. It wasn't a precise move, but it was vicious. Even as the bullet struck home in his forehead, the knife slid away from Thomas Lacey's flesh, leaving a fountain of blood pouring out in its wake. Red splashed down Lacey's chest, soaking the upholstery of the chair, spilling down onto the floor...*

Laura drew in a breath, her eyes wide open. Her head felt like it was splitting open. It took everything she had not to drop the gun and clutch her head. She couldn't shoot. That much was clear to her now.

So then what?

"You've got me, Agent Frost," Ed Bronston said. His voice was a dry croak, like he hadn't had a drop of water in the whole time since she'd seen him last. It was sepulchral, eerie, like he wasn't of this earth any longer. "But I've got him. What are you going to do?"

Laura clenched her jaw for a moment, trying to think. She couldn't shoot.

"Drop the knife," she said. It was worth a try.

"You drop the gun," he replied.

As she had expected.

The easy route wasn't going to be an option here.

She couldn't shoot. She couldn't just stand here without breaking the status quo; Thomas Lacey needed medical attention.

There was only one thing she could do.

Laura slowly lowered her gun until it was pointing at the floor.

"What are you doing?" Bronston asked, a moment of panic in his voice. It was almost funny. The fact that he wasn't about to get shot was worrying him.

"Ed, you don't need to keep the mask on. I know who you are." Laura's tone was weary. She wanted to try to capture some kind of rapport with him, build it up like they had a special relationship. He clearly thought they did.

There was a moment of silence. Then, keeping the knife where it was, Ed reached up and pulled the mask off his face in one smooth movement. His skin was red, imprinted with patterns from the inside of the mask all the way from his high forehead to his square chin. His dark eyes didn't move from her.

"So, you figured it out."

"I knew it was you as soon as I saw you'd been released." Laura gave him a wry, lopsided smile. "Listen, Ed, it's over, you know? I'm not the only one who figured it out. Even if you get away from here, the FBI is going to be after you. It's time to stop."

"I don't think so," Ed said, a sneer breaking across his face. "Not when I have you right where I want you."

Laura felt a bead of sweat drip down her spine, even as she tried to stay outwardly calm. It was one thing to know that he was targeting her. But hearing him admit it made it all the more real.

There was a gasp; Ed and Laura both looked down to see Thomas Lacey's eyes flying open. He was breathing, taking ragged and rapid inhales through a rough throat.

"Don't move," Ed snapped immediately, pressing the blade against Thomas's throat until the man stiffened and stopped moving. He continued to gasp for breath, his wide eyes fixed right on Ed.

"Let him go," Laura said. "You'll still get what you want. We'll make a deal."

Ed's narrowed eyes shot back toward her. "What deal?"

"If you cut his throat, I'll shoot to kill. You've been watching me. You know I'm a good shot." Laura paused, letting that sink in. "If you let him go, I'll put the gun down. It'll just be you and me. That's what you want, isn't it? Revenge? This isn't about him at all."

"Pl-please," Thomas wheezed, his voice barely understandable, but Ed hissed and pressed the knife against his throat hard enough that a drop of scarlet ran from the tip of the blade.

"I'm not stupid," Ed snapped. "If I let him go, you'll shoot me anyway. You put the gun down first."

Laura opened her mouth to tell him that she couldn't, that it wasn't smart, but a stab of pain ricocheted through her head and—

*Ed's face changed before she had a chance to react. He sliced through Thomas's throat and ducked at the same time, and when Laura fired, she missed. He sprang up again before she had a chance to recover from the recoil, whirling around, pointing it at him—but it was too late—he was close enough to knock her hand upward and bury the shot in the ceiling—the knife was at her chest—*

Laura blinked, sweat running freely down her back now and beading on her forehead. The visions were coming so fast she barely had time to prepare. If she didn't get this right, she was going to die anyway. She and Thomas both.

"All right," she said, cautiously, moving slow. She didn't want to startle Ed, and she didn't want to miss the warning of another vision. But as she slowly crouched to the floor and let go of her gun, nothing happened.

When she stood again, her hands raised by her sides to show that she wasn't holding anything else, Ed's grip on Thomas loosened. He moved the knife away slowly, leaving Thomas free, whimpering in his chair.

"Now kick the gun over to me," Ed said.

Laura didn't need a vision to tell her that Ed was still close enough to stab Thomas if she didn't comply. She drew back her foot, making eye contact with the young man. "Run," she told him, as she gently scooted the gun across the ground toward Ed.

He planted one boot on top of it, watching with the knife outstretched as Thomas struggled to his feet and then darted past Laura, down the hall. Though he was still fighting to get enough breath, it must have been adrenaline powering him. He was gone in a moment, leaving them alone together.

"Well, well," Ed said, grinning. He leaned down to pick up the gun with his spare hand. "Isn't this—"

Laura didn't wait for him to finish his sentence. The second his eyes were off her, she sprang, leaping toward him with her arms outstretched. She tackled him to the floor, rolling with the momentum and ending up under him, then on top again. Ed grunted with the impact, then growled low in his throat, his gritted teeth bared as he tried to throw Laura off him to the side.

She kept hold of his shoulders, wrapping her legs around his waist, using his momentum to keep the roll going. They both hit the side of a coffee table, crying out with the impact, and rolled back. Laura's back connected with the floor and stayed there.

Laura had to get the upper hand to survive this. She reached lower down his arm to try to restrict him, pulling her legs under her to try and flip him over so that she could keep him down, but his other hand whipped around, the knife still in his grasp. She felt it slash over her left arm, slashing through both her jacket and shirt and then the skin, and drew back her right arm to punch him in the face. He took the blow full on the nose, forcing a sound of pain and surprise out of him as the impact pushed him back.

Laura didn't have time to register how badly her arm was bleeding or how much it hurt. She yanked with her feet again, pulling one of her own legs back up toward herself, knocking him further backward. He hit the coffee table again, dislodging a rain of coasters and old magazines and the bottle of beer Thomas had been drinking.

Ed snarled as he looked down on her, recovering his balance enough to plunge forward, the knife outstretched in his hand. He had her now. She was trapped, pinned down—he lunged downward—

Laura twisted to the side, but it wasn't enough. She didn't have enough leverage, enough room to get out from under him. But the trick with the coffee table had given her what she needed to stop the knife plunging into her heart. Instead, it hit her ribs, glancing off them. Ed left it stuck in her, like it was all over.

"I've got you now, Agent Frost," he croaked, his voice calling as if from the grave. "Now all that's left for you to do is die."

And he was right. She wasn't fatally wounded, but that didn't matter. She would bleed out here, from her arm and her side, and Ed wouldn't let her get help. It would be slow, and maybe he would get impatient and speed things up a little, raining down more wounds on her exhausted body. But it was a sure thing. She was going to die.

The gloating smile on his face showed her he was sure he had won.

But he didn't know she had backup.

## CHAPTER THIRTY THREE

Laura felt the shadow of death filling the room. It made her as sick as the pain did. Burning in her arm, her ribs. It was so close and so strong that she couldn't even work out where it was coming from. From Ed? From herself?

But then she saw a flicker of silent movement over Ed's shoulder, and she knew.

Nate was here, and the shadow of death around him was so strong she could feel it even without a touch. This was it. This was the moment that he died.

Nate made some kind of noise, kicked some small thing that had fallen off the coffee table and rolled toward the door, hard to see in the dark. Within a flash, Ed's sneer was no longer above her face, and Laura realized that he had snatched up the gun and moved quick as lightning.

He stood above her now, facing Nate. Her gun in his hand. Pointing at her partner.

"Looks like the cavalry's here," Ed rasped, and Laura could see him now: her brave, loyal, strong partner, holding his gun up in front of him, the two of them locked in a Mexican standoff.

"Drop the weapon," Nate barked. He was steady and true, but Ed was unhinged. He had his revenge. There was no way to know if he cared about his life anymore.

"You first, Agent," Ed said. "Or your partner here doesn't get the help she needs to survive."

Laura saw with absolute clarity how it would play out. She didn't need a vision. She knew Nate too well. He was going to look at her and see the blood, and he was going to put down his gun. Just like she knew beyond a shadow of a doubt that Ed wouldn't play fair.

The second Nate let down his guard, Ed would kill him.

The shadow filled the whole room, making it hard for her to concentrate on anything else. The air was thick with it, like it was a visceral smoke she would breathe in when she inhaled. It was happening now.

She couldn't let Nate die here.

Laura found some last reserve of strength, reached with her right hand for the blade that was still sticking just out of her ribs. She grabbed it, gasped with pain and the renewed spurt of her blood as she pulled it out. She couldn't wait. Couldn't let the pain take over. Couldn't acknowledge that yes, in return for saving Nate's life, she might be ending her own.

She sat up. She stumbled to one knee, then the other. She pushed herself upright. Her vision went black for a moment, but she fought through the nausea, the dizziness, the pain.

She brought her right arm up, and just as Ed's muscles moved, signifying his hand tightening around the gun, she stabbed the knife into his back.

Her aim was true. She knew the right angles to use, had been through all of the training. She didn't hit a rib. She hit his heart. She twisted the knife as she dragged it down, opening it up wider, causing more damage.

The first thing she felt was the warmth of his blood, splattered over her and beginning to pour down from the gaping wound in his back.

The second was the weight of his body as he fell backwards onto her, pinning her back to the floor.

And the third was relief, when she heard Nate calling her name and rushing to her side.

***

"You're lucky," the doctor said, which made Laura want to laugh in his face. "With these stitches, I don't think you're going to have a scar on your arm. Just make sure to keep it clean, and get yourself to your local hospital next week for a check-up. As for the wound on your side, it will take a little longer to heal, and you'll have a scar—but it's sewn up and clean, so if you keep it that way, I don't foresee any complications."

"I know the drill," Laura said, which was unfortunately true.

"Better than most," Nate added. She was grateful for the backup. "Thanks, Doc. She going to need anything else?"

"That should do it." The doctor nodded, moving to the door of the private room. "When you're ready, you should be good to check out."

"Thanks," Laura said, belatedly, as the door closed. She felt like her timing was a little off; lag, maybe, from all the visions and the headaches and the physical fight. She'd come straight to the hospital from the scene, no time for a break or decompression, and it had been a whirlwind of assessment and stitches and blood transfusions. And all the rest. The fear for Nate. For Amy. The need for a drink. The need, always unfulfilled, to see Lacey.

It was a wonder she wasn't permanently lagged.

"How are you doing?" Nate asked, seeming to read her mind. He stood awkwardly by the bed, his arms folded across his chest.

"I could do with sleeping for a week," Laura said. "How did it go while I was getting my stitches?"

"Sheriff's handling the crime scene." Nate shrugged. "Bronston didn't tell Thomas anything. Looks like he was just… insane. Like you said. Targeting you. He must have fooled the psychiatric tests to get himself released. We've got local cops going to examine his apartment, see if they can find anything else, but it seems like everything is just about wrapped up."

"That's good," Laura said. She rested her head back against the pillows, wishing she could stay longer. She had only been at the hospital a few hours, but if the doctor said she was well enough to travel, then she was well enough. Still, she could sleep on the plane. Then at home, hopefully. She would get a day off to cope with the injury, at the very least.

And mandatory counseling to deal with having stabbed a perp to death. Laura didn't want to think about that. She'd have to deal with it when it came to it.

"Look, uh…" Nate hesitated, sitting down on the edge of the bed and reaching for her hand. Laura flinched it away, trying to pretend that she was coincidentally just getting up as he sat down, swinging herself around to sit facing in the opposite direction. "Laura, you just did it again."

"Did what?" she asked, reaching for her watch from the surface by the bed and busying herself with doing up the strap. She couldn't bear for him to touch her. She didn't want to know. She was so afraid. She had always felt the shadow of death was further off, not gathering pace with the investigation. And if she hadn't just saved his life from the real danger…

She couldn't face it. She didn't want to feel that shadow of death hanging on him again. Not yet.

"Avoided me." Nate sighed. "You've been acting weird this whole case. And that's saying something, because you're always weird as hell."

Laura flinched again—at his words, this time. His opinion mattered to her. Hearing him describe her that way, like he saw her just as everyone else did…

"Which is one of the things I like about you," Nate added quickly, reacting to her expression. "I like that you have that mysterious edge, that you're different from other agents. I love that we can trust each other. It's just that, this time… I'm worried about you."

"I'm just a little sore," she said, making to hop off the bed.

"Laura." Nate's voice was hard and flat. It was unusual enough for him that she froze and looked at him, turning over her own shoulder. "Stop. I… I've known for a while that the things you do are… strange. The insights you get. You always chalk it up to luck, but it's just not possible for that to be the case so often. I don't know how you know, but you know things I don't. Things no one knows."

Laura bit her lip. "Nate," she said, shaking her head, her voice cracking. "I can't—"

"I know you don't want to tell me," Nate said. His voice was steady and soft, washing over her. "I'm a patient man. I can wait. But if we're going to stay partners, you need to let me in. Sooner or later, you have to let me in."

Laura's shoulders slumped. Privately, though she wasn't going to admit it out loud, she knew he was right. She had lost partners before because she would not open up. They had become suspicious of her, in the end, thinking that she had some confidential informant or other trick up her sleeve that she wasn't letting them in on. They would grow jealous, call her a bitch who was only out to further her own career. Then it would be over.

Nate was different, had always been different. They had managed to get along this far. But she had always known, at the back of her mind, that this day would probably come. Maybe it was time. Maybe telling him now would be the right thing to do.

Nate's hand landed on her shoulder, and even though Laura froze in anticipation of that awful shadow of death coating everything around her, it was faint this time. Soft and indistinct, like gauze. Disappointment was tempered with relief. She had somehow managed to delay it, to push it further off in to the future. But still, it was there. The sickening reminder that he was going to die.

*That's why I can't tell him.*

And a second wave washed over her, the feeling coming on thicker and murkier than before, like someone had thrown a heavy curtain across the window.

"I'll see you outside," Nate said, getting up and taking his hand away. The color returned to the room, and Laura gulped in a breath as he left her on her own.

Laura pushed her hands against her forehead, trying to keep down a burst of nausea. What did this all mean? She'd been considering telling him, and the shadow had eased off a little. But the moment she decided not to, it had come back in full force.

Was he supposed to know?

Was telling him about her ability the one thing she would be able to do to change his fate—and save his life?

She picked up her cell phone from the table beside the bed as it rang out, startling her.

"Agent Frost," she said, breathless from the exertion and from the shock of getting a call that she hadn't been expecting. Still, instinct kicked in. She guessed it was probably going to be Division Chief Rondelle, or—

"Laura."

Laura's breath caught in the back of her throat. Of all the people she would have thought likely to call her, he was one of the last. "Marcus?"

"I had a call from the hospital," he said. His voice was strained and tight, like he was begrudging having to talk to her at all. "Apparently, I'm still your next of kin. Something happened to you?"

"I'm sorry," Laura said, her voice restrained and subdued. "I'll update my records. I'm… I'm fine."

"You get blackout drunk again, Laura?" Marcus asked accusingly.

"No!" Laura said, hating the fact that even the denial itself would make her sound like a liar. She only had herself to blame, she knew. All the times she had lied in the past to cover up her alcohol problem. "No, I'm out here working a case. Things got a little… hairy with the suspect. I took a few knocks, but I'm okay. They're discharging me already."

Marcus made a noise that sounded like he wasn't sure whether to believe her, but before he could say anything else, another voice interrupted.

"Is that Mommy?" The girl in the background of the call was faint, but Laura heard her. It was Lacey. Her sweet, beautiful daughter. She was close by. She was almost close enough to talk…

"Lacey?" Laura burst out, shouting it loud, wanting to make her voice heard over the speakers on the other end. "Lacey, honey, can you hear me?"

"Shut up," Marcus snapped at her. "No, Lacey, it's not Mommy. Go back and finish your breakfast, okay?"

"Okay, Daddy."

"No! Lacey! Please, Marcus, please—" Laura gasped, tears spilling down her cheeks.

"I told you," Marcus said heavily. "Not until I'm ready."

Then the line went dead.

Laura felt hot tears streaming over her face, sobs racking her body as she leaned forward, covering her eyes with her hands. Her daughter… she'd been so close. But so far.

Laura cried herself dry. She only had so much within herself. It was partly self-preservation: the harder she sobbed, the more her ribs ached. She managed to lied back on the pillow, breathing deeply and looking up at the blank ceiling, finding enough of a calm inside herself to stop the tears.

Just not the grief.

Laura breathed out heavily, rubbing her head. She needed to do something, anything, to make this feeling diminish. She needed to do some good. She looked back through her contacts and dialed another number—this time, for Dean Marsters, the FBI tech who'd said he would help.

"Yeah?" he said, picking up after only a couple of rings.

"Dean. Please tell me you have something."

"Oh, Frost. As a matter of fact, I was going to call you," he replied. His voice sounded chipper, like he was pleased with himself. "I didn't know if you wanted to be disturbed while you're recuperating. I heard through the grapevine you were injured early this morning."

"Please disturb me," she said. She caught the irony in the words as soon as she'd said it. The more disturbing the dirt he'd managed to find on Governor Fallow, the better.

"Well, turns out he's had a couple of run-ins over the years," Dean reported. "As far as I can see, they mostly involve people being paid off to sign NDAs and keep his bad behavior to themselves. I don't have any exact details just yet, but I have the names of a few people who received suspicious amounts of money. It could lead nowhere if they're not prepared to talk, but if you need to take him to court, this could be something you could lean on. Get full disclosure from his lawyers, or something like that. Even if you can get a look at the agreements to see what it is they've signed off on not talking about."

"Got it," Laura said, even though she felt her heart sinking. It sounded like a lot more work. She'd been hoping for something concrete, something she could use to immediately have Fallow declared an unfit father—or at least rock his position in office. But she was going to have to work with it. Amy needed her to. "Send me everything."

"Will do, Frost. Don't forget that coffee and muffin you owe me."

"Next time I'm in the office," she promised, ending the call.

She lifted her phone, thinking she would dial another number. When her finger hesitated over the call button for Governor Fallow's residence, a spike of pain hit her in the forehead. She knew what was coming even before it—

*Amy. A close-up of her face. Crying.*

*"Daddy," she said, sobbing through tears that shook her whole frame, blowing a bubble of snot under her nose. "No!"*

Laura surfaced with a gasp, finding her hands shaking. Short but sweet. It told her everything she needed to know.

She ignored the pain in her head—and everywhere else, it seemed—as she got up out of the bed and reached for her clothes. She had to go—and now.

She dressed quickly and headed for the exit. Out there she found Nate already waiting with the car, ready to drive them both to the airport. It was time to leave here, and Laura was champing at the bit to be in the air already.

There was one other person who was still waiting for her to contact them, she knew. VirginiaMan383. She wished she could just sit here in the hospital and actually rest, but it felt like her timescale kept moving up. Amy couldn't wait; she needed help as soon as possible. And now that she knew there was something going on with Nate's death, something connected to the very knowledge of her visions, she needed advice.

Meeting up with someone who experienced the same things she did might help her to decide what to do. To make sense of it all. Maybe she could get some answers.

She fired off a message through the forum's personal messaging system from the passenger seat, her fingers flying over her phone's keyboard as quickly as she could make them.

*Hi, VirginiaMan383. I'm coming back into town. Let's meet on Thursday at the café next to the Y on W Street. 1:30 okay for you?*

She hit send without pausing. Now wasn't the time for second thoughts. It was the time for pushing forward.

And there was one thing left—the most important thing yet. She had to get on a plane—and the moment she landed, she knew exactly where she was going.

# CHAPTER THIRTY FOUR

Laura hammered on the door, stepping back to glance up at the windows of the home above her. The governor's mansion was an impressive structure, but that wasn't what her attention was focused on now. She was looking for movement, for any sign of life.

The door opened promptly, revealing an Hispanic woman wiping her hands on a long apron. Even as she opened it, she was glancing over her shoulder, which had Laura's hackles up immediately.

"Hi, FBI," she said, immediately showing her badge without preamble. "I'd like to come inside."

The housekeeper hesitated. Her face was pale, and her eyes darted from Laura's face to the badge to back over her shoulder again.

"I'm not supposed to…" she began, trailing off as she gnawed at her own lower lip. Laura watched her hands and realized they were shaking.

"If I have cause to believe that someone in the house is in danger of harm, then I have the right to enter the property without permission or a warrant," she said, keeping her voice low but her words urgent. "Do you understand?"

The housekeeper turned and looked at her again. "Yes," she said. She paused, clearing her throat. "I… think you might have heard someone scream a moment ago. I heard something as well."

"Thank you," Laura said fervently, stepping over the threshold and charging through the house.

She had to force her hand not to stray to her gun.

She followed her gut, not sure of the layout of the house. But it wasn't hard to guess; straight through to a wide-open kitchen, sunlight streaming in through French doors. A cursory glance there revealed nothing, as Laura had expected. The housekeeper's domain, or a cook if they had one. Not where the master of the house spent his time.

Back to the main hall; stairs leading up, which Laura had to assume would take her to Amy's bedroom. But first, two doors on either side. Laura took one at random, finding herself in a comfortable and lavishly decorated sitting room, complete with an American flag curling over the fireplace; a room where the governor could receive guests. It was empty.

The next door along was another sitting room, but this time smaller and more intimate; photographs of the family lined the walls, and not just the posed and political kind.

That was where she found Mrs. Fallow.

"You," the woman gasped, quickly dashing her hands over her face as Laura burst in. That didn't hide the tears she had been crying at all. "You're—you're not supposed to be here. We don't... want you!"

Laura stared at her for a fraction of a moment. Even now, when she tried to say it strong and loud, it didn't ring true. Not with the tears still drying on her face, black mascara crusted under each eye.

Laura ignored her and turned away. A mother who allowed her daughter to be abused. Her most precious thing. The one person in the world it was not only her duty, but her *privilege* to protect.

Most of all, Laura hated her because she was just like Laura. Trapped by her own fear and pain until she had let her daughter down.

The very failings that Laura would never, ever, if she lived for a thousand years, be able to forgive herself for.

She charged up the stairs, knowing there were only two people to find, and knowing by the tears on Mrs. Fallow's face that she was likely to find them together.

She ran at full tilt, taking the stairs two at a time and then nearly falling at the top, but not stopping as she raced along the corridor. A room at the end of the hall was spilling light from the windows in a diamond pattern out on the floor, and Laura recognized it. She knew the door, the carpet and wallpaper she could glimpse inside.

She knew the silhouette of the man who stood there, belt raised in his hand.

Raised high, as if to strike.

"Fallow!" Laura yelled, calling on something deep down inside of her; what came out of her mouth was a screech of righteous fury, like she was possessed by a demon. He faltered and turned to look at her, the belt dropping by his side.

Her momentum could not be interrupted. Just two moments later Laura staggered to a stop in the doorway, looking past him, past his dumbstruck face and the belt hanging loose at his side.

Past him, at Amy.

The little girl was curled up into a ball in the center of her bed, crying, her body shaking up and down silently as she sobbed hard. Her mouth was hanging open, snot trailing down from her nose.

"You can't be in here," the governor said, finding his voice.

Laura looked straight at him and moved her hand to her hip, to the grip of her gun. She waited until his eyes flicked down and took in the silent threat.

"Amy," she said, keeping her eyes on him a moment longer, but softening her voice. "Amy, do you remember me?"

"Ye-yeah," Amy sobbed, wiping the back of her hand over her nose. "My a-angel."

"Come here to me," Laura said. She stepped into the room with her hand outstretched, planting herself between the governor and the bed. "Come on, now. It's going to be okay."

"You can't be in here," the governor repeated. "You've got no right."

When Amy slowly stumbled from the bed and then to Laura's side, Laura was quick to take hold of her arm and pull her back toward the door. She kept her eyes on the governor; his eyes flicked down to her hip over and over again. He was slowly reddening, even further than he had been when she arrived.

"Let's go," Laura said quietly, turning and picking Amy up, lifting her from the floor and setting her on the opposite hip—away from the gun—to get her out of there quicker. Her heart was beating a mile a minute in her chest. Whether it was fear they'd be caught and stopped, or anger at what Governor Fallow had done, she could no longer tell.

"I'm going to have you fired," the governor said, raising his voice as he followed them. "You hear me? I'm going to make a call and get the cops here. You're going to be stripped of your badge. You won't get away with this."

"It's going to be all right," Laura said lightly, brightly, glancing into Amy's eyes. The girl clung to her, her arms going around Laura's neck. Even though she was clearly still distressed, she was no longer crying. She kept looking at Laura, not around or back at her father. Like Laura was her rock.

And that was all Laura had ever wanted to be.

Governor Fallow was shouting and screaming behind her, his voice on crescendo after crescendo, threatening her with legal action, telling her everything she was going to lose. Laura didn't care. She stopped listening.

At the door, she turned back. There was no one else in sight. The housekeeper had disappeared. Mrs. Fallow had not emerged. Even she had to know that this was what was best for her daughter.

It was only her and the governor.

"You," she said, her voice quiet and low, aimed directly at him like a bullet between his eyes. "If you make a fuss about this, if you so much as make an offhand comment to my boss, I will end you. I will testify in court about what I've seen, and so will others. And I won't even need to. With the footage I've seen from that room, no one would let this defenseless, innocent little girl back in a room with you. And you can kiss your political career goodbye, too. One word—and everything you have goes up in flames. Do you understand me?"

She didn't wait to hear if he understood. She took in his wide eyes, red face, his spluttering mouth, and turned away. She carried on walking, marching Amy right to the car and setting her inside, putting on her seatbelt in the backseat.

As she walked back to her door and got behind the wheel, Laura dared to take one look back at the house. The door was gaping empty, the governor gone. He'd either believed her, or he hadn't. The wide-eyed look he'd had when she threatened his career was at least promising.

Implying that the FBI had been secretly recording him had been inspired, if a complete falsehood. Psychic visions couldn't be submitted as evidence of wrongdoing. If the governor ignored her warnings and tried to retaliate, Laura would be in serious trouble. She could be fired for this. Arrested for kidnapping.

But for now, Amy was safe in the back of her car. And, as she drove away, Laura couldn't be worried about that. She could only be relieved.

She had no idea where she would take her, what she would do next, but as she put distance between their car and the mansion, she knew that distance was everything.

Hell would rain down on her.

Let it.

Laura had no idea what came next. What her next move would be.

But for now, the girl was safe.

And that was all that mattered.

## NOW AVAILABLE!

### ALREADY SEEN
### (A Laura Frost FBI Suspense Thriller—Book 2)

"A MASTERPIECE OF THRILLER AND MYSTERY. Blake Pierce did a magnificent job developing characters with a psychological side so well described that we feel inside their minds, follow their fears and cheer for their success. Full of twists, this book will keep you awake until the turn of the last page."
--Books and Movie Reviews, Roberto Mattos (re Once Gone)

ALREADY SEEN (A Laura Frost FBI Suspense Thriller) is book #2 in a long-anticipated new series by #1 bestseller and USA Today bestselling author Blake Pierce, whose bestseller Once Gone (a free download) has received over 1,000 five star reviews. The series begins with ALREADY GONE (Book #1).

FBI Special Agent and single mom Laura Frost, 35, is haunted by her talent: a psychic ability which she refuses to face and which she keeps secret from her colleagues. While Laura gets obscured glimpses of what the killer may do next, she must decide whether to trust her confusing gift or her investigative work.

**When a female acting teacher turns up murdered in Tacoma—the second such death in two months—FBI Special Agent Laura Frost is called in to determine if it is the work a serial killer. Yet, what Laura finds is more disturbing than even she can imagine—leading her to a race against time to save the next victim.**

Laura's talent leads her deep—too deep—into the twisted minds of serial killers. Will it lead her to catch a killer? Or will it take her down a road of confusion, dead ends—and her own destruction?

A page-turning and harrowing crime thriller featuring a brilliant and tortured FBI agent, the LAURA FROST series is a startlingly fresh mystery, rife with suspense, twists and turns, shocking revelations, and driven by a breakneck pace that will keep you flipping pages late into the night.

Book #3 in the series—ALREADY TRAPPED—is now also available!

## Blake Pierce

Blake Pierce is the USA Today bestselling author of the RILEY PAGE mystery series, which includes seventeen books. Blake Pierce is also the author of the MACKENZIE WHITE mystery series, comprising fourteen books; of the AVERY BLACK mystery series, comprising six books; of the KERI LOCKE mystery series, comprising five books; of the MAKING OF RILEY PAIGE mystery series, comprising six books; of the KATE WISE mystery series, comprising seven books; of the CHLOE FINE psychological suspense mystery, comprising six books; of the JESSE HUNT psychological suspense thriller series, comprising fifteen books (and counting); of the AU PAIR psychological suspense thriller series, comprising three books; of the ZOE PRIME mystery series, comprising six books; of the ADELE SHARP mystery series, comprising ten books (and counting); of the EUROPEAN VOYAGE cozy mystery series, comprising six books (and counting); of the new LAURA FROST FBI suspense thriller, comprising three books (and counting); of the new ELLA DARK FBI suspense thriller, comprising six books (and counting); of the A YEAR IN EUROPE cozy mystery series, comprising three books (and counting); of the AVA GOLD mystery series, comprising three books (and counting); and of the RACHEL GIFT mystery series, comprising three books (and counting).

An avid reader and lifelong fan of the mystery and thriller genres, Blake loves to hear from you, so please feel free to visit www.blakepierceauthor.com to learn more and stay in touch.

## BOOKS BY BLAKE PIERCE

**RACHEL GIFT MYSTERY SERIES**
HER LAST WISH (Book #1)
HER LAST CHANCE (Book #2)
HER LAST HOPE (Book #3)

**AVA GOLD MYSTERY SERIES**
CITY OF PREY (Book #1)
CITY OF FEAR (Book #2)
CITY OF BONES (Book #3)

**A YEAR IN EUROPE**
A MURDER IN PARIS (Book #1)
DEATH IN FLORENCE (Book #2)
VENGEANCE IN VIENNA (Book #3)

**ELLA DARK FBI SUSPENSE THRILLER**
GIRL, ALONE (Book #1)
GIRL, TAKEN (Book #2)
GIRL, HUNTED (Book #3)
GIRL, SILENCED (Book #4)
GIRL, VANISHED (Book 5)
GIRL ERASED (Book #6)

**LAURA FROST FBI SUSPENSE THRILLER**
ALREADY GONE (Book #1)
ALREADY SEEN (Book #2)
ALREADY TRAPPED (Book #3)

**EUROPEAN VOYAGE COZY MYSTERY SERIES**
MURDER (AND BAKLAVA) (Book #1)
DEATH (AND APPLE STRUDEL) (Book #2)
CRIME (AND LAGER) (Book #3)
MISFORTUNE (AND GOUDA) (Book #4)
CALAMITY (AND A DANISH) (Book #5)
MAYHEM (AND HERRING) (Book #6)

**ADELE SHARP MYSTERY SERIES**
LEFT TO DIE (Book #1)

LEFT TO RUN (Book #2)
LEFT TO HIDE (Book #3)
LEFT TO KILL (Book #4)
LEFT TO MURDER (Book #5)
LEFT TO ENVY (Book #6)
LEFT TO LAPSE (Book #7)
LEFT TO VANISH (Book #8)
LEFT TO HUNT (Book #9)
LEFT TO FEAR (Book #10)

**THE AU PAIR SERIES**
ALMOST GONE (Book#1)
ALMOST LOST (Book #2)
ALMOST DEAD (Book #3)

**ZOE PRIME MYSTERY SERIES**
FACE OF DEATH (Book#1)
FACE OF MURDER (Book #2)
FACE OF FEAR (Book #3)
FACE OF MADNESS (Book #4)
FACE OF FURY (Book #5)
FACE OF DARKNESS (Book #6)

**A JESSIE HUNT PSYCHOLOGICAL SUSPENSE SERIES**
THE PERFECT WIFE (Book #1)
THE PERFECT BLOCK (Book #2)
THE PERFECT HOUSE (Book #3)
THE PERFECT SMILE (Book #4)
THE PERFECT LIE (Book #5)
THE PERFECT LOOK (Book #6)
THE PERFECT AFFAIR (Book #7)
THE PERFECT ALIBI (Book #8)
THE PERFECT NEIGHBOR (Book #9)
THE PERFECT DISGUISE (Book #10)
THE PERFECT SECRET (Book #11)
THE PERFECT FAÇADE (Book #12)
THE PERFECT IMPRESSION (Book #13)
THE PERFECT DECEIT (Book #14)
THE PERFECT MISTRESS (Book #15)
THE PERFECT IMAGE (Book #16)

THE PERFECT VEIL (Book #17)
THE PERFECT INDISCRETION (Book #18)
THE PERFECT RUMOR (Book #19)

**CHLOE FINE PSYCHOLOGICAL SUSPENSE SERIES**
NEXT DOOR (Book #1)
A NEIGHBOR'S LIE (Book #2)
CUL DE SAC (Book #3)
SILENT NEIGHBOR (Book #4)
HOMECOMING (Book #5)
TINTED WINDOWS (Book #6)

**KATE WISE MYSTERY SERIES**
IF SHE KNEW (Book #1)
IF SHE SAW (Book #2)
IF SHE RAN (Book #3)
IF SHE HID (Book #4)
IF SHE FLED (Book #5)
IF SHE FEARED (Book #6)
IF SHE HEARD (Book #7)

**THE MAKING OF RILEY PAIGE SERIES**
WATCHING (Book #1)
WAITING (Book #2)
LURING (Book #3)
TAKING (Book #4)
STALKING (Book #5)
KILLING (Book #6)

**RILEY PAIGE MYSTERY SERIES**
ONCE GONE (Book #1)
ONCE TAKEN (Book #2)
ONCE CRAVED (Book #3)
ONCE LURED (Book #4)
ONCE HUNTED (Book #5)
ONCE PINED (Book #6)
ONCE FORSAKEN (Book #7)
ONCE COLD (Book #8)
ONCE STALKED (Book #9)
ONCE LOST (Book #10)

ONCE BURIED (Book #11)
ONCE BOUND (Book #12)
ONCE TRAPPED (Book #13)
ONCE DORMANT (Book #14)
ONCE SHUNNED (Book #15)
ONCE MISSED (Book #16)
ONCE CHOSEN (Book #17)

**MACKENZIE WHITE MYSTERY SERIES**
BEFORE HE KILLS (Book #1)
BEFORE HE SEES (Book #2)
BEFORE HE COVETS (Book #3)
BEFORE HE TAKES (Book #4)
BEFORE HE NEEDS (Book #5)
BEFORE HE FEELS (Book #6)
BEFORE HE SINS (Book #7)
BEFORE HE HUNTS (Book #8)
BEFORE HE PREYS (Book #9)
BEFORE HE LONGS (Book #10)
BEFORE HE LAPSES (Book #11)
BEFORE HE ENVIES (Book #12)
BEFORE HE STALKS (Book #13)
BEFORE HE HARMS (Book #14)

**AVERY BLACK MYSTERY SERIES**
CAUSE TO KILL (Book #1)
CAUSE TO RUN (Book #2)
CAUSE TO HIDE (Book #3)
CAUSE TO FEAR (Book #4)
CAUSE TO SAVE (Book #5)
CAUSE TO DREAD (Book #6)

**KERI LOCKE MYSTERY SERIES**
A TRACE OF DEATH (Book #1)
A TRACE OF MUDER (Book #2)
A TRACE OF VICE (Book #3)
A TRACE OF CRIME (Book #4)
A TRACE OF HOPE (Book #5)

Made in the USA
Monee, IL
09 March 2023